CHANGES

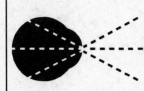

CHANGES

PAMELA NOWAK

THORNDIKE PRESS
A part of Gale, Cengage Learning

GALE
CENGAGE Learning·

Detroit • New York • San Francisco • New Haven, Conn • Waterville, Maine • London

GALE
CENGAGE Learning®

LIBRARY OF CONGRESS CATALOGING-IN-PUBLICATION DATA

Nowak, Pamela.
  Changes / by Pamela Nowak. — Large print edition.
    pages ; cm. — (Thorndike Press large print core)
  ISBN 978-1-4104-6447-7 (hardcover) — ISBN 1-4104-6447-4 (hardcover)
  1. Women librarians—Fiction. 2. Native Americans—Fiction. 3. Large type books. I. Title.
PS3614.O964C49 2013b
813'.6—dc23   2013031182

Published in 2013 by arrangement with Pamela Nowak

For my mom, Vauna,
who fostered imagination and play,
encouraged my dreams and goals,
and taught me to work for them.

CHAPTER ONE

March 29, 1879

A freezing blast of March air hit Lise Dupree squarely in the face. She looked up from the main desk of the Omaha Public Library and her half-organized stack of law books to see Thad Spencer skid toward her.

He crashed into the desk, and the books tumbled to the floor in a succession of echoing thuds. The thirteen-year-old leaned on the oak desk, his heavy blond hair drooping over his face. He shook his head and gulped for air. "That Indian teacher, Miss La Flesche, sent me and said to come quick. She's at the Indian Wigwam store with her pa." He drew another breath. "They said it's about your Aunt Rose."

"Aunt Rose?" Memories of Aunt Rose's hearty laughter flooded Lise's mind. Then Uncle John had hung from a gallows and Aunt Rose had been banished to the Santee Sioux Reservation near Dakota Territory.

7

Susette La Flesche didn't know Aunt Rose.

"Yeah. How come an Indian teacher knows somethin' about your aunt?"

Lise's heart pounded. Susette was the only person in the area who knew about Lise's part-Sioux heritage. She couldn't allow anyone else to find out.

"I don't know. My aunt lives hundreds of miles from here." None of this made sense. "Why didn't Miss La Flesche come here herself?"

"I don't think they have passes — they're hidin' in the back storage room at the Wigwam. Do you think they know somethin' about those Ponca Indians that got arrested on the Omaha Reservation last week?" Eager excitement shone in his blue eyes. "Once you get done talkin' to 'em, I want to find out what the Poncas did and if there was a fight."

The implications set Lise's stomach churning. The Poncas shared the Santee Reservation with the Sioux. Lise had no idea what would bring them so far from their home to visit Omaha tribal lands. But she did know the La Flesches could be jailed for leaving the Omaha Reservation without passes. Whatever news Susette had gathered about her aunt from the visiting Poncas must be serious for Susette and her father to travel sixty miles without proper paperwork.

Lise dropped her wire spectacles on her desk and shoved her ink jar into a drawer. Standing, she grabbed the winter shawl she'd draped over the back of her chair.

"You ready?" Thad's voice was impatient and he shifted from one foot to the other. "Should I clear out the customers?"

"It's empty." Lise frowned. Her rising concern about the urgency of the situation battled her practical nature and ingrained responsibility to close the library properly for the weekend. "Get the drapes." She issued the brisk order, then picked up the law books, ruing the bent pages as she stacked them in a pile on the desk. The wrinkled pages could wait but at least she'd saved the spines from permanent damage.

Thad raced across the room and whipped the heavy green velvet draperies shut. The room darkened, closeting the heat inside to keep the rooms warm until Lise reopened on Monday morning. "Now you ready?"

"Let's go." On the chance she'd need a reason for her visit to the Wigwam, Lise grabbed a volume of *The Adventures of Tom Sawyer* from the shelf behind her desk and tucked it under her arm, then followed Thad out the main door. She turned her key in the sturdy lock, rushed down the narrow stairwell, and flipped the *open* sign to *closed.* Swinging the bottom door shut with a slam, she locked it and marched off without another word.

She hurried down the slope of Dodge Street, clutching at her shawl. The cold biting at her fingers and cheeks was nothing compared to the clenching knot of worry that refused to leave her. She increased her pace.

Thad remained at her side. Their rapid steps echoed on the wooden sidewalk of the thoroughfare. Ahead of them, startled Saturday afternoon shoppers parted to clear a path.

Lise glanced at the boy and smothered a sigh. She didn't need the gossipy teen meddling any further in her affairs. Passing for white was the only way to keep what she'd struggled so hard to gain. She had a job she needed and treasured, a library to tend, readers to nurture, and a growing collection of law volumes that could forge change for native peoples. She'd come too far to lose it all, again. As a white, she could transform the world, or at least one small part of it. As an Indian, she would be stripped of her dignity and her job.

"Thad —" she began.

"If you're gonna tell me to go home, don't. Somethin's going on and I'm not goin' anywhere 'til I find out what it is."

It was clear there'd be no getting rid of him. Uneasiness coursed through her. She'd need to find a way to talk to Susette alone.

She turned onto Fourteenth and hurried past the wooden structure that housed the firearms shop. The proprietor stood in the entrance, demonstrating a pistol to two deputies. He fired a shot into the air and Lise jumped. She'd seen the skinny deputy before and didn't trust the way his eyes lingered too long on women. Her skin prickled at the memory. She dropped her head and hoped they hadn't caught his attention.

Thad's long legs kept easy pace with her as she crossed the dirt street and strode past the Omaha National Bank and the busy Caldwell Block building. They rounded the corner and stopped before the Indian Wigwam. "Where did you leave Miss La Flesche?"

"Inside. C'mon. There's been all sorts of talk about those Poncas. Let's find out what they did."

Lise shook her head, resisting the urge to defend the peaceful Ponca tribe. No white woman would do that.

11

They approached the store. The owner, Julius Meyer, traded in Chinese, Japanese, and Indian curiosities. He sold cigars and tobacco and advertised himself as an Indian interpreter. The place was known for being full of natives with passes from their reservations. Susette and her full-blooded Omaha father, chief at the Omaha Agency, would blend in. No one should ask for their passes.

Lise's brown hair was just light enough for her to pass for white but dark enough that she'd never before risked a visit to the Wigwam, a place white women didn't enter without legitimate reason. She clutched the novel against her chest, glad she'd thought to bring it. Delivery of a book would explain her presence if the issue arose.

Thad brushed past several buffalo hides hanging near the Wigwam's door, pulled them back, and waited for Lise to enter. She threw a glance over her shoulder, unable to shake the feeling that they were being followed, and rushed inside.

The store was dim, the afternoon sun blocked by the array of animal pelts that hung from the ceiling, an incongruous silk kimono in their midst. Lingering smoke filled the air, cigar and pipe tobacco blending in a hodgepodge of aromas. Lise wrinkled her nose at the discordant smell.

"This way." Thad pointed to the back of the shop.

They wound their way down the aisles, past several Omaha Indians in faded dungarees, a few in buckskins. While some sported bear-claw necklaces over calico work shirts, others had abandoned their native adornments altogether. They peered at her with furtive glances. At a counter, Julius Meyer and a well-heeled white man examined a jade figurine. When neither gave her notice, Lise released a relieved breath. Thad stopped before a rough wooden door.

"Stay here," Lise instructed.

"But —"

"Thad, please." She glanced at the other customers, then at the boy. "Maybe you can get some information on the Poncas from some of the customers. I really need to talk to Miss La Flesche privately."

"Aw." He stared at her, then shrugged. "I guess," he muttered.

"Thanks." She pushed at the door, found it stuck, and threw her full weight against it. It grated open, and she slipped into the room.

Inside, Susette paced. A fashionable, travel-worn gray dress emphasized her curves. She looked like any other young woman of Lise's acquaintance . . . except

13

for the ruddy complexion that drew disdain from the white population. A bedraggled pink ribbon hung in her jet black hair. Seeing Lise, she moved forward, arms extended. "Thank goodness you're here."

Lise stepped into Susette's embrace and touched her friend's dirt-covered face. "What is it and why all the secrecy? Tell me you haven't chanced travel without a pass?"

Susette grasped Lise's hands. "There wasn't time. Standing Bear and his band of Poncas were staying on our reservation. They were arrested by the Army. When the soldiers took them to Fort Omaha, they made a list of everyone in the group. Father was given the list only this morning." Her eyes softened. "Your Aunt Rose was with them. In all the time they were with us, we didn't know she was there."

Lise's heart skipped a beat. Rose was arrested with a band of Poncas? She didn't understand why her elderly aunt, a Sioux, would have traveled almost a hundred miles away from her home with the Poncas. "She wouldn't have left the Santee Reservation. She loved it there."

"She was with her Ponca stepson and his family."

"But the Poncas have been at the Omaha Reservation almost a month. Why didn't she contact me?" Lise rubbed the goose bumps on her arms. "What's wrong? What happened?"

Susette offered a compassionate touch. "She's ill, Lise. Her mind is sick. She doesn't realize where she is. If I had known sooner, I would have —"

"Ill? Where is she? I need to go."

"At Fort Omaha. Father and I just came from there." She nodded across the room. Joseph La Flesche, Omaha tribal chief, sat in a dark corner, his black eyes staring at them.

Lise nodded in respect and set her personal items on the table, waiting for the chief to join the conversation. Fort Omaha was four miles from town. She'd go there as soon as she left the Wigwam.

Joseph stood and stepped into the light. "I do not understand these things," he said. "Our cousins the Ponca have done no wrong yet the Army will not let them live in peace. We ask General Crook for help, but he tells us there is nothing to be done. They will be sent away. Susette says we must make things happen ourselves in a court of law. She says your books will tell us how."

Lise's thoughts shifted back to her aunt. "Right now, I need to see Aunt Rose."

Joseph gestured for his daughter to answer.

"I think General Crook would allow that," Susette said. "You're her niece, and Crook is a good man. He would respect your wish, and your privacy."

"How ill is she?"

"She . . . she had a very high fever, Lise. She lived through it, but her mind is not the same."

"General Crook said she is be . . . befuddled," Joseph said.

"Did you see her?"

Susette shook her head. "No, but the general —"

"The general is detaining her. What do you suppose he would say?" Lise faced her friend. "I'm going to the fort."

"Miss Dupree, wait." Joseph's commanding voice brooked no argument.

"What is it?" she asked, her voice edged with frustration. The Poncas were not her concern. She'd already risked too much by entering the Wigwam, and she resented Joseph using news of her aunt to lure her here so he could ask her help with legal research.

Susette offered a brief smile of understanding. "General Crook said the order to move them will come any time. If we don't take action before that happens, the Army will immediately put them on a forced march back to Indian Territory or to prison."

A chill crept up Lise's spine. *Just like Minnesota.* Aunt Rose had already spent her time in prison. She'd already been forced to move to a land that was not her own. She would not survive a second time.

"Aunt Rose is Sioux. She's not part of this — she can go back to the Santee Reservation." But the words sounded futile, even to Lise.

"She made herself part of it when she married into the Poncas," Joseph reminded her. "She chose to stay with her husband's people."

"But surely they won't remove those who are ill."

Joseph gripped Lise's shoulder. "All of them, my friend. They did it before. They will do it again. They will march even weak, tired people through the snow and the spring rains and they will not care what happens."

A sharp rap sounded at the door. As one, the group stiffened. The door opened with a rasp, and Julius Meyer stuck his lean face through the crack. "Deputies. We'll stall."

They hurried toward the darkened shadows at the back of the room, their glances skimming the crates and boxes for a suitable hiding spot.

The door jerked open and a deputy entered the room. His clothes hung on him like a shapeless potato sack. Buck teeth dominated his thin face.

Lise froze as she recognized the leering eyes of the skinny deputy she'd seen outside the firearms shop. She shivered and glanced toward her friends from the corner of her eye. Joseph had stepped in front of Susette, shielding her. Lise prayed she had retreated far enough into the shadows to avoid detection.

"That her?" the deputy asked someone behind him. "She don't look like no Indian princess."

"Shut up, Hank." A second man entered, old and balding, with a scaly patch of skin centered atop his head. He shut the warped door, frowned at his partner, then looked at Lise. "Who're you?"

Lise's gaze darted to the Mark Twain book across the room, on the table under her shawl.

Hank ogled her, his mouth gaping. "I don't like Indians what put on airs. We're gonna have to teach this one a lesson, huh, Clem?" He stepped further into the room.

Her skin tingling, Lise fought to stay calm. She shouldn't have come. White women didn't enter such places. Hank would haul her off to jail, she'd be fired from her job, and she'd have to move on again.

Hank licked his lips and approached her.

Lise swallowed as she read the intent on his face. Once that man had her in a cell, she'd be at his mercy. She drew back, panic rising in her throat.

"The white librarian brings her foolish books and tells me the Omaha children need to read them." Joseph stepped forward from the darkened corner of the room, drawing Hank's attention. "Take her away. We have no need for the white man's words."

Taking Joseph's cue, Lise drew a breath and jutted her chin forward. "I am Miss Dupree, the librarian. And you are . . . ?"

"Deputy Clem Jenkins, ma'am," said the second deputy. "Leave her alone, Hank."

Hank glared at his partner, then shifted his attention to Joseph. He sauntered through the room, stopping in front of him. "Where's that Indian princess, chief?"

Joseph's eyes revealed nothing as he stood, silent.

Hank looked at Lise, his gaze roaming over her. "How 'bout you, librarian? You seen her?"

Lise fought to keep from shivering and

stared back at him. "Seen whom?"

"Hold on there, Hank. Let's have us a look-see back by those hides."

Clem moved farther into the room, scanning the cluttered inventory. Hank grabbed Joseph and pulled him along, into the shadows.

Lise's gaze followed, stopping when she saw Clem pointing at Susette's pale pink hair ribbon on the floor next to the pile. *Dear Lord.* Her heart skittered, and she held her breath. She didn't want to think about what Hank would do to her friend.

The trio reached the hides. Joseph wrenched his arm away from Hank and swung at Clem. Hank stumbled against the pile. Pelts slid to the floor, stirring dust as they formed a heap.

Susette crouched behind the hides, cornered.

Hank emitted a long, low whistle and moved over the hides toward her.

Susette. Lise ran to the table, grabbed the Mark Twain book, and threw it at Hank.

Hank jerked in surprise, then stumbled face-first over the remaining pile. His hands clawed at the hides, scattering them.

Susette stood and dodged around the other side of them while Joseph feinted toward Clem.

Clem moved forward, his eyes on Joseph. "Get up, you idiot," he shouted at Hank.

Lise rushed toward Hank and planted her left foot on his back. "Run," she urged Susette.

Clem pulled his gun and closed in on Joseph while Susette scrambled toward the closed door. She pulled on the knob, fighting to get the stuck door open.

Hank shoved himself up, knocking Lise aside. She staggered, then righted herself and stepped into his path. Hank advanced, and she moved with him, mirroring his steps. He lurched to one side, grabbed Lise, and shoved her against the table. She slammed into it. Pain shot through her hip and she bit her lip. The coppery taste of blood filled her mouth.

Hank rushed for the door and caught Susette's wrist. He slung her against the wall and ground against her as his hands skimmed her body. Her dark eyes flashed and she clawed at his face.

"No," Joseph shouted. He lunged toward his daughter, and Clem's muscular grip closed around his arm. They grappled for a moment before Clem raised the gun and cocked it. Joseph drew a breath and stilled. "Don't hurt her."

Lise sprang toward Susette, nausea rising

in her throat as Hank groped her friend.

"Far enough, Miss Librarian," Clem threatened. "You stay out of it and no one gets hurt." He shook his head at Hank. "Take your paws off her and tie her up."

Lise stopped, weighing options and consequences. She didn't like either but continued resistance would only make things worse.

Hank threw a snide glance at his partner, then lifted his roaming hands. He twisted Susette's arm until she turned, then grabbed the other and tied her wrists together. He yanked the door open, shoved her from the room, then turned and leered at Lise. "Unless they've got passes, it looks like the Chief and the Indian Princess here get to spend a night in jail. Plenty of time for gettin' to know her later."

Lise tightened her jaw and drew her shoulders back, anger driving her after the exiting deputy.

Thad Spencer and a small crowd of Indians stood in the store, their stances nervous and edgy as Hank forced Susette through their midst. Julius Meyer shook his head at them, and at Lise.

"Miss Dupree," Joseph called from behind her.

She turned to his authority.

Joseph emerged from the back room, Clem behind him with his gun shoved into Joseph's back. Hatred for the deputy flashed in his dark eyes.

"General Crook can still issue the passes. Go to him. It is in your hands now."

District Attorney Zach Spencer sat behind his desk in the cramped "guest office" provided for him in the Douglas County Courthouse and stared at his younger brother, Thad.

The kid was winded and babbling.

Zach pulled a half-finished peppermint stick from his mouth and ran a hand through his heavy blond hair. "Slow down, Thad. You're not making sense."

"They barged in and took 'em away, Zach." Thad paced the tiny room, then pivoted. "They can't do that, can they?"

Zach exhaled in frustration. Thad's biggest problem in life was that he couldn't leave anybody else's problems alone. He'd wager two bits that Thad had been meddling again. "Who barged in? Where? And who was taken away?"

"The deputies." Thad stared at him as if the matter were clear as spring water. At least he'd stopped pacing. "They muscled their way into the Indian Wigwam and took the La Flesches off to jail."

Joseph La Flesche, the tribal chief at the Omaha Agency, was the only connection that came to mind. But, with Thad, you couldn't make assumptions. "The Omahas?" he asked.

Thad nodded.

"For no reason?" Zach leaned forward and rested his chin on his palm. Making sense out of kids was difficult at best.

"Well . . ." A trace of uncertainty filled Thad's voice.

"Thad?"

Thad shrugged. "They didn't have passes was all."

Zach rubbed his forehead. Indians without passes seemed to be a growing problem in the past week, but it was not unusual. Leave it to Thad to get worked up about it. "They were off the reservation without passes?"

"I guess." Thad shifted feet, his impatience returning.

"Then they broke the law, kid. You break the law, you get arrested. That's the sum of it."

"Does that entitle the officers of the law to make threats of violence?" came an indignant feminine voice from the doorway. "And to take indecent liberties with a woman because she's an Indian?"

24

A slender woman stood in the doorway, her sour tone in striking contrast with her mouth-watering coloring. Sarsaparilla hair hung in loosened strands around a honey-glazed face. Her chocolate eyes simmered.

Zach swallowed and damned his insatiable sweet tooth. It skewed his observations at the most awkward times. He stuck the pep-permint stick back in his mouth and lifted his eyebrows, an attorney trick Gramps had taught him years ago.

She met his gaze and raised her own brow in response.

Zach smiled, appreciating her challenge. He'd never been particularly fond of docile women. Intrigued, he set the candy on the desk and rose. What was she doing follow-ing his little brother around? He gave Thad credit — the kid had good taste. Maybe he could wrangle dinner with her before he went back to Lincoln. He crossed the room and extended his hand. "District Attorney Zachary Spencer, ma'am."

"Head Librarian Lise Dupree." She shook his hand with firmness that matched his own but offered no reciprocal smile. "My question was a serious one, Mr. Spencer."

"And a rhetorical one as well, if I'm not mistaken." When she still didn't smile, he glanced from the gutsy librarian to his younger brother.

Thad fidgeted, showing respect for his elders but clearly ready to burst in at the first chance. Whatever had happened, it seemed to be weighing heavily on both of them.

"Will one of you please explain?" Zach stepped back and gestured to a couple of empty chairs.

Lise Dupree moved into the room, graceful determination in every step. She settled into one of the stiff wooden captain's chairs and leaned forward. "Mr. Spencer, I haven't time to waste."

"I told her she should see you first thing," Thad announced, pride and purpose colliding in his excited voice. "You can have them out in less than an hour, huh?" He plopped onto the arm of the other captain's chair with a self-important air.

"Thad. Quiet." Zach issued a warning stare to his brother.

Thad's shoulders slumped. *Hell.*

Zach tipped his head toward the door. "Why don't you run downstairs to the jail and see what you can dig up? Tell whoever's in charge I sent you."

Thad stood, his chest puffed with importance, and slipped from the room.

Zach turned to Lise. "Tell me what happened."

Her mouth stretched into a thin line and she released a small breath. "Two deputies burst into the Indian Wigwam and arrested Joseph La Flesche and his daughter, Susette."

"Charging them with being off the reservation without passes?"

"Yes."

He'd hoped there was more to it. The mix of anger and worry in the librarian's face told him she had more than a casual interest in the situation. She wasn't going to like what he had to say. "It's cut and dried, Miss Dupree. It's an illegal offense. If caught, violators are arrested and held until the Army returns them to the reservation."

She crossed her arms and leaned back in her chair, staring at him. "I understand the illegality, Mr. Spencer. What course of action is available in regard to the criminal behavior of the deputies?"

Her controlled, indignant tone conveyed a perception of the law he hadn't expected. Disconcerted, his concentration wavered. "Criminal behavior?"

Her lips pursed. "I stood right there and watched that man put his hands on Miss La Flesche, then threaten to take further liberties once she was behind bars. Is there no recourse to prevent that?"

Zach frowned. The thought of the deputy's action sickened him. It was an abuse of power and an insult to the woman. But Miss Dupree was here for legal redress, not his sympathy or moral outrage. He doubted she was going to like this answer much, either. So much for dinner. He sighed.

"The law defines the consequences for those accused of breaking the law. It does not allow for dismissal of charges if the accused feels threatened by officers of the law." He paused, trying to gauge her reaction. Angry and insulted, as he'd expected. He shifted tack. "Should one of the deputies take advantage of Miss La Flesche, it would then be a crime, with legal redress. The law doesn't provide for what 'might' happen."

She stood and glared at him. "What do you mean 'might' happen? He's already taken liberties. I'd say he's already edged over into cruel and unusual punishment."

"Ordinarily, Miss Dupree, you'd be correct." He ran his hand through his hair and wished she didn't know her law so well. "But Miss La Flesche is an Indian. The law defines her differently."

She slammed her hands onto his desk and

leaned forward. "That's poppycock, Mr. Spencer, and you know it. You're talking in circles, avoiding the fact that there's no legal difference between groping an Indian woman and actually ravishing her, just the white perception of the law. All persons have basic rights, Mr. Spencer, all of them."

Zach choked back the threatening wave of empathy. The Law was a strict taskmaster. It made no room for sentiment, made no allowances for the heart.

"Case law has restricted certain persons. Pursuing it would be a waste of time. Indians aren't citizens. They have no legal rights."

Her nostrils flared but she held her temper in check. "But Hank and Clem wouldn't know that, would they?" she asked.

Zach blinked. The unexpected response had thrown him. Damn, her thought process was intriguing. "Hank and Clem?" he asked.

"The two deputies. The threat would be enough to stop them if you delivered it."

He nodded, understanding her strategy. "They'd —"

"Just what we thought," Thad interrupted, bursting in from the hallway. "No passes. They're gonna hold 'em overnight then transport them back to the reservation." He paused only momentarily. "I was thinkin',

29

do you suppose that's what the Army's holding those Poncas for?"

Zach nodded. "Same situation. From what I've heard, they left Indian Territory without permission. They'll be returned."

"But can't you do somethin'?" Thad pleaded. "Take somebody to court or somethin'?"

Zach drew a tired breath. No matter how many times he explained it, Thad seemed to expect him to do the impossible. "Look, Thad, I'm a district attorney. I work for the government. I don't take cases on my own. I don't fix things."

He glanced at Lise Dupree and fought the twinge of compassion she stirred. Compassion was a prosecutor's worst enemy. He searched his memory for the government's standard legal response and drew his mouth into a hard line. "And even if I did, it wouldn't be either of these. Everyone knows Indians are more secure where the government puts them instead of wandering around the country on their own. The law views them as children. They're better off under the government's care."

Her face stiffened, her chocolate eyes turning bitter. "For a lawyer you have an incredibly poor sense of justice."

She turned and walked out, leaving Zach

30

with regret for his harsh words and a resolve
to not involve his heart with the Law.

CHAPTER TWO

Lise reined in her borrowed horse and dismounted. Against the fading light of early evening, a middle-aged, pot-bellied private stood at attention, blocking official access into Fort Omaha's grounds. Lise eyed the huge open spaces around the fort's large parade ground, wondering where the Poncas were being kept, then returned her gaze to the solitary guard.

"State your name and business, ma'am." His tone was efficient, polite, and blessedly non-confrontational.

Lise breathed a sigh and offered the soldier a smile. "I'm Lise Dupree, librarian at the Omaha Public Library. I have a message for General Crook."

The soldier appeared unimpressed. "General Crook is at mess, ma'am. You'll have to wait."

Lise fought to conceal her impatience and stilled her foot from tapping against the cold ground. She'd already wasted enough time arguing with that unyielding blue-eyed district attorney back in town. She needed Crook's military authority to get Susette and Joseph released. Nightfall was approaching and Hank had made his plans for Susette clear. "The message is urgent."

"I'm sure it is, ma'am, and I'd be happy to relay it to him, but I ain't going to usher you into his dining room and interrupt his dinner. You can wait or not, your choice."

She shivered in the cold air. "May I do so in his quarters?"

"Next door, in headquarters, ma'am. Across the parade ground, there."

Lise followed his gesture, noting the solid brick structure as well as the more impressive building beside it, the newly built Crook House. "Thank you, private."

"Lt. Bourke, his aide, will be inside. State your business and he'll relay it to the general as soon as mess is finished."

She nodded and led her horse across the brown stubble of the parade ground. Three Ponca lodges had been erected at one end of the open space. Buried memories flooded her mind. Her uncle had awaited his death sentence inside a similar lodge. This wasn't Minnesota. There was no crowd shouting for revenge. No one was going to hang this time. Still, her heart pounded, urging her to detour toward the lodges and find Aunt Rose.

She swallowed, hard, practicality and sentiment warring. Pressure built behind her eyes. She turned away. Her own desires would have to wait.

But as soon as she got a release order for the La Flesches, she'd find a way to free Aunt Rose. And when she did, she'd throw it in the face of the arrogant, irritatingly handsome district attorney. She wasn't about to be lulled by his slow smile or his Nordic charm. His blind allegiance to "the Law" was the kind of attitude that allowed injustice to continue.

She shifted thoughts to the task at hand, and strode toward the headquarters building. Halfway there, she stalled and gazed at Crook's private residence. In the time it might take for the general to finish his meal, darkness would fall. And with it would come the opportunity for the slimy Hank to slip into the cell and finish his earlier threat to Susette.

Polite waiting would cost time they didn't have. She veered to the right, threw the horse's reins over the hitching rail, marched up the stairs of the Crook House, and pounded on the front door.

34

Inside, footsteps sounded. Another private, dwarfed by the white cotton apron that marked him as an officer's cook, or striker, opened the door. "What the blazes is going on?" he demanded.

"I need to see General Crook. It's urgent."

"General's eating. Wait next door."

She stepped into the entry. "I'll wait here. Tell him I have a message from Joseph La Flesche."

"No sir, ma'am. You wait at headquarters. This here's the general's private quarters."

Lise's impatience swirled into anger. She stepped forward and glared at the soldier. "In the past hour, I have learned a loved one is ill, watched my friends get manhandled and hauled off to jail, been given a mission I didn't want, and have ridden four miserable miles in the wind. You can either tell him I'm here or I'll tell him myself." She moved past him and entered the oak and walnut paneled hallway. "Where's the dining room?"

"Can't let you do that, ma'am." He stepped forward and grasped her elbow. "Let me take you over to headquarters."

Lise struggled and his grip tightened. With surprising strength for his size, he spun her around and shoved her toward the door.

"Private Hodges. Release that woman."

The soldier lowered his head and his hands slid away. "Yes, sir, General Crook, sir."

"You are dismissed."

The private disappeared down the hallway as Lise turned and faced Crook. Heat crept up her neck along with the realization that she'd let her emotions dictate her actions. She hated losing control, especially in the presence of a man as powerful as General Crook. She choked back the embarrassment and raised her eyes.

Crook stood at the end of the hallway, knee-high leather moccasins on his feet. He wore civilian clothing and a ragged brown beard. His expression was stern.

Lise swallowed and met his gaze. "General Crook, sir."

"You've interrupted a fine venison steak. It better be important."

"Joseph La Flesche sent me."

Crook's expression shifted. Concern filled his gray eyes. "Joe? Then this isn't hallway chatter." He glanced toward the dining room. "Come in." He turned and led the way down the elegant hall.

Lise followed, uncertainty jumping in the pit of her stomach. Crook had a reputation for fairness but she hadn't expected his gruff exterior. Clearly, he wasn't a man who

36

stood on formality.

They passed a small table with a bowl of rose hips whose heady fragrance filled the air, complimenting the hand-painted tea roses on the wallpaper. "Mary's roses," Crook explained, turning. "She's back East, picking out dishes to match." He rolled his eyes and moved toward the massive carved walnut table, then glanced back at her again. "You eaten yet?"

The scent of roasted venison and brown gravy rose from the table. Lise's stomach growled. "N . . . no, sir."

"Then sit and help yourself. Might as well tackle two things at once." He pulled out a chair, waited for her to sit, then settled into his own chair. "I've seen you in town. You're Miss Dupree, the librarian. Joe's girl mentioned you. What's going on?"

Lise stifled her remaining discomfort and smoothed her simple wool skirt. "Joseph and Susette were arrested for being off the reservation without passes. Joseph told me to contact you." As Commander of the Army's Department of the Platte, Crook had considerable influence. She frowned, recognizing she should have come to him immediately instead of wasting time pleading with the unsettling district attorney.

"Damn." He chewed for a moment, then

37

bellowed. "Hodges!"

The striker appeared in the doorway, still clad in his apron. He held an extra place setting in his hands. "Sir?"

"Go get Bourke."

The private arranged the china and silverware in front of Lise, then exited the room.

"Eat up, ma'am," Crook advised. "It's going to be a busy evening."

"Yes, sir." Lise lifted a slice of venison from the platter. She cut into it and brought it to her mouth, chewing the gamey meat while she pondered how best to solicit Crook's intervention.

"They hurt them?"

The question caught her off-guard. Lise pushed a tendril of dark brown hair behind her ear and opted for the direct approach. She looked straight at Crook. "They were roughed up and the deputy manhandled Susette. I don't think it will end there."

Crook nodded, understanding in his eyes. "I'll have them out as soon as possible. I respect Joseph La Flesche. One of the finest Indian leaders I've met. Too damn stubborn, though. He should have told me at the start they didn't have passes. Now, I'll have to issue a military order. Messy." He shoved a bite of potatoes into his mouth, swallowed it down, and stared at her. "They have time to talk to you?"

"They did. They told me about Standing Bear's group of Poncas."

"Joe's girl said you know one of them."

"I . . ." she paused and shifted in her chair. She'd gotten Crook's promise to intervene on Susette and Joseph's behalf but she wasn't sure how far he could be trusted with the knowledge of her relationship to Rose.

Crook's gray eyes softened. "It doesn't leave this room."

"My aunt."

"I'll arrange a visit as soon as we're through here. Joe and his girl say anything more?"

"General Crook, I'm not sure we should be discussing these matters. You're holding my Aunt Rose under arrest with Standing Bear." She laid her fork on the table, pushed back her chair, and began to rise. "I've delivered the message. I really should —"

"Sit. Whole thing's complicated, Miss Dupree. Are we clear on nothing leaving this room?" He stared at her, waiting.

She nodded and sat back down, more than a little surprised that he seemed as uncertain as she was. She met his gaze and nodded again.

"You have a stake in this, enough of one

that I'll take that nod as your solemn word." He paused. "I'm a general in the U.S. Army. I follow orders. I don't always like or agree with them. Last week, I was ordered to arrest Standing Bear. Joe confirmed what I heard from Standing Bear. The arrest didn't need to happen. There were fairer ways to handle it."

Lise wrinkled her brow. "There were other options?"

"I think so, yes, but it comes down to orders."

"So they remain here, as prisoners?"

"Right now, I *should* have Standing Bear's band under escort back to Indian Territory. But somebody was in a hurry. The order was to arrest. Only to arrest. Out of respect for what they've been through, I ignored the full intent of the order. But, as soon as Washington figures out the second half of the order wasn't articulated, I'll be marching those desperate people back to that godforsaken hellhole. Until then, they'll remain well-fed and as free from abuse as I can keep them. I figure we have a matter of days, at most."

"Then there's time to fight the orders?"

"Not much. We need a plan and someone to head it up. Tom Tibbles, over at the *Omaha Herald,* would be a good start. I'll take care of freeing Joe and his girl, then schedule a meeting with Tibbles. We'll send word to you, later tonight, as soon as it's set." He looked across the table and held her gaze. "We'll need you, too."

Lise stared back at him and the knot in her stomach tightened into a hard lump. "Me?"

"Joe's daughter said you know law. She said you could dig up something in those law books of yours that might buy more time. Unless we do, those Poncas will be on their way back to Indian Territory, your aunt included."

The lump in her stomach churned. How in the Sam Hill was she going to find a way to fight the U.S. Army without losing her career in the process?

A half-hour later, Lise crossed Fort Omaha's parade ground and neared the small encampment of Indian lodges beyond the south end. They were arranged as Crook's aide had described. Her heart pounding, she neared the one he had indicated, pushed aside the heavy buffalo robe, then entered the darkened lodge. She paused, waiting to be acknowledged. The smoky smell of sage lingered in the air.

She breathed it in, the scent evoking bits

41

of her childhood before the uprising. She'd nearly forgotten how sage smoke wrapped its way around a person. She let the unexpected comfort surround her as she thought about what she would do. If she could talk Aunt Rose into leaving the Poncas and returning to the Sioux Reservation alone, there would be no reason to get involved in fighting Standing Bear's battle.

"Come in, child." The kind female voice crackled with age.

Lise gazed at the unfamiliar old woman. She sat to the right, a young man at her side. Her wrinkled hands adjusted a worn blue and yellow blanket over a sleeping form. Lise's heart skipped a beat. Aunt Rose lay beneath the blanket, thin and pale, so much older than Lise remembered her.

"You are so like her. Come." The woman beckoned with a tired gesture. "I am Naomi. And this is Albert."

Lise smiled at the woman Aunt Rose had often mentioned as a friend in her hesitant, misspelled letters, then at Albert, Rose's stepson. Moving with soft steps, Lise circled the warm fire and neared her aunt. She knelt beside her. "She looks so weak."

Albert grunted. "We are all weary."

"It is why we stopped to rest with the Omaha. Too much hunger and sickness in

42

the cold." Tears welled in Naomi's tired ebony eyes.

"Damned Army has moved us around for four years. We can move no more." Albert's voice was filled with hatred.

Lise's chest tightened. She'd felt the same way when the Army had hung her uncle and banished Aunt Rose and her son. She nodded in agreement at Albert, then turned back to Rose. "Can we wake her?"

"She will waken, but . . ." Naomi shifted and glanced at Albert.

"The fever has taken her mind," he said. "She no longer knows any of us."

A tear crept into Lise's eye. She reached out to touch Rose's sleeping form. She stroked a lock of graying hair from her aunt's face, hair she had once delighted in braiding. Her hand brushed a small sloppily beaded pendant that hung from Rose's neck. Lise choked back a gasp. The bright blue and red of the beads had not faded, not in all the years since Lise had made it. The tear slid down her face.

Naomi patted Lise's hand. "She talked of you all the time."

"I never went to visit." Regret stung her.

"Rose chose the Indian way. Your mother chose the path of her white husband. Rose understood that."

Albert glanced up. "At least you had a choice. The Poncas are pawns of the white man. We were peaceful farmers, living in houses like the white man wanted until they sent us away."

Naomi nodded. "One by one, the elders have died. Rose is one of the few left. She was so proud of her house. Albert was a good provider. They did not even let him bring his tools."

Lise frowned. "But, why?"

"The government made a mistake." Albert expelled a heavy breath and stood. "At Fort Laramie, they gave the Santee Sioux land that they had already given the Poncas. No one would listen when the tribes tried to tell them."

"When Rose came to Ponca land, she was my enemy, one more Sioux to take away our land." Sadness, then acceptance, showed in Naomi's face. "Then our sons suffered together. Our spirits shared pain and gave each other strength."

Aunt Rose had written much the same thing about Naomi. A half-smile pulled at Lise's mouth. "I'm honored to meet my aunt's good friend. And my cousin Albert. She sent me many letters about you and all you have done for her."

Naomi smiled back and took Lise's hands

in her bony, gnarled fingers. "I am honored the Great Spirit has put us in each other's paths this day. Rose would say it is a special sign that you are here in this place where we have come to rest. In time, we will all know the reason for this good fortune."

Albert paced the lodge. "We've come to rest because we have been arrested. We should have kept going."

"We want only to return to the home of our ancestors," Naomi said, her huge eyes full of a lifetime of sorrow. "Is that so wrong?"

"No, Grandmother," Lise said, using the traditional title of respect. "It is not wrong." She glanced at Naomi, then Albert, unsure of how much they really knew about their situation. "You know the Army will not allow that?"

Albert nodded. "Standing Bear will bury his son along the Niobrara. Then, we will return to live here, among our Omaha cousins."

"They intend to send you back to Indian Territory. Another long march." She eyed Albert. Indian Territory lay south of Kansas, nearly four hundred miles away while the Niobrara River, Rose's home, was just over a hundred miles north. "They would not force Rose," she said. "They would allow

45

her to return to the Santee."

"No." Vehemence filled her cousin's voice and his face hardened.

"I've thought it through. I could get her released. She could go home."

He shook his head. "She is Ponca now, my mother. My father willed this, when he took her as his wife. There is no one among the Santee to care for her — not since the Great Spirit took her own son. I will not send my mother to strangers. Who would care for her? Feed her? Bathe her? She has no one there."

Lise touched her aunt's face. She had forgotten this custom. The Great Spirit had linked Rose's destiny to the Ponca tribe. She drew a breath, then released it. "She will not survive a forced march."

Albert approached and touched Lise's shoulder. "Cousin, look at her. Her body lingers but her mind is gone. I will not leave her."

Next to them, Rose shifted. She opened her eyes and smiled blankly at Lise, then at Albert. "Oh, good," she said in Lakota, her voice full of throaty cackles. "Gooseberries."

Lise's throat constricted as she realized the truth in Albert's words. Tears slid down her face. She let them fall. *Let yourself weep only once.* Aunt Rose's words filled her mind. *There is no room for tears, my child. The Great Spirit has other plans for us.*

Crook had made it clear he'd schedule a meeting soon. There was much to do if she was to have a suggestion to secure the release of the whole Ponca band. It was now the only way Aunt Rose would ever return to the Niobrara and the gooseberry bushes she loved.

Zach Spencer eyed the fresh-baked cake on his mother's cherrywood breakfront and tried to figure out the best way to learn more about Lise Dupree without sending Thad off on a tangent about Indians. Ever since he'd walked in the door and smelled the chocolate, he hadn't been able to get his thoughts off the dark-eyed librarian.

The floor of Abigail Spencer's modest dining room squeaked and Zach winced. He'd remained at the office long enough to avoid coming home in time to feed Gramps, telling himself he needed to finish reading an important legal brief. Ma didn't need to find him lingering with nothing to do.

Thad's voice, with its steady stream of encouragement, drifted from the bedroom down the hall. The kid was good with the old man, that was for sure.

Zach moved away from the sound and

stepped into the kitchen. Ma thrust a platter of chicken into his hands and nodded toward the dining room. They paraded out, the steaming foods offering comforting smells along the way, and Zach took his customary seat at the polished table. Faded scratches gave testimony to the long life of the table and brought a smile to Zach's face.

Ma caught his expression as she sat next to him. "You made that one," she chided.

"Didn't mean to," Zach offered.

Ma shook her head. "No. You boys were handful enough without even intending." She smiled back at him.

Thad plopped into the chair next to Zach, grabbed a plate, and piled it full of crispy fried chicken and steaming sweet potatoes. "Gramps ate good, Ma. Always does when you fix sweet potatoes."

She nodded at her younger son. "Thank you for feeding him. It means a lot to him when you boys spend time with him." She stared across the table, catching Zach's gaze.

Zach shifted in his chair. He knew what she meant with that look. But damn it all, it hurt to sit there and watch saliva dribble from the sagging corner of Gramps's mouth.

"You hear me, Zach?"

"Yes, ma'am." Guilt prickled at him. "I'll take him in some cake for dessert." Maybe

48

tonight would be a rare good night, one when Gramps's cloudy blue eyes would light with shared memories instead of frustration and anger over his debilitated condition and that his body no longer responded to commands from his still-active mind.

Ma smiled. "He loves you, Zach. You're his pride and joy and it tears him up that he can't sit and talk law with you anymore."

"I know, Ma. I promise I'll spend some time with him before I head back to Lincoln." He'd squeeze it in before his meeting with retiring Senator Adam Foster. Last month, Foster had offered to back Zach as his replacement. Maybe Gramps would perk up if they talked about the campaign. He'd wanted Zach to run for office, to follow in his footsteps as a senator as well as an attorney.

"Good intentions do not make good deeds unless they're carried out."

"I know, Ma." He leaned over to Thad and nudged him in the ribs. "You paying attention, kid? Learn early or she'll be nagging at you when you're twenty-eight, too."

Ma rolled her eyes. "Age and maturity are not the same thing."

"They should have made Omaha the capital," Thad said. "That way, you wouldn't

49

have to go back and forth to Lincoln."

Zach ruffled his brother's hair, thankful he'd changed the subject. "Maybe we can ask the legislature to change it."

"Don't be ornery, boys."

It was as good a time as any, Zach guessed, to see what Thad knew. "Thad tell you about the fuss this afternoon?"

"About the Indians?" Abigail drew a heavy breath. "It was all he could talk about."

Thad's eyes gleamed, a sign the kid was about to latch onto the subject again. He licked his greasy fingers, readying himself.

"Thaddeus Spencer, you use your napkin!"

"See what happens when you don't mind your manners?" Zach winked at his mother, made a show of using his own napkin, and grinned. "Well, kid, since we've both heard all about the Indians, why don't you tell us about the librarian?"

"What about her?"

Abigail arched her eyebrows. "Yes, what about her?"

"You know her well?"

Thad shrugged. "She's pretty nice."

"Has she been at the library long?" Zach prompted.

"A few months. Why?"

"It's been awhile since I've had cause to

50

visit the library here. She doesn't seem much like a librarian."

Thad's brow wrinkled. "She wears glasses," he finally said.

Zach tried to picture her chocolate eyes framed by glass, like the mouth-watering candies in the display case at the Douglas Street Confectionary.

"Zach? You all right?"

"Sure, kid. I guess it's that the librarians I know are all quiet and mousy."

"Not Miss Dupree. She's smart and she knows what everybody likes to read. She treats me like a grown-up."

Ma sighed and set down her fork. "She's a bit forward-thinking from what I've heard." She dabbed her mouth with her napkin and smiled at him. "She's been working with Andrew Poppleton to set up a law section in the library, and she's talked him into moving his own collection over there. I think she'd rather be a lawyer than a librarian."

Zach grinned. "Been gossiping, Ma?"

"Just keeping my ear to the ground."

His interest sparked, Zach fished for another question, one that wouldn't encourage the wheels that were likely spinning in Ma's head.

"You see her around much, besides the

library?"

"She goes to city council meetings," Thad supplied. "I heard old man Barnes complaining about it at church."

"Don't be disrespectful, Thaddeus," Ma said.

A sharp knock interrupted any further discussion. Zach glanced at his mother. "Expecting someone?"

She shook her head, rose, and left the room to answer the door.

Zach glanced at his brother. "She'll be mad as a wet hen if that's some pal of yours."

"I know the rules. I ain't stupid."

"I know, kid."

"Zachary." Abigail stood in the doorway, frowning. "The caller is for you. He said it was business. Be brief."

Zach bit back resentment as he rose and stepped into his mother's parlor. Being disturbed at supper didn't make him receptive to whatever his visitor had to say. He should have waited until Monday.

Indian Agent Rufus Christy stood at the window, spiffed up some in a brown wool suit, but rough all the same. The smile on his face as he peered out the glass at the lingering neighborhood children seemed incongruous with all Zach had heard about him. The agent clenched a wrinkled hat in his hands, worrying it back and forth.

Zach shook his head and cleared his throat.

Christy turned, his smile fading behind an artificial, businesslike expression. "So sorry to bother you, Mr. Spencer, in your own home. Or, I guess, in your mother's home." He expelled a short laugh.

"Yet, you have." Zach paused, letting the silence work. It wasn't so much that he cared whether or not folks dropped by. He'd learned a long time ago that business had to be kept separate from the rest of his life. And Rufus Christy wasn't here as a friend. That much he knew. So, it was business. Which meant it belonged at the office. "I don't mean to be rude, Mr. Christy, but couldn't this wait —"

"It's . . . well, I heard you was leavin' for Lincoln again and I didn't want to miss you, you being in Omaha only once a month."

Zach's patience thinned. "What is it, then?" He motioned to a chair.

Christy sat and drew a breath. "I figured I ought to talk to you about them Indians."

Zach settled into a chair and crossed his legs, then leaned back and stared at Christy, the way Gramps had taught him. *Never let 'em see anything but power, boy.* He tipped

53

his head slightly and smiled. "I thought 'them Indians' were your department, Mr. Christy."

"Well, Mr. Spencer, in fact, they are." Christy shifted in the chair. "But, as one government official to another, sometimes we gotta get our hands messy if we're gonna handle business."

Messy hands didn't mesh well with senate campaigns. Zach looked at Christy, wondering what the little man had up his sleeve. Tired of the game, he sighed. "Why don't you just tell me why you're here, Mr. Christy."

"Them Poncas, the ones what are runnin' all over the place. Old Crook ain't escortin' them back where they belong. I wanna know what the district attorney can do about it."

The Poncas. What was it with folks and Indians lately? Zach's mind shifted to Miss Dupree . . . he'd rather debate the issue with her than Christy.

"Isn't that an Army matter, Mr. Christy?" This was a hot potato he didn't want.

"Crook ain't followin' orders."

"Then I suggest you wire his superior officer."

"Them Indians are causin' a disturbance in this city. They could be ordered removed.

It took me months to get them hauled to Indian Territory where they belong. They ought to be put back there."

"Those Indians are on Army land, Mr. Christy. Fort Omaha is not part of the city."

"They're causin' laws to be broke. The Omahas are driftin' down from their reservation without passes and causin' problems. Several of 'em were arrested."

"So I've heard. And I also heard they were issued passes by General Crook, albeit after-the-fact. Something about his aide forgetting to return them when they left the fort."

"Crook shouldn't be stickin' his nose into it. Indian agents issue passes, not generals, and you know it."

Christy was mostly right, but Zach didn't care for his attitude. The man had a reputation for grabbing power wherever he could find it. Though Army officers didn't normally get involved in these issues, Zach was aware that they had the authority to do so. He suspected Christy knew it, too. The agent wasn't as ignorant as he pretended to be.

Zach leaned forward. He wasn't sure what Christy was up to, and it'd take a lot more time to argue the issue than he had the patience for at the moment. Besides, this wasn't something he needed to get involved with.

"Mr. Christy, it makes no difference. No laws have been broken. My hands are tied." He stood. "Now if you'll excuse me, my supper is getting cold."

Christy pondered a moment, then rose. "What if there was laws bein' broke? What if some of them redskins got out and made their way into town, causin' trouble? Seems to me that could be a threat and that you ought to take action to force Crook to move them savages."

"It's not a civil issue, Mr. Christy. If it were, my office would take the necessary action to see that laws are obeyed. In the meantime, if you have a problem with Crook's actions, I suggest you contact his superior officer."

Christy nodded. "Then I guess I'd best be on my way, Mr. Spencer. I got a telegram to attend to."

CHAPTER THREE

Images of Aunt Rose's empty gaze and toothless smile haunted Lise as she walked through Omaha's dark, deserted streets.

Beside her, former mayor Andrew Poppleton pulled his greatcoat tight around him. "There aren't many young ladies who could coax me out of my warm house at midnight on a Saturday night."

"I know, Mr. Poppleton. And I appreciate you coming." The soles of her shoes crunched on the frozen ground as she kept pace with him. As the major benefactor of the law library, he'd spent many hours overseeing Lise's work and had become a friend in the process. She hoped she could convince him to help develop a plan to free Aunt Rose and her companions. One that didn't include Lise risking the secret of her identity.

"And this was Crook's idea?" he asked.

"Well, sort of." Lise glanced at the balding attorney. She shrugged her shoulders. "The meeting was Crook's idea. I suggested you could help. With his approval, of course."

"Crook and Indians, you said. I guess that explains the urgency, though I'm not sure I appreciate clandestine midnight meetings. Ah, Tibbles has the lamp on."

Lise looked ahead to the offices of the *Omaha Herald* and noted the weak light shining from the second story window. They neared the building and Poppleton pulled open the door, wincing as it creaked. Lise smothered a smile. Although fussy and proper at times, Poppleton would be the perfect person to pursue a case on behalf of the Poncas. She hoped her idea had enough merit to tempt him to accept the case.

Thomas Tibbles stepped down the stairs with cat-like quiet and nodded to them. "Come on in. We're upstairs. Brrr, it's a chilly night. It's a wonder you two aren't frozen."

Lise's spectacles steamed and she pulled them off as she and Poppleton followed the editor up the narrow staircase. The heavy scent of printer's ink lingered in the darkness. Somewhere in the building, a lone press thudded in a steady rhythm. They turned down a bare hallway and entered a small dim office.

General Crook stood near a scarred wooden desk, tamping a pipe. Seeing them, he lifted it in salute.

Lise crossed to the general, her heels clacking on the worn floor. "They're free?" she asked.

"And safe. Deputies didn't like seeing those military passes. The skinny one tried to argue but the sheriff shut him up."

"They didn't —"

"Didn't harm a hair on her head. They're at the fort. Thought it best they stay out of town for a while."

Lise released a breath and hooked her glasses back onto her ears. Becoming aware of the other curious gazes, she mouthed a "thank you" to Crook and slipped into a straight-backed chair.

Crook nodded to the attorney behind her. "Andrew. Good to see you. Miss Dupree is a resourceful woman."

Poppleton crossed the room and shook Crook's hand. "I didn't expect you to be here in person. It explains the late-night tromp."

Crook looked at each of them, his face serious. "No one can ever know I was here."

If Lise's plan was accepted, Crook would never meet with the group again. As the officer holding the Poncas under military arrest, he shouldn't be with them, planning to secure the band's release. That he would risk exposure and court martial said much about the man's sense of justice and his honor. His reputation of fairness in dealing with Indians was clearly well-earned.

Tom Tibbles closed the door and approached the group. "I think we all realize the delicate nature of your involvement, General. And respect it." He waited for agreement, then sat behind his desk. "Shall we explore our strategy?"

Poppleton cleared his throat. "Miss Dupree tells me this is about the Poncas you're holding up at the fort. Peaceful tribe, if I've got my details right?" He selected a vacant chair and sat.

Lise nodded. "They're related to the Omaha, sir, but lived on a reservation with the Santee Sioux along the Niobrara River, near Dakota Territory."

Crook leaned forward. "You also heard of Rufus Christy?" He spat the name out. "Indian agent. A damned poor one. Four years ago, the murdering coward got a bug in his butt and moved the Poncas. Some kind of personal vendetta."

Poppleton knitted his brows. "I understood the removal was related to treaty issues."

"Christy claimed the Poncas were illegally on Sioux land and should be relocated," Tibbles explained. "Standing Bear and a party went down to Indian Territory but decided they didn't like the lands Christy showed them."

Crook slammed his fist against the editor's desk. "The son of a —" seeing Lise, he cleared his throat. "Beg pardon, ma'am, but the damned idiot refused to bring them back."

Lise smiled at his vehemence, then turned to Poppleton. "They walked home. All the way back to the Niobrara."

Tibbles shifted in his chair. "Before long, Christy's got the commissioner's ear and the Army's involved. They marched those poor people down there again, with no supplies, and left them there with nothing."

Resentment clawed at Lise. "They suffered from pneumonia and fevers." High fevers that left sweet old women lost among the gooseberries in their minds. "They lost about a third of the tribe."

"Christy said he couldn't get them medicine. Most likely, he didn't even try." Crook paused, his jaw twitching. "He's an ignorant coot. Claims he wants to civilize the Indians but there seems to be more to it."

"Christy followed them up here," Tibbles said, "then sent word to Washington."

"Next thing you know, I get orders to arrest those poor, tired people." Crook shook his head in distaste, his brow wrinkled with private thoughts. "The orders were incomplete. I told Miss Dupree she has precious little time to poke around them law books and figure out a way to stall Christy's plans."

Lise glanced at the lawyer. "Mr. Poppleton, we need an attorney."

"Yes, I can see that you do."

Tibbles sat behind his desk, cleaning his glasses. "Andrew, the simple fact is that we need you. You've got clout. You're a founding father of both Omaha and Nebraska, with a distinguished legal and political career."

"And a very demanding current position. Or have you forgotten my responsibilities at the Union Pacific?"

"It shouldn't take too much of your time. Wouldn't we just need to clarify the lands guaranteed under the treaty?"

Poppleton drew a breath and looked at Lise. "Are you familiar with treaty law?"

"Constitutional law, sir, and some case law."

"You won't find the details of treaties in

case law books. We'd need to order copies of the Ponca treaties from the Commissioner of Indian Affairs. I think there are four. Then there are the Sioux treaties, as well. We'd have to dig through all of them to find a way to fight Christy's claims."

"What if we found another attorney to assist you?" she asked.

Poppleton shook his head. "It's useless, my dear."

"But —"

"It's not just the research time. I suspect all those copies of treaties being ordered by an attorney in Omaha would be enough to tip the commissioner off. Even if we did find a loophole that would allow us to petition for overturning one of them, the commissioner would throw a political wrench in it before we could even get the case prepared. Once the government sends those people back to Indian Territory, there won't be enough of them left to fight."

Silence settled over the group while Lise and Poppleton stared at one another. Despite Poppleton's awareness of her interest in law, Lise had expected this argument. In fact, she'd considered the point herself earlier, when she'd sat in the library amid a pile of books. "Then we take a different angle."

Poppleton raised his eyebrows again. "Such as?"

"The arrest itself."

"Were your orders issued properly, General?" He glanced at Crook.

Crook nodded. "I'm afraid they were."

Lise's mind drifted to her meeting earlier with Zach Spencer. Forcing away the image of the district attorney's pale blue eyes, she concentrated instead on what he had said. Susette and Joseph could be held because they had been charged with breaking a specific law. "Did the order to arrest the Poncas mention specific charges?"

"No." Crook's stern visage softened with curiosity. "But they left Indian Territory without passes."

"Did they *need* passes?"

Lise glanced at Poppleton and waited. His gray eyes glittered and he motioned for her to continue.

"Two issues," she began. "First, was the order to live in Indian Territory legal in the first place? Second, if they haven't been charged with a crime, can they be detained?"

Poppleton chuckled. "Good heavens, my dear! It's so simple I didn't see it. A writ of *habeas corpus.*"

Lise nodded.

"Which is?" Crook asked.

Tibbles stood, excitement filling his face. He paced behind his desk. "One of the basic rights we have in this country is that *no one* can be imprisoned without being charged with a crime."

"We sue for a writ, a document, that explains exactly what crime the Ponca have been accused of committing. They can't hold them if there was no crime," Lise explained. "If there was a crime, we demand a trial to establish their guilt or innocence."

Poppleton stroked his chin. "Filing for the writ will be fairly easy. If it's granted, the government will challenge and we'll go to trial. I'm not sure how the government will approach the challenge so we'll need to come up with an argument for the charge. They'll likely focus on them being off the reservation. I don't have the time for that, not with my duties at the U.P."

"If we find another attorney, will you be co-counsel?"

"We'll need someone willing to put in the time, for free, and risk his reputation. Representing Indians against the U.S. government is not going to win any votes, not unless we work damn hard to change public opinion. Not with Custer's massacre still recent enough to make folks' skin crawl."

"What if Mr. Tibbles works on changing public opinion?"

"I'm not sure —" Tibbles began.

"Susette La Flesche could help you," Lise said. "The articles she wrote for the *Herald* about reservation life were well received, weren't they?"

"Well, yes. As a matter of fact, we had a very good response. She does have a way with a pen." Tibbles's eyes lit, as Lise had suspected they would. "And Joseph La Flesche's good name will stand us well. Local folks respect his tribal leadership. If Miss La Flesche will assist, I'd be willing to take on the task. In the right hands, we could make it work."

Lise smiled. Susette had spoken well of Tibbles. In fact, his sense of fairness had sparked her friend's admiration.

Poppleton cleared his throat, drawing their attention. "If we file for a writ, will Standing Bear be willing to have his name on the suit? Will he be a good candidate to represent his people?"

Crook nodded. "The man has integrity. He'll do it."

"So, we sue the government?" Lise glanced at the others.

"We sue the government's representative. In this case, the person who is illegally detaining the Poncas." Poppleton's gaze settled on his friend. "We sue George Crook."

Crook's eyes were solemn. "That's the only way to handle it?"

"It is."

"Then this will be my last meeting with you."

Tibbles placed his hands on his hips and beamed at them. "Now, all we need to do is locate co-counsel."

"If we can find someone to do the research, I believe I can talk John Webster into joining us," Poppleton said.

Tibbles glanced at Lise. "What about you? With Webster on the treaties, we'll still need someone working on the case law? Can you do the legwork?"

Lise sighed. Researching the idea had been personal, a way to help free Aunt Rose without becoming too involved. The more closely she was associated with actual legal action, the more likely it was that someone would discover her heritage. From there, it would be a matter of days before she lost her job and all she'd worked for.

She glanced at the editor, then at Poppleton and Crook.

"A wonderful idea, Tom," Poppleton said. "I should have thought of it myself. If Miss Dupree will agree, so will I."

"And I," said Tibbles.

A spark of tender understanding filled Crook's eyes. "And I." He smiled and drew a breath. "Seeking justice is a risk. For some of us more than others." He stared at Lise.

She glanced at the general and swallowed, knowing what he meant, and that she had no choice.

Late Monday morning, Zach stuffed the last few folders into his leather case and glanced around his office in case he'd forgotten anything. Seeing a few scattered papers, he unbuckled the straps of his case and rose from his chair. This afternoon, he had a meeting in Lincoln with three of the state's most influential men about backing his candidacy. He had a half-hour to get to the train station.

His office door opened and Senator Adam Foster peered around it. "There you are. Good news. Ezra Millard's agreed to speak to his board of directors on your behalf."

Zach set the papers down and smiled. Millard was head of the Omaha National Bank and was known for his substantial support of select candidates. His contribution would set an example other businessmen would be likely to follow. "And in return?"

"And in return, you simply legislate justly. With an eye toward a good business climate, of course."

"Of course."

"Look, Zach, these pledges of support, they're just formalities. You understand that, don't you? You're my hand-picked successor, just like you were for district attorney."

"I don't like to take that for granted, Adam. Nothing's guaranteed."

"Well, this pretty much is, my boy. As long as you keep your nose clean, the senate seat — your granddaddy's seat — will be yours."

"Right now, the only seat on my mind is waiting on the Union Pacific's twelve-ten."

"You need me there for the meeting?"

"Nah. You've laid enough groundwork. I'll be fine."

"Excuse me, Mr. Spencer, Senator Foster." The clerk of court stood in the doorway. "I thought you might want to see this before you left." He slipped into the room and thrust a thin envelope into Zach's hands. "Just filed, sir." He turned and exited without a sound.

"I'll read it on the train. Time's marching."

"Here. Gather up your things. I'll open it

69

up for you." Zach tucked the last few papers into his case while Foster unwound the string from the envelope's closure and slid the contents out. He handed them to Zach.

Zach opened the papers and scanned them, intending to tuck them into the case if they required his attention before he returned to Omaha. Halfway down the page, he paused. "Well, I'll be —"

"What is it?"

"Some Indian just filed for a writ of *habeas corpus.*"

Foster raised his thin eyebrows. "A writ? An Indian?"

"Standing Bear is suing the U.S. government for his immediate release. What the hell?" Zach sighed, exasperated. It was a cut-and-dried case but it pricked at him. From all Thad had said, the Poncas were just victims of the way the government conducted its business. Law or no law, he didn't relish being the one to enforce it.

"An Indian? They haven't any standing." Foster grabbed the papers and scanned them.

"It'll get tossed out," Zach said. If he was lucky, it'd never make trial. "But not until I make a case to do so and a district court judge officially dismisses it. In the meantime, it'll tie up my time and energy."

The senator shook his head. "I'll wire Lincoln, reschedule the meeting. Pressing legal matters."

"Not that pressing, for pity's sake. I'll plan on coming back next month as usual. I can handle the trial preparations from Lincoln."

"You can, but you need to do it here. Why waste the good exposure?" Foster set the papers on the desk and chewed on his bottom lip for a moment, then paced the room. "It's an opportunity, boy," he said. "I've heard murmurings all over town about those damn Indians. We'll build on it, get you some press coverage, drum up your willingness to defend the law, show the public you won't stand for any shilly-shallying." He smiled and nodded with conviction. "If folks don't know your name now, they will when you send that savage back to where he belongs."

Zach stared at Foster and swallowed. "That's what I'm afraid of."

Lise closed the cover to the heavy book on constitutional law and plunked her elbows on the table. Monday's late morning sun shone through the high library windows. Squinting, she set her chin on her palms and sighed.

"Tired?" Susette asked from the doorway.

Lise turned and gave her friend a smile. Susette was the first close friend she'd had since her boarding school days with Miriam and Sarah, and she was the only person in Omaha aware of Lise's parentage. Though full-blooded Indian, Susette had been well-educated and shared Lise's determination to use her skills to help her people.

"My eyes feel like they're about to fall out of my head." Lise told her. She pulled her glasses off and rubbed her temples. "I've cited every case in here that has anything to do with *habeas corpus.*" She glanced at her crisp notes. She had only one more thing to do before the government responded — persuade Susette to help with Tibbles's newspaper campaign.

Susette approached, her footfalls a quiet padding in the stillness of the empty room. Her plain green skirt swayed with understated grace. Pulling out a wooden chair, she sat next to Lise and folded her hands in her lap. "General Crook gave me a new pass and your message. I'm not sure I understand."

"He told you about the writ?"

Susette nodded. "And about Mr. Poppleton and Mr. Tibbles. But he also told me you needed me to come back to Omaha instead of going home to the reservation."

Lise tucked an errant brown tendril behind her ear and drew a breath. With Susette, the direct approach was usually best. "We need your help," she said.

"My help?" The corners of Susette's mouth lifted in amusement. "You have already wasted time repairing problems I have made. I don't think I would be of much *help*. Besides, I have a schoolroom full of children waiting for their teacher."

"They'll understand. And I suspect they won't mind missing class for a few days." Lise grinned at her friend.

Susette shook her head. "I need to return home. I know nothing about law. I've told you and you have secured Mr. Poppleton. There's nothing more for me to do."

Lise had expected this sort of answer. Though self-confident, Susette had little concept of her own abilities beyond teaching. And this was an opportunity her friend needed to seize. "Your sister can take your classes. Tom Tibbles needs you."

"T . . . Tom?" Color rose in Susette's cheeks and she turned away.

"He plans to launch a campaign in the newspaper," Lise explained. "He needs a good writer to help. He wants you."

Susette's head whirled as she faced Lise again. "Me? Why?"

"He already knows you can write. You know how to reach people. Your articles about the school on the reservation received positive response from the *Herald*'s readers."

"He was kind to let me write them. Most white men would not have done so."

Lise touched her friend's arm. "He needs someone who knows the Poncas, someone who can write from their perspective, someone who can interview Standing Bear in his own language."

"Standing Bear has an interpreter. Mr. Tibbles will manage well without me."

"Mr. Tibbles has an entire newspaper to run, Susette. He can't focus entirely on Standing Bear. He needs help." She drew back, secure that she had Susette's attention. "You know how important public opinion is. Do you think there's any chance the Poncas will be released if the public is against it?"

"But if the law says —"

"The law isn't as pure as it appears. Interpreted, it gets colored by witnesses and public officials, and the people on the street. You know that. You have a Nebraska teaching certificate that is useless to you in white schools, even though the law says you are qualified."

Susette stood and paced the room. "You're right. And Tom . . . Mr. Tibbles . . . is a good man. I will work with him."

"Good. He's started on things already. There was an editorial in this morning's edition of the *Herald.*" She studied her friend with deliberation, wondering if she should mention Tibbles's obvious interest in her. She shook the thought away. Tibbles was a white man, a professional white man. Susette was full-blooded Indian. Such interest only led down one avenue, and it wasn't one Lise should encourage.

"The men have been busy," Lise said. She straightened her stack of notes into a neat pile and smiled at Susette.

"I saw Poppleton go into the courthouse earlier."

"He was probably filing the writ." Lise opened the small watch she wore pinned on her bodice and pulled on the delicate chain until she could see the clock face. "He said he would do it before noon today."

"What happens next?"

"Poppleton and Webster prepare the case and present it. You and Tibbles reach the public. The case goes to trial." She shrugged her shoulders.

"And what about you?" Susette asked quietly.

"I wish Aunt Rose a safe and happy journey back to the gooseberry bushes along the Niobrara."

"Just like that?" Susette leaned forward. "It's that easy?"

Lise lifted her gaze. "Barring any legal complications, it will be."

"But you will research more if it is not?" Susette's dark eyes were dead serious.

Lise patted the stack of notes. "More than this? I'm sure the attorneys can take it from here."

"But if we need you, will you help us again?"

"I can research more if needed. Anything else, you know I can't be involved in."

Susette straightened and shook her head. "Can't or won't?"

"Both." Lise slammed the notes into a drawer, stood, and walked across the room, evading Susette's probing eyes. Her friend Sarah had been much the same, pushing issues easier left alone. She didn't know what Susette was so worried about, anyway. The research was done. She'd been thorough. There was nothing more to do.

Susette still stood at the main desk. "So you're telling me," she said in a muted tone, "that what happens now to the Poncas is not as important."

Anger rushed through Lise and she pivoted sharply. Susette's grandmother had been Ponca, and she couldn't let her friend think her reluctance was about indifference. "That's not true and you know it."

"What I know is that you are ashamed of who you are."

"Don't you dare say that." Tears stung Lise's eyes and she forced herself to remain calm. Susette had tried to discuss this with her before. Out of habit, Lise glanced around the room, then remembered it was empty. She moved toward her friend, her jaw clenched. "You don't know what it was like."

Susette's expression softened. "I am Indian. I know what it's like."

Lise closed her eyes, seeking the words. She drew a breath and looked at her friend. "At least the Omaha are seen as peaceful."

"We're still Indian. Tell me how much a woman like you knows about reservation poverty and always being second class. You don't even live the truth."

Lise stared at Susette, knowing she should have told her friend the full story a long time ago. She needed to make her understand that keeping the secret was not due to shame.

"My mother was half Sioux and she left

77

the reservation when she was old enough," she began. "But her half-brothers and half-sisters remained there. Their children starved while they waited for annuities that never came." Her voice flat, Lise stared at the rows of bookshelves that lined the far wall. "After the uprising, they lynched my uncle because he was a reservation Indian. Townspeople burned my parents' store, even though they had saved white lives. Twice after that, my father was driven out of business and my mother said we must never again speak of her family. Doing so meant being shunned, being driven away with nothing. I couldn't even acknowledge people I loved."

She shivered and bit her lip, then swallowed. All these years, she'd told this story only to Miriam and Sarah. Her heart ached at the memory of the treasures her mother had buried deep in the bottom of a worn wooden trunk — soft doeskin dresses and moccasins, her grandmother's beadwork, a broken coup-stick. She turned and faced Susette again, her jaw tight to keep it from trembling.

"Don't you see? If anyone knew I was part Sioux, they wouldn't let me keep working in their library with their children. I was 'let go' from my position in Spirit Lake because

I tried to live both lives, just as Mother warned I would be. I love my job, shaping young minds. And I love creating this law library so justice has a chance." Her voice leveled. "But I need the job, too. It's the only support my mother has since my father died. This is the only way open to me."

At the desk, Susette's dark eyes were sure and steady. "I understand fear. I've known it, too, though for other reasons." She crossed to Lise and touched her cheek. "But I also understand that it's not good to bury who you are. We do not always choose our own paths." She dropped her hand and held Lise's gaze. "We may need you again. Will you help us?"

Lise lifted the corners of her mouth in a small smile. "All right. There's no reason I can't give Poppleton the support he needs. It's just research, after all."

CHAPTER FOUR

Lise shoved a wooden cart full of leather-bound books down the second aisle of the fiction section, her thoughts on Susette's comments. In the months they'd been friends, Susette had never before questioned Lise's resolve to keep her background a secret. This morning's assertion that she was ashamed of her heritage had hurt.

She fingered the beaded necklace that hung from her neck, hidden under the bodice of her dress. Last night, she'd stood in front of the mirror, thinking about the girl child she had once been, a tiny mixture of white and Indian, wearing calico and moccasins, brocade and beads. Whether her hair had been in braids or curls, she had known who she was and where she had come from. After the uprising, her mother had tucked away everything but the beads. From time to time, she'd brought the other items out so that Lise would not forget, but they were always stored away again, out of sight.

Lise squeezed her eyes shut and swallowed. She wasn't ashamed. She wasn't.

The door creaked open, then closed with a quiet click.

Lise drew a breath, settled a tattered, musty-smelling copy of *Uncle Tom's Cabin* on the shelf, and crossed through the lingering dust motes to the front of the library. The white-haired Balton sisters were snoring in their sun-warmed chairs by the window.

Zachary Spencer lounged against the edge of her desk, his arms crossed in front of him and a lazy smile on his chiseled Nordic face.

Lise narrowed her eyes and strode toward him. "I thought you were headed back to Lincoln today," she said. "Thad told me you only came home for a few days." She blanched at the brusque tone of her voice.

"Looks like Thad was wrong."

She reminded herself he was a patron and offered him a polite smile. "May I help you find something?"

"I'll need to take a look at that law section of yours. Turns out I have a case to research before I head back to the main office." He flashed a grin. "I could use a little help."

"That's what I'm here for," she told him. "What are you researching?"

"Indians. And *habeas corpus.*"

Lise stared at him, professionalism forgotten. "Indians?" she choked out.

"Yes, Indians."

She narrowed her eyes. "On Saturday, you seemed pretty determined not to get involved in anything that involved Indians." His abrupt rejection of Susette and Joseph's plight had been clear. An offer of help now was pointless. What was he up to?

"I was. Still would be if it weren't my job." His eyes twinkled with a flirtatious warmth that was hard to resist. "That band of Poncas Thad was going on about has filed a writ of *habeas corpus* against the government. The district attorney represents the government. First time I've been on the defense side of the law for quite awhile. I could use your help."

She stared at him in disbelief, tense anger brewing inside her. He'd be defending the government's actions, working to send the Poncas back to Indian Territory, and he had the nerve to come into her library and flirt with her, then ask her for *help?*

"That's what you're here for, remember?" he coaxed.

"Well." She drew a breath. "The law section is over there." She pointed across the room. "Help yourself."

"What about some assistance?"

Lise sighed. She couldn't very well refuse him use of the library, but she'd be hog-tied if she was going to make it easy for him. He could flutter those long lashes at her all day long and it wouldn't change a thing. Not only was he irritating and uncooperative, but he was now officially the enemy.

"I've got a stack of books to re-shelve," she said. Guilt over the unprofessional response pricked her.

"They'll wait."

She squinted at him. "You need help to walk across the room?"

He laughed. "I might need your skill in locating the right volumes."

"The books are organized in standard form. If you've used a law library, you shouldn't have any problem."

He smiled and shook his head. "Maybe I'd like the company." A soft invitation filled his voice.

"I'm not here to socialize, Mr. Spencer. I have things to do, and these books need to be re-shelved this afternoon."

"Yeah, I can see folks beating down the door to get at them." His gaze darted around the near empty room. Aside from the dozing women, there was but one other patron, a teenager at the far table, thumbing through a fashion magazine. "Won't take you but an hour to put those away. Plenty of time left in the day." He rammed his hands into his front pockets and grinned. "Help a fellow out?"

Lise battled the urge to banter with him. The man was a rogue and obviously used to getting what he wanted. She pinned him with a sharp stare. "The way you helped me the other day?"

"Is that what this is all about?" He exhaled. "I'm a district attorney. I prosecute cases. The La Flesches had been arrested. Helping them would have been a conflict of interest."

Lise straightened, mocking his stance, and faced him. "A district attorney has the power to intervene if he suspects abuse of power by the authorities."

"Insofar as the law permits."

"That's a very narrow interpretation and you know it."

"It's not my job to interpret the law. I apply it."

Lise glared at him. "Even at the cost of trampling on an individual's rights? Of putting a person in danger?"

"I don't make the law, Miss Dupree."

Zach moved away from her with slow, calculated steps and approached the law library shelves. "And sometimes, I don't agree with it. But I respect it. And I enforce it."

"Because it's your job?" She followed him across the room.

"Because I believe in our legal system," he clarified. "Come on, help me out?" He turned and winked at her.

Heat filled Lise's face and she bristled at her reaction to his flirting. Zach Spencer was a dangerous man. Deep down, she knew he wasn't being antagonistic. He had as much right to use the library as anyone else, even if he was going to use it to prepare a case against the Poncas. But she didn't have to like it.

She weighed her options. She knew the books both from her own research and from the meticulous catalog she'd nearly finished. Piles of neat little note-cards were stacked in the back room, waiting to be filed in drawers. She could find many of the cases even without the cards.

As librarian, she couldn't refuse him her assistance. It didn't mean she had to tell him about the catalog.

She pointed to the shelves. "Starting on the left, state statutes followed by state case histories, organized by year. Then, federal statutes and case histories, also in chronological order."

"Cataloged?" he asked. He lifted one corner of his mouth and a small dimple appeared.

Lise drew a breath. Opposition seemed to make him more determined. Misdirection might be a better choice, and a little distraction might be the way to accomplish it. She plunged ahead, before second thoughts changed her mind. Smiling up at him, her eyes grew wide. "Well, they're all right there on one section of the shelf."

"They're not cross-referenced by issue or case name?"

"I think each volume has an index." She shrugged.

Zach stared at her. "You're telling me I'll need to go through every index?"

"Or you could use the tables of contents."

"Right. If I want to spend the next year here."

"Isn't that how you normally do it?" She batted her eyes.

His brow knit. "How long did you say you've been a librarian?"

"Are you questioning my skills?" She allowed a saucy tone to fill her voice, then sobered. "There's only so much a person can do. The law library is new. You'll have to make do with the indexes for now. Of course, if you'd like to come back in six months, I might have the cataloguing done."

"Will you show me the books?" His voice had softened, a quiet urging.

Lise exhaled a breath she hadn't realized she'd been holding. The plan had worked. He'd shifted enough of his attention to her that he would lose focus. As long as she flirted back, the diversion would succeed.

"Every minute I spend helping you sets me back one minute on the catalog." And, if things went well, it would set him back three minutes on his research. "You do realize that, don't you?"

"Please," he urged again.

"Do you want a list of volume and page numbers or would you prefer to check each reference as I find it?"

"List it," he told her, and grinned.

She grinned back, thinking about how much time it would take him to decipher her notes.

Rufus Christy paused at the top of the narrow stairway and peered through the glass door into the library. The secretary at the courthouse had said Spencer would be at the library and sure enough, there he was.

Right across the room with that uppity librarian.

He'd expected the man to be halfway back to Lincoln by now, but it was just as well he'd stayed around. If Crook became a problem, it'd be handy having a district attorney ready to send a report to the Department of the Army. General Sheridan would respect that. Sometimes, the little dwarf wasn't responsive to Rufus's reports.

Rufus shrank into the shadow against the wall, reached into his coat pocket, and pulled out a wad of tobacco. He bit off a chunk and stuck the rest away. He rubbed his hands together and blew on them.

It was cold in the icy stairwell. He'd mosey in, soon enough, and find a stove. Miss Dupree was a high-falutin sort — the kind of woman who'd insist on the county spending money on coal so she could stay comfortable.

Right now, though, she looked like she was plenty warm, if Spencer's sappy grin was any indication. Damn idiot would be lucky if she didn't have him marching down the aisle before summer. He was an upstart greenhorn, no matter how hard he'd tried to be a big bug the other night.

Rufus opened the door and stepped into the room. Two old biddies looked up at the blast of cold air and gave him the evil eye. He sneered back at them and chewed his plug with enthusiasm. Satisfaction rippled as they lowered their gazes, discomfited.

The librarian looked over, too, and her saucy smile faded.

Spencer looked like a kid caught with his hand in the cookie jar.

Rufus chuckled and crossed the room.

"May I help you find something?" the librarian asked.

"Just trackin' down Mr. Spencer, here," Rufus told her, looking around for a spittoon. "Wanted to let him know where things stand, long as he's still in town. You mind lettin' us have a minute — it's a mite complicated."

"I'm sure Miss Dupree would understand it with no problem, Mr. Christy," Spencer said.

Rufus glanced at the pile of books on the table. Sheets of note-filled papers were scattered next to them. Bunch of chicken scratch.

The librarian stood next to the table, biting on her lip.

"I sent that telegram," he announced, "like we talked about."

Miss Dupree's face pinched up and she glared at Spencer.

"Crook ought to have new orders by now," Rufus continued. "Them Indians'll be goin' back where they belong, courtesy of U.S. Army escort." If the government had put them all in Indian Territory to begin with, his life would've been different. The scars on his back itched at the thought. Now, it was time for all of 'em to pay for what they done, to him and to his family.

He swallowed a mouthful of tobacco juice, not wanting to spit on the floor, and grinned at Spencer. "Didn't expect to find you here. I was all fixed to leave a message in your office."

Spencer lifted one eyebrow. "You haven't heard?"

"Heard what?" He eyed Miss Dupree's sashaying backside as she stalked to the shelves and began ramming books into place.

"The Poncas have engaged an attorney," Spencer said. "They've filed for a writ of *habeas corpus.*"

"A what?"

"They're suing Crook for unlawful imprisonment."

"That's a crock of bull crap." Rufus caught sight of a spittoon and aimed a stream of tobacco juice into it. The librarian winced when it pinged against the brass pot.

"Likely so," Spencer agreed, "but the Poncas won't be going anywhere until they have their day in court. Trial's set for the first of May."

Rufus rubbed his cheek, found he'd missed a spot when he shaved, and frowned at Spencer. "Who the hell would take on a case like that?"

"Andrew Poppleton and John Webster."

"Idiots, both of 'em. Damn savages don't belong in no courtroom."

The librarian slammed another book against the back of the shelf.

Spencer looked at her and lowered his voice. "That's what I'm looking at — whether they have the right to even bring suit."

"You?"

Spencer nodded. "I'll be defending Crook and the government's interests."

"Why ain't the Army defendin' him?" Worry crept through Rufus. The Army he knew, like he knew all the folks in the Interior Department. Outsiders like Spencer were unpredictable.

"The writ was filed with Judge Dundy," Spencer explained. "He issued it. And since he's a district judge, the government is represented by the district attorney."

Rufus frowned. The kid would ruin the

whole case if he didn't quit chasing skirt and get down to business. Things could get out of hand if someone didn't take charge. "Sounds convoluted."

"I'll approach from the angle of the tribe's standing, whether they even have the right to sue."

"What about the treaties and what the Army's already done?"

"I'll need to research that." He gestured to the books on the table.

The librarian returned from her shelving. "I'm sure it's all here, somewhere." Like every woman Rufus had met, she twittered like a bird. Spencer's gaze settled onto her. Hell. If someone didn't get that boy out of here, he'd spend hours waiting for that simple-minded woman to find what was obvious to anyone with half a brain.

He reached for the lawyer's arm and caught his attention. "Ain't no reason to look in books to find that out," he said. "I've been Indian agent longer'n you've been out of short pants. Time you and me have a long talk, boy. Pick up your papers and we'll head over to Krug's Brewery. We'll have a beer and I'll tell ya everything I know. Those Indians ain't got a chance in hell."

Zach and Rufus Christy were deep in

conversation when the library door creaked open, and Lise glanced up from checking out the *Harper's Bazaar* to the timid teen. A trio of familiar giggling youngsters slipped into the library and waved to her as the teen exited. She expected they'd have their usual list and she'd need to help locate the books and wait while they argued about which volumes they wished to take home. She crossed the room and offered her assistance.

Sometime later, she was in the middle of searching the shelves for Edgar Allan Poe stories — an odd choice for the girls — when Zach approached.

"It seems I'm off to learn the history of the Poncas, Christy style," he said.

A chill crept up Lise's spine. The blunt Indian agent gave her the willies. And, according to General Crook, he'd been the man responsible for sending the Poncas to Indian Territory. Evil emanated from him like skunk spray.

Twin twinges of fear and resentment edged into her thoughts. She didn't have to deal with him, and it shouldn't matter to her if Zach Spencer did. He was the enemy, after all. She needed to remember that.

Zach shifted his weight. "Biased as the man is, it will help my research to get some background information. Maybe it will narrow my search for relevant statutes if he can offer any dates."

"He's a bitter man who should have been relieved as an Indian agent long ago." She glanced across the room and frowned. Christy was jabbering with the girls, a smile on his face, all traces of evil vanished. "How can one man have two such different natures? Look how he acts when he's around kids. You'd never know how venomous he can be when he talks about Indians."

"I heard his family was attacked on their way west. He and a sister were tortured and taken captive."

It was a reasonable enough explanation, but Lise's mind refused to wrap itself around it. Or maybe it was her heart that balked. She wasn't sure. "He's judging a whole people for the actions of a few."

Zach drew a breath and nodded. "Most folks do." His pale blue gaze settled on her face. "I need to go. May I stop back tomorrow?"

Lise shivered, feeling his inspection, and licked her lips. "You may. I think I can find the time to help again." She paused. "If you need me."

"I was hoping you'd be available." His mouth lifted into a smile. Lise's own mouth tipped up in response.

"Spencer?" Christy interrupted. "You gonna yammer with that librarian all day?"

Zach glanced at the Indian agent, then tipped his head. "Duty calls. See you tomorrow." He turned and headed for the door, passing Susette on her way in. He looked back once, then slipped out and disappeared down the stairs. Christy followed, a scowl on his face as he stepped around Susette.

Lise handed the two volumes of Poe to the chattering sisters and admonished them to keep their voices down, then neared her friend.

"You look pleased," she said.

Susette's black eyes danced. "I am." With an eye on the other patrons, she lowered her voice. "I'm staying in town for awhile — with the Meyers. Tom . . . Mr. Tibbles . . . has spoken to some of the ministers. They'll let him speak to their congregations on Sunday. We're also planning an extended article for the paper. We interview Standing Bear tomorrow."

Lise glanced around. The chatty girls were involved in a spirited debate over which book to choose, and the elderly Balton sisters were engrossed in the daily paper. "I thought Tibbles was too busy," she whispered to Susette.

Her friend smiled with pride. "I've offered

to write his regular articles. Now he has the time." She sobered. "His zeal is good for the Poncas, as is his honor. Not like that squirrel who just left here."

"Christy?" Lise spat the name out.

"What was he doing here?"

Lise picked up two children's primers she'd been holding for Susette and recorded return dates on the small cards inside their front covers. "The blond man who left with Christy is Zach Spencer, the district attorney handling the case against Standing Bear." She handed the books to Susette. "I think Christy's trying to manipulate things with him."

Her friend leaned across the desk. "The man who looked at you with stars in his eyes? The man you gave such a coy smile?"

"I'm wrapping him around my finger," Lise explained with a wave of her hand. "He came in to research the case. I can't tell him no, not if I want to keep my job, but if I can distract him, I can slow things down."

Susette caught Lise's hand and gripped it. "And if he distracts you instead, my friend?"

Lise shrugged her shoulders. "He won't."

Susette straightened and crossed her arms, shaking her head. "Won't he?"

Rufus stood at the top of the landing,

puzzled. Something was haywire. He'd hung back, since Spencer said he had to drop his books off at the courthouse, and crept back up the stairs. A white woman and a squaw, looking around to make sure they wouldn't get caught, lent itself to all sorts of worrisome thoughts. But to allow an Indian to reach out and touch her . . .

It was clear that attorney had fixed his mind on the librarian. He'd seen that. But what if she had Indian sympathies? Well, that was somethin' else.

The little book-lady was gonna have to be watched. And it wouldn't hurt things none if he paid a visit to that senator that was nursin' the boy's campaign along. Wouldn't hurt a bit.

CHAPTER FIVE

"I think you need to make a public statement, Zach," Senator Adam Foster said from across the room. "The *Daily Bee* can run it on the same page as the stories on those attacks down in Texas."

Zach shook his head. Adam had been saying the same thing for two days, ever since Rufus Christy had toted two pints of beer home after their meeting at the Krug Brewery and hand-delivered them to Adam with a generous helping of his advice. Christy was a meddlesome little man and Zach wasn't sure he liked the sway Christy seemed to have with Adam.

"I don't think it's a good idea to stir up a hornet's nest. Texas has nothing to do with Nebraska. Besides, the Comanches surrendered two years ago. It's old news."

Adam leaned forward in his chair, his dark eyes shrewd as they narrowed. "Those murders took place just a day's ride from

San Antonio, a city comparable to Omaha, by renegades who refused to stay put in Indian Territory. Now, *we* have renegade Poncas. Who's to say they won't do just what the Comanches did?"

Zach sunk his forehead into his hand and propped it with an elbow on his desk. "Oh, for crying out loud." He paused, then looked at Adam again. "You don't really believe that, do you? That ass Christy was going on about the same thing at Krug's. He gave me a lesson on treaty history, all from his point of view. Then I had to sit through an hour of gory atrocity stories, including what happened to his ma and sister." Zach's gut tightened at the memory of Christy's tale, but the stab of pity dissipated as he recalled the agent's face when he explained what needed to happen to the Indians.

"The man has a bias," he told his advisor. "He probably shouldn't even be an Indian agent. If he's been prodding you, you need to know he doesn't see things clearly."

"I know all about Christy and his hatred of the red man. Everybody does. But there are a lot of folks who believe the same things. Those are the people we need to reach."

Despite Adam's words, Zach still wasn't

sure the senator hadn't been unduly influenced by Christy. "I went out to Fort Omaha yesterday, to have a look at the Poncas and hear Crook's version of events. Those exhausted Indians have been through hell. They aren't going to rape and murder or steal anybody's kids."

"Hell, Zach, I know that. Your average man on the street, though, he hears the rumor and he's scared. You've got Tom Tibbles running stories about how peaceful and good the Ponca are. If you don't put any other view out there, the public is going to swallow that crap and you're going to be the villain." He pointed a finger at Zach. "When the case comes up, we need to take the law and order stance. Tibbles has raised the stakes. Now, you don't have a choice. If you want to be senator, you need to generate fear, then let folks know you stand to protect them."

Zach ran his hand through his hair. Adam was right. The campaign had changed how he needed to view issues. Still, it turned his stomach to think about accusing those tattered people of impending violence. He didn't believe it. "They're sick and hungry," he said. "They're not going to hurt anyone."

"Doesn't matter." Adam stood and began shuffling through the papers he'd laid on

Zach's desk. He raised his gaze and offered a wry smile. "The world revolves on what people think, not the truth."

Zach's gut clenched. He hated Adam's insincerity almost as much as accusing the Poncas of motives that didn't exist. "I don't like it."

"You don't have to." Adam located what he was looking for and extended a scrawled outline toward Zach. "I already talked to Ed Rosewater at the *Bee.* He's willing to run a series of articles, reminding the public of what can happen when Indians get out of hand. A couple of those former captives were recovered in the last year or two. Ed'll use their stories." He tapped the paper for emphasis.

Zach glanced at the outline. He recognized the information from one of Christy's tales. Comanche and Apache raids had taken their toll on the Texas frontier during the sixties and early seventies. A lot of deaths, a lot of captives. "Old news," he repeated.

"Then he can run a feature on Custer and his boys or the Nez Perce War. A history of Indian violence."

Uneasiness rumbled through Zach. It wasn't right and it had the potential to backfire on him later. Vocal politicians always encountered argument sooner or later, usually when it was least expected. He didn't want to have to defend a position he'd never espoused in the first place. "Going on record that the Ponca are anything near that sort of danger is risky. I won't do it."

Adam scooped the papers together and stuffed them into a folder. "You can't be a politician if you won't play politics. Your granddaddy would tell you the same thing."

"Gramps would quote the law and say he stood behind it. I'm comfortable with that."

"If asked by the press, you would state that applying the law fairly is the best way to protect the public?"

Zach shifted in his chair. Ed Rosewater could easily twist his words around. He'd have to be careful. "All right," he agreed, "but I'm not going to answer any direct questions about the Poncas being a threat."

"I'll let Ed know he can use that quote." Adam picked up the folder and headed for the door, then turned back to Zach. "He can do it up as an interview, rather than a released statement. He's good at getting to the root of things. He'll know what to do."

Lise sat outside Aunt Rose's threadbare lodge, fighting tears. The late morning sun warmed her skin. Across the prairie, grass was starting to green and, if it weren't for the melancholy that had wedged itself around her, the burgeoning beauty of the day would have pleased her.

Instead, she just felt useless and defeated.

The tepee flap lifted and her cousin, Albert, emerged. He touched her shoulder as he settled next to her. "She is asleep. Naomi will sit with her."

Lise shivered despite the sunlight. "I didn't mean to upset her." Moments earlier, Aunt Rose had exploded in a weak fury, shouting disgraceful things before collapsing against her pallet.

"It happens, cousin. No one knows why." Albert adjusted his worn tan dungarees, stretched out his legs, and lifted his face to the sun. He leaned against a small pile of wood and gazed out toward the prairie. "Perhaps she is fighting against what has happened to her," he said.

Lise felt guilty. "I should have visited, been a part of her life."

"She would have liked that." Albert turned and smiled at Lise. "But she also understood."

A soft breeze brought the scent of stewing meat and the mouth-watering aroma filled the silence that stretched between them as Lise considered how to best ask her cousin about life on the Dakota border. She didn't want to ignite the anger he'd displayed during her last visit, but she needed to know Aunt Rose had not suffered. "Was she happy?" she finally asked.

"Our life was good. My father gave her much. She had a log house and many gooseberry bushes." Memories drifted across his face. He straightened and rolled up the sleeves of his faded red cotton shirt, then picked up a rounded stone and worried it in his hand.

"The men still hunted. We brought home buffalo meat and hides until the buffalo were no more. But we also farmed the land we were given so there was other food, and we did not have to starve if the annuities were late. She told us how important this was."

Lise looked away briefly, remembering how the Sioux in Minnesota had lived their lives dependent on the government supplies.

"She helped my father learn the white ways she had known before she came to us. She sewed us shirts of calico and taught us how to weave the old ways with the new ways and to accept our enemies." Albert tossed the stone away and drew a breath.

"And were all the families doing this?"

Lise asked, her mind seizing the information.

He nodded. "That is why we did not understand when the Indian Agent Christy told us to move. We were already living our lives like white men. We no longer hunted the plains and we lived as neighbors with people we had once hated. Many of us had not lived in lodges for years. The Sioux and the Ponca had found a way to live with the white man's mistake." He stared at her and his voice hardened. "There was nothing that needed to be fixed."

Lise absorbed the information, thinking about what she knew of Rufus Christy. "I'm not so sure that he was trying to fix things so much as he was trying to punish you for being Indian," she said.

Albert stood and grabbed a chunk of wood. He stalked toward the stew pot and tossed it onto the open fire beneath the tripod that held the stew. Sparks flew into the air as the new firewood sizzled. He turned back, scowling. "But we were not being Indian. We were being white. Only our skin color made us Indians. That and a few customs and the language we kept alive to remind us who we were. Forcing us away was not right."

Lise rose and moved toward her cousin.

"Had Christy visited the reservation?" she asked.

Albert stirred the pot with an iron ladle. The aroma of cooking meat and vegetables filled the air. He let go of the ladle, released a heavy breath, and stared at the stew. "He came to our houses. He saw our fields and our clothes and our tools. He wrinkled his nose and said we were dirty Indians and must move away from land that was not ours."

Next to him, Lise stood silent, unable to make sense of what had happened. She no longer had any doubt that Christy's actions had been personal rather than professional.

"He told us we must move to a new place so we could learn to be white. The new land could not be farmed — it was dry blowing dirt and swamps full of mosquitoes. There were no houses for us to live in and no tools to make a living. There was no food, only gray army blankets full of lice and disease. The other tribes did not want us there." He looked straight at Lise. "And we did not want those things. We wanted our old lands and to be left in peace."

Lise watched him move back to the woodpile. With quick darts of movement, he restacked the scattered logs into a solid pyramid.

"Did the Sioux want you removed?" she asked him.

"The Sioux were like the Ponca. We saw that the white man had been stupid when he put us both in the same place, but we lived together because we had no choice. Now, we have overcome our differences and there is no reason for anyone to be moved."

Her mind sorted through all Albert had told her, examining the neat pockets of information she had categorized it into, no longer searching for any understanding. Grasping at a detail, she held Albert's gaze. "Standing Bear and those who are with him, all of you were living in houses, on farms?"

"Yes. Some of the others had not left their lodges. They chose to stay on the new lands in Indian Territory. They did not care that the new land was no good for farming. They will hunt for game that is not there and wait for the government to bring annuities. Standing Bear's band does not wish for that life."

"Just to clarify, cousin . . . you *want* to live on farms?"

"Yes. We do not understand why we cannot return to our lands. But if we cannot, we will return only to bury Standing Bear's son along the Niobrara. We will then live with our cousins on the Omaha Reservation and work the land there."

Lise pondered his words, feeling the uselessness lift. She needed to go back to the library and do more research, but she was positive a legal precedent had been established that released Indians from the requirement to live on reservations if they had chosen to forsake tribal ways and live as whites.

What Albert had told her indicated that Standing Bear's people had been living that way for years. If Standing Bear publically severed tribal relationships on behalf of those he represented, they could not be forced to stay in Indian Territory. They would be free to live as whites.

All they had to do was convince Standing Bear to say he was no longer Ponca.

Susette looked up from the counter of the *Omaha Herald.* She squinted in the afternoon sunlight and pushed a stray lock of hair behind her ear as she reread the story she'd just written. "What do you think?" she asked.

Tom Tibbles glanced at her from the other side of the counter and burst into laughter.

Susette shifted her feet and stared at him, suddenly unsure she should be in the newspaper office. Perhaps it would be better for her to return to the reservation, where she was secure in her role. "What are you laughing at?" she asked.

"You have ink smeared all the way across the side of your face." Though amused, his voice held no trace of mockery, and Susette breathed easier. She had done nothing the daughter of a chief could be ashamed of.

She eyed her hand. A streak of black ran the length of her thumb, fading like a comet's tail as it reached her wrist. She peered down her nose and scrunched up her cheek.

"Here," Tom's hand reached toward her face and a long index finger traced a fiery trail from her nose to her ear.

Susette shivered and shied away. It was the second time that day she'd felt the dangerous tingle. Earlier, their hands had collided above a block of print. Her fervid reactions were uncalled for. Tom Tibbles had treated her with more respect than any other white man ever had. She mustn't forget they were of two different lives, with little in common. Tom was a white man, one who spoke well of his wife. She swallowed.

"War paint," she joked.

"Apropos," he said, and pulled his hand away with a faltering quickness. "Let's have a look." He took the handwritten article from her and skimmed the contents. "Excellently written," he told her, "and a nice rebuttal to that garbage Ed Rosewater is spewing in the *Bee*."

Pride surged through her and she couldn't hold back the smile. Ever since she could remember, she'd wanted to write articles for the white man's paper. Her father had told her she could do anything she wanted, had insisted she attend the missionary's school so she could learn the ways of the white man. Now, she taught the children on the reservation those same skills. Still, she'd longed to have her words in print.

Tom Tibbles was the only editor who'd ever given her that chance. His praise meant a great deal.

"Mr. Rosewater enjoys the attention. He is not so concerned with the facts," she said.

"He never has been." Tom's gaze softened. "I like your attention to detail here." He pointed to the third paragraph. "While I'd thought about an article on those boys who didn't want to leave the Comanches, your idea to make the public aware of Standing Bear's character is much better. It keeps the focus on the real issue. You pulled a lot from the interview we had with him."

Susette shrugged, unsure of how to handle

the compliment. She was not used to praise from men. "Your questions were good ones."

"As were the ones you added." Tom gathered the papers into a neat pile, then stared at her. "Have you ever thought about making a career of journalism?"

Her cheeks warmed and she fiddled with the lid of the ink jar, disconcerted by the genuine interest in his tone. "You did not notice I am Indian?" she asked. "Or that I am a woman?"

"I can't see any of that when I read the paper."

"Ah, but who would be interviewed by an Indian woman?"

His silence told her that she'd hit the truth. She placed the ink jar on a shelf, then reached for a rag to wipe the traces of printer's ink from the counter. She'd learned several days ago that cleanliness was a constant battle here.

"When we were at the interview, Standing Bear didn't call you Susette," Tom said. "You have an Indian name?"

His interest caught her by surprise. "A nickname, like my father. He is also known as *Esta-maza,* or Iron Eye. If you have seen the steel in his gaze, you would know how this came to be."

"And you?"

"When I was a girl, someone said I should be *Instha Theamba,* or Bright Eyes."

"Bright Eyes. It fits the sparkle you have. Your eyes and your nature."

She shifted under his gaze, wondering if there were things she did not understand about white culture. His words were direct, even intimate. With her people, there would be much meaning to them. "You are teasing me."

"I'm saying what is, Susette." He touched the back of her hand, stilling her cleaning. Again, his touch jolted through her. "You have a way about you that shines. It's hard to resist."

She pulled her hand away and hung the rag on the nail next to the shelf. Perhaps coming here had been a mistake. Perhaps she had stepped into a situation that could become dangerous.

"Would you come with me tomorrow," Tom said, "when I speak to the Chamber of Commerce about the Poncas? After we visited Standing Bear, I watched you tell Lise all about it. Your energy was infectious. I think you'd make an impression on those businessmen."

She faced Tom and forced a calm that had long ago fled. "I think they'd laugh at me."

112

He shook his head. "They'd swallow up everything you said to them."

The tinkle of the bell over the door interrupted his coaxing. Even as relief washed over her, Susette felt disappointment that their private conversation was over.

Lise entered the newspaper office, her face lit with excitement. She strode to the counter and smiled at both of them.

"What is it?" Susette asked.

"I've found the angle we need."

"The angle?" Susette asked.

"Newspaper jargon, Bright Eyes," Tom explained. "Take notes."

"Never mind him," Lise said. "The case. I've found a way to make Standing Bear's case."

Tom crossed his arms, his hip against the counter. "Well, don't leave us waiting."

"If Standing Bear has forsaken his tribal ties, he is no longer bound by law to live with the tribe. He does not have to go to Indian Territory with them."

"It's that easy?" Tom asked, looking skeptical.

"All we need to do is convince Judge Dundy that Standing Bear doesn't consider himself to be a Ponca."

Susette stared at her friend, unable to fathom what was so easy about it. "I don't think he will do this. He is very proud to be a Ponca." He was like her father, a man who defined himself by his heritage.

Lise persisted. "He lived like a white man before being forced to Indian Territory, correct? He doesn't want to live with the tribe in Indian Territory, correct?"

"But I don't think that means he does not wish to be Ponca. There is a difference."

"All we need is for Poppleton and Webster to make enough of a case that Dundy is convinced."

Tom pondered the idea, then nodded. "We can focus on that. It will dovetail perfectly with Susette's article on his good character."

Still unsure, Susette glanced away and a slight movement outside the window drew her attention. Rufus Christy was emerging from the *Herald*'s seldom-used outside entrance to the print room. The door, at a right angle to the front of the main part of the building, gave Christy a direct view into the office. He stared at them through the window, then stepped into the shadows and disappeared around the strange addition. Apprehension tumbled inside her. "Tom? Lise?" she said. "We have a problem."

"I don't think it will be one, Bright Eyes," Tom said.

"No. Outside." She pointed. "I think that

114

Indian agent has been in here spying on us."

Zach adjusted his shirt collar and started up the stairs to the library. The narrow stairwell was darker than it had been the last time he'd visited. It looked like Lise Dupree had hung some cloudy sort of cloth in front of the door's big window. He smiled. It was the sort of thing his ma would do though it was a mystery why a person would decorate a perfectly good window and make a stairway dark in the process.

He pushed open the door and walked inside.

She was there, as he'd anticipated. Her hair was wound up like a caramel roll at the back of her neck. Just above the lace at the top of her collar, her coffee-and-cream skin whetted his appetite. He swallowed and started across the room.

Lise looked up from the card catalog and said something to the patron next to her. The balding man nodded his head and waved her away. She crossed toward Zach, smiling.

He smiled back, taking in her smart spring-green dress and the way it hugged her curves.

"You look like a mint gumdrop," he said and instantly regretted the words. Most women didn't take kindly to being compared to candy.

She raised her eyebrows. "Is that a good thing or a bad thing to look like?"

He lifted his own brow in response. She hadn't slapped him and that was a good sign. "A good thing. Don't you like gumdrops?"

"It's not a matter of like or dislike. I'm just not sure looking like one is a compliment." She gestured for him to follow her to the legal section and walked across the room.

"It is," he told her, following the sway of her hips. Her skirt flowed out behind her.

"And mint is good as well?" she asked, over her shoulder.

"It is." Lord, what a lame response. She must think he was an idiot.

"Then, thank you." She stopped at the shelves and turned around. "It's one of the strangest compliments I've ever received."

He shrugged. "I've got a sweet tooth. It colors the way I see things."

"Mm hmm." She crossed her arms and tipped her head to one side.

Zach swallowed and stared at her. She was an enigma. Sassy and sophisticated, playful and professional. He was fascinated.

"I brought a list of cases I'm looking for,

along with approximate dates." He lifted his leather satchel and silenced a groan. Any fool with experience in a law library could locate what he was asking for. She'd think he was brainless, too.

"That should narrow your search considerably. If you know your numbers like you do your colors, you can find those on your own." She began to move away.

His mind scrambled for another task. "I'll also need citizenship cases, as applied to non-whites."

She stilled. "Those would be a bit harder to locate. I'll need to explain the system."

"I also want everything you have on the origins of *habeas corpus* and application under British case law."

"Definitely difficult. Those will take some time. I'm not sure I have anything like that catalogued yet."

He set his satchel on the nearest table and rummaged inside. "Should we start with citizenship then?" he asked. If memory served him right, there was no citizenship case law. He'd be able to ask for a simple dismissal of Standing Bear's suit, based on lack of legal standing. If the Indian had no right to file a suit, they could dispense with the trial, and the publicity Adam was so intent on pursuing.

Lise watched him, pointedly ignoring his question. "You don't happen to *have* any mint gumdrops, do you?"

He smiled and shook his head. "Not today."

"Lemon, maybe?" Her molasses eyes grew round.

"I've got a peppermint stick."

She leaned forward and whispered, "With you?"

"Right here in my pocket." Zach patted his coat and winked at her, content to play the game. Research wouldn't take long anyway.

She drew back. "With your pocket lint?" Mock shock graced her voice, reeling him in.

"My pockets don't have any lint." He reached into his pocket and pulled out one of his ever-present candy sticks. He unwrapped the brown paper, broke off a two-inch piece, and handed it to her. "Here."

She took the candy, put it in her mouth, and sucked on it, pleasure filling her eyes.

Zach's heart skipped a beat. *Good God.* He shook his head and glanced at the notes he'd pulled from his satchel, then cleared his throat. "We were talking about citizenship cases."

"Were we?" she asked. "Did you want the

list I made the other day?" She pulled a folded piece of paper from the hidden pocket of her dress and handed it to him.

Tearing his gaze away from her, he focused on the paper. Tiny creases remained after he'd opened it. Scrawling words filled the page, none of them readable. "You have lousy penmanship for a librarian."

She shrugged. "My hand was tired."

His body hardened at the double entendre, and Zach's concentration tumbled again. He glanced at her, unable to detect any trace that she understood what she'd said. She picked up the glasses that were hanging on a chain around her neck and put them on her face. He shifted his stance; figuring out whether a vixen existed under that prim and proper façade could be a fascinating process.

"Miss Dupree," he asked, "are you deliberately trying to distract me?"

"Now, why would I do a thing like that? You were distracting me." She peered through her glasses, then moved toward the shelves, her eyes searching the titles. "Are you thinking along the lines of Dred Scott? I think there's a Louisiana case concerning a German girl who was sold into slavery." Her voice had shifted, brisk and business-like.

"I think that would sidetrack things. Slavery isn't the issue here. We'll need to stick to Indian cases only."

She turned. "Most of the Indian case law deals with issues of sovereignty and right of occupancy. There's an implied recognition of the Indians' right to treaty for transfer of land within those rights of occupancy and sovereignty." She gestured to the top shelf. "See Peters, *United States Statutes at Large,* Volume VII volume vii. Specific cases related to sale of land would be the *Fletcher v. Peck* and *Clark v. Smith.*"

Her abrupt shift in demeanor hit him like a cyclone. Hell, she sounded like a defense lawyer. Feeling he'd been tossed in the air and dumped hard on the ground, he stared at her. "And citizenship?"

"Ownership of land would imply one is a citizen, would it not?"

"Not necessarily."

"I disagree." Her expression was far removed from the flirtatious siren of a few moments earlier, but it lit her eyes up all the same.

He pulled at his collar, wondering when it had gotten so hot in the drafty room. Damn, the woman was attractive.

"And the court?" he queried.

"The courts haven't addressed the issue.

Not specifically."

He grinned at her, unable to resist. Sparring legal points with her would make law a whole lot more exciting. "Did you know your face lights up when you argue?"

"I'm not arguing."

"Discussing, then."

She looked over the rim of her glasses. "Do you want me to pull the Dred Scott material or not?"

"Are you sure you're not a lawyer?"

"I'm a librarian, Mr. Spencer."

A librarian and a lot more. He had no doubt she could match wits with any of his colleagues and could probably put more than a few of them in their places. Good God, his heart was pounding. What a mixture in contrasts she was — smart and sassy, sexy and savvy. A chocolate-covered cherry with a crisp outer shell that promised to melt in your mouth and a tart yet sweet inner core that almost always snuck up on him, surprising in its liquid satisfaction.

"Mr. Spencer? Would you like me to pull the Dred Scott material?"

The candy image faded from his mind and he stared at her. "I'd rather you came to dinner with me."

"I can't bring books to dinner, Mr. Spencer. Reading at the table isn't polite."

He laughed, drawing the attention of the bald-headed man. Researching this case was going to take a hell of a lot longer than he'd anticipated. "Then leave the books here," he told her. "We won't need them."

If he had to, he'd request a delay.

He didn't think Judge Dundy would have a problem setting the trial date back a couple weeks.

CHAPTER SIX

A soft knock sounded on the door of Lise's boarding-house room. She glanced up, curious, and placed a thin ribbon in her book before setting it on the small table next to the rocking chair. She crossed the room and peered out. Susette stood in the dim hallway, concern etched across her pretty face.

Alarm shivered up Lise's back. She quickly let her friend in. "What's wrong? Aunt Rose?"

"Rose is fine. I didn't mean to worry you. I just needed to talk."

"Has Christy done something more?"

Rufus Christy had been seen staring into the newspaper office with undisguised malice on his face, the sort of malice that precipitated spurts of action. That seemed like enough. With Christy, it was hard to tell what direction it would take, or what the consequences would be. The threat had nagged at Lise since they'd seen him.

"No," Susette said, setting her wrap on the bed. "The typesetter says Christy was asking about a job, for a friend."

Lise shrugged. "It's hard to believe that was all there was to it."

"He insists Christy came in the service door and they spoke for awhile, then Christy left." She paced the room, distracted. "Tom did coax a little more from him — that Christy kept moving toward the inside doorway, as if he wanted to get closer to the office area, where we were."

"Do you think he heard us?"

"Not with the press running. I think that's why he looked so angry when he left."

"The man makes my skin crawl." Lise's stomach knotted. "I think he was watching us from the library window when we were talking the other day. I didn't see anyone there but I felt like we were being watched. I thought I was imagining things. But, after we saw him at the newspaper office, it made me wonder if he was spying at the library, too. I put a curtain up."

Her friend nodded. "Tom says we need to watch him closely."

"Maybe I should be less involved." It wouldn't take much for Christy to question her interest in the case and, along with it, her identity. She'd given the information to

Susette and Tom Tibbles. It was time to distance herself from the case, before Christy's mind started making connections she didn't want made. If he did, she'd lose everything.

"I was thinking the same thing about myself." Susette's voice wavered and deep lines formed on her forehead.

Lise took Susette's arm and guided her to the bed, then sat beside her. Something was seriously wrong.

Susette sat in silence, then caught Lise's gaze. "I don't think it's a good thing that I am working with Tom," she said.

"Has Christy threatened you in some way?" If that Indian agent had done anything to her friend —

"This isn't about Christy. It's about Tom and me and what happens when I'm with him."

Lise's disquiet deepened. Had she been so uneasy about Christy that she'd misjudged Tom Tibbles's intentions? "Has he tried something?" she asked.

"No," Susette shook her head back and forth in denial. "I just think it would be better if I weren't at the newspaper office. People might presume things."

Lise stared into Susette's dark eyes, saw the pooling tears, and drew a breath.

"People might think all sorts of things. You've never worried about that before. What's going on?"

"He . . . I . . . it's better for me to return home."

"What is it that you're not telling me?"

Susette swallowed. "I'm drawn to him and I think he feels something, too. It's like being pulled underwater whenever I am with him."

"Oh, Bright Eyes." She reached for Susette's hand and squeezed it. She knew the feeling. Hadn't she almost drowned under Zach's gaze, melted a bit when hunger had flickered there? Except with Zach, she was only playing. For Susette, it was clearly not a game.

"It was foolish of me to even go to the newspaper office," Susette said.

"Foolish?"

"I didn't think I would feel such things, but I was wrong." Susette lowered her head. "How could I be so stupid?"

"You're not stupid."

"I'm an Indian woman. A white man tells me how good I write, how much he admires me, and I become soft and weak. I believe every word because my mind is clouded. If we hadn't been interrupted, how long would it have taken for him to pull me into his

126

arms? Or his bed? And how willingly would I have gone?"

"He wouldn't have —"

"My heart was beating so fast, even though my mind shouted at me. Even though I knew it wasn't good, that he is married, a white man of power and I am nothing more than a squaw."

Lise reached for her friend's chin and turned her face until her dark eyes held Lise's gaze. "And from all I have heard of him, he is a white man of integrity with a solid respect for our people. One who would never use the word 'squaw' the way you just did. I don't think he asked you to work with him in order to take advantage of you."

"Didn't he?"

Lise drew a breath. "He asked you because I suggested it."

"You what?" Susette's eyes flashed.

"He balked, said he couldn't spare that much time. I suggested you as an assistant."

"An assistant. But not a writer."

"He obviously thinks you write well or he wouldn't have perked up at the mention of you helping him."

Susette smiled wryly. "Perhaps it wasn't my help that he perked up about."

Lise smiled at the double entendre, pleased Susette could still find humor in

127

the situation. Seconds later, she sobered. "Are you sure, Susette? About the undercurrents?"

"I am sure."

"If you go back to the reservation, can you continue your work by mail?"

"It would take too long. There's too much that must be done as it comes to light."

"Can he do it without you?"

"Of course he can. But he cannot run his paper at the same time."

"Then . . ."

Susette sighed. "I will not go home. It's too important that I do this work. Standing Bear has put his faith in us." She smiled at Lise and drew her shoulders back. "But I won't dishonor myself. If Tom Tibbles asks that of me, I will refuse him, and Standing Bear will have to find other ways to tell his story."

Adam Foster stared across his desk at Rufus Christy. He despised the little worm but was finding him useful, in spite of his distaste. "And you're sure there's a connection?" he asked.

"Clear as day," Christy said as he squirmed in his chair. "First, there's that rumor that the librarian tried to help the La Flesches escape from the Wigwam the day

128

they got arrested. Then I see them talkin'
all cozy-like in the library. Don't take no
huge leap to put two and two together when
they're clustered together at Tibbles's news
rag."

Adam knitted his brow, examining all the
angles. "Coincidence, perhaps?"

"Coincidence, hell."

Adam leaned back in his chair and thought
about the information. If the librarian was
in cahoots with Standing Bear's supporters,
it stood to reason that he needed to think
about all the time Zach seemed to be spending on research.

Still, he wasn't sure about Christy's motives. "Let's just assume, for a moment, that
there is some link between the librarian, the
La Flesche woman, and Tibbles. Why would
that be of any concern to me?"

Christy shifted his chewing tobacco from
one cheek to another. "You ain't noticed
how often your boy Spencer heads over to
the library?"

"The only law book collection in the city
is located there, Mr. Christy. I hardly see
any reason to —"

"She makes puppy-dog eyes at him and
he laps it up."

Adam kept his face impassive at this new
bit of knowledge. He'd have to tread care-

fully. "Oh, for Pete's sake, Mr. Christy. You make it sound as if he's a school boy."

"If the shoe fits, Mr. Foster . . ."

"For argument's sake, suppose he is interested in the woman." He stared hard at Christy. "Why does that involve me?"

Christy chuckled. "You ain't stupid, Senator." He chewed again at the wad in his mouth, his gaze never straying. "The whole state knows you're backing Spencer for senate."

"And?"

"What happens when Spencer starts talkin' about the case with her? She'll milk him for all the information she can get and feed it to La Flesche and Tibbles who'll pass it on to the damn Poncas' lawyer." He shook his head. "Bad news for the people of this country, bad news for your boy Spencer. Losing a case like this wouldn't look good. Lettin' them no account redskins go is bad for everybody. Next thing you know, tribes all over will be leavin' reservations and we'll have a damn mess on our hands. Massacres all over the place."

"I see." He stood and offered his hand to the agent. Useful news, all in all. Maybe Christy wasn't as stupid as he seemed. "Thank you for your concern, Mr. Christy."

"Wait on here a minute. Thank you? Ain't

you gonna do nothin'?"

Adam dropped his hand. He stepped around the desk and stood above Christy, gesturing for him to rise. "I'll take it into consideration. Perhaps alert Mr. Spencer."

Christy pushed back his chair and stood. "Now that don't make no sense whatsoever," he told Adam.

"I beg your pardon, Mr. Christy, but I believe it does."

"It'd make even more if you used the situation instead of ignorin' it. A few well-placed friends and you'd be collecting information that would help Spencer win the case." He grinned. "Put a typesetter in Tibbles's shop and listen in."

Adam pondered the suggestion. It wasn't his usual style but, then, neither was plotting with men like Christy. While it might not solve the librarian complication, it would keep the Standing Bear trial from becoming a problem. "The idea might have some merit," he said.

"Shouldn't be too tough to grease a palm already there or get a new hand hired on. I put a bug in the foreman's ear already."

Adam frowned. He suspected all Christy had done was create suspicion. "Of course, I should hate to get involved directly."

"Ain't nothin' I can't handle on my own."

Christy looked excited about the prospect, as Adam had suspected. "Could even send a warning note to that uppity librarian," Christy added.

Adam shook his head, unwilling to leap too far into the abyss. "I don't think that will be necessary, Mr. Christy. After all, we wouldn't want to tip our hand, now would we? Not if gathering information is our goal." He edged Christy toward the door. "You leave the librarian to me. I'll find a way to deal with her."

Already, an idea had begun to form in the back of his mind. If he wasn't mistaken, Zach had mentioned his little brother, Thad, spent a lot of time at the library. Maybe he'd see if the kid wanted to do a few odd jobs for him, as well. Shouldn't be too difficult to get the kid talking about Miss Dupree's activities. Not at all. And no one would suspect a kid.

He smiled at Christy and opened the door. "If she has a weakness, I'll find it," he said. "After all, the easiest way to conquer a foe is to aim for the soft underbelly."

That evening, Lise and Zach entered the Grand Central Hotel and stood in the warm cherry-paneled lobby. Well-dressed patrons crossed the thick oriental carpets and lounged in the deep leather chairs. Soft lamplight filled the quiet, and subtle mouth-watering aromas filtered out of the dining room. The atmosphere was refined without being ostentatious. She liked it immediately.

Zach pushed his blond hair away from his eyes and winked.

A quick shiver of appreciation for the boy-ish masculinity of the gesture rocked her. Apprehension followed. What in heaven's name was she doing here?

She'd come with the intent of finding out exactly what he planned for the case. She'd fooled herself into thinking she was in control of her relationship with Zach. It wasn't simply that she was intrigued by his quick wit and intelligence. The moment his hands touched her shoulders to remove her wrap, she knew she was kidding herself. She was attracted to the man.

"Let me take this," he said, his breath caressing her ear. He slid the wrap off, then stepped back, his gaze lingering momen-tarily on her tight bodice before meeting her eyes. "You look beautiful."

Heat filled her face and she glanced away.

He steered her across the lobby and into the dining room where a myriad of scents beckoned. Beside her, Zach breathed deeply. "They've got the best apple pie in town, next to my ma's."

Lise smiled at his familiar reference to food, intrigued all over again. She glanced at his fashionably cut brown serge suit and noted the nods of recognition from others in the room. The professional image was at odds with the blond hair threatening to fall over his blue eyes, and his sweet tooth was the last thing she'd have expected from a district attorney.

The itch to dig deeper into his personality, to explore the conflicting sides of him, badgered her common sense. She should be in her room, buried in research, instead of breaking bread with the enemy. She reminded herself to remain hidden from him, distract him as necessary, and focus on getting details about the case. That was what she was here for, not chasing some silly notion of friendly companionship. His mission was to destroy the Poncas, after all. He wasn't her friend; he couldn't be.

She broadened the smile. "I should have known you'd focus on dessert," she said as they neared a table.

He grinned and pulled out her chair. "It gets in the way sometimes. Right in the middle of preparing a brief, I'll get stuck on thoughts of fudge."

"It's a wonder you stay so trim." Lise

hoped the dim evening light would hide her blush. Being coy was hardly her forte.

Zach's eyes twinkled. "If thoughts added weight, I'd be in trouble. You didn't wear your glasses."

"I . . . I didn't think I'd need them." Vanity, she thought, hating that she'd caved in to it. Still, it had drawn his attention. If he saw her as a flirt, his guard would be down and he'd be more willing to discuss the case. Wasn't that why she was here? She widened her eyes. "Of course, that might mean I'll have to ask you to read the menu to me."

"How about I just select something for you?"

She agreed, and he ordered stuffed pheasant in mushroom sauce. He possessed a smooth ease with the attractive waitress, who tipped her head and offered a slow, inviting smile before asking if he'd like his usual dessert. Frowning, Lise busied herself with adjusting the crisp linen napkin on her lap and tried to ignore the woman's blatant flirtation.

His gaze moved back to her. "I can't figure you out, Lise Dupree."

The comment startled her. "Oh?" she asked.

"You shift constantly." He shook his head and stared at her in momentary silence.

"The minute I have you marked as prim and professional, you become teasing. Now you're irritated, preoccupied."

His astute observation made her as uncomfortable as his steady gaze. She'd revealed too much. It was hardly any of her business if the waitress flirted with him.

"Unpredictable and fascinating," he continued. "The fact that I can't work out what's going on in the pretty little head of yours is bewitching."

Lise set the goblet down, drew in a breath, and placed her hand back in her lap. Composed, refined. He was interested, just as she'd intended, but she was the one who'd become distracted. "I'm hardly unpredictable. I'm a creature of habit, my behavior fitting into neat little categories."

"I beg to differ. There's nothing neatly categorized about you. And if I didn't know it, I don't think I'd have classified you as a librarian at all."

The trim blond waitress approached. Plates of fragrant roast pheasant and vegetables steamed in her hands. As she set them down, Lise pondered his words. Though he'd easily identified her recent behavior, he hadn't a clue to how she really thought. She needed to keep it that way. It was past time to redirect the conversation away from her and to the matter at hand.

The waitress served their wine, then moved away. Lise cut into a candied plum, releasing its heavy aroma. Zach's nostrils flared in appreciation.

"And if I didn't know you were the district attorney, I wouldn't have pegged you as a prosecutor. Where I would expect a hard edge, there's a man with a sweet tooth." She relaxed and bit into a tender piece of pheasant. "Why did you choose prosecution instead of defense?"

"You might say it's in the blood. Gramps was a prosecutor, as was my pa, before he passed on." He chewed, pride and enjoyment mixing in his expression. "I was brought up to follow in their footsteps."

"The senate as well?"

He nodded. "Gramps served two terms."

"And now you're poised to do the same?"

"God willing. It'd mean a lot to him." A wistful tone entered his voice.

"He's still with you then."

"Yeah. At times." He set his fork down and glanced away.

"I'm not sure I understand."

Zach swallowed and returned his gaze to her. "He had a stroke," he said.

"He means a great deal to you, doesn't he?"

"He shaped my life. There's no other way to put it. My pa died when I was still at home. Gramps took us all in."

"He raised you?"

"Took me fishing, sat under the stars, and showed me the constellations. He took me to his office, to the courtroom, taught me respect for the law. He's everything to me. I wanted to make him proud, still do. I guess I want to be like him." The memories brought a melancholy smile to his face.

Lise smiled back. "And now you are."

"I'm not sure how much he's aware of." He leaned forward, both elbows on the table. "Every now and then, his mind seems to work. I don't know which is worse, watching him sit there, propped up by pillows, staring at nothing, or seeing him frustrated because he can't tell us what he's thinking."

"But it's clear he is thinking?"

"Sometimes."

At least Zach had that to hold onto. Aunt Rose's mind would never come back. Lise had researched the effects of fever in one of the library's large medical texts. There would be no periodic moments of clarity, no recognition. Lise fought against the pressure behind her eyes.

She stared at Zach's chiseled features and

138

thought about the day she'd gone to his office. He'd made comments she'd tried hard to ignore, comments she'd told herself were not important. Yet, they were. It suddenly mattered a great deal whether the incredibly handsome, sensitive man across from her really believed Indians were little more than children who were incapable of caring for themselves. Her mouth pulled into a frown.

"Lise? What's going on in that head of yours now?"

"Do you really believe what you told me about Indians?"

He sat back, amused surprise in his eyes. "What did I tell you?"

"That they aren't citizens," she said. "That they can't think for themselves."

He nodded once. "I believe I said that *the law* specifically does not include them as citizens."

"And what about them being no more than children?" she pressed.

"The law views them as children."

She expelled an exasperated breath. "The law?"

"Yes, the law. You came to me for a legal answer. I gave you one."

"And what about your beliefs?"

"My beliefs don't matter."

She crossed her arms and stared at him, letting an edge of anger slide into her voice. "Do you believe Indians are better off on reservations, Zach? Do *you* think they're children?"

"Since the law has established reservations, there would be less conflict, fewer episodes of violence if they did not challenge the law." He paused to stare at her.

"And?" she asked.

He shook his head and went back to his meal. "My opinion on the rest doesn't matter. As district attorney, I represent the law and uphold it."

Lise watched him, sensing his unwillingness to separate himself, seeing the conflict drift across his face. Her heart tightened for him. Still, she had to know. "It matters to me."

"Lise, I really can't —"

"Can't? Or won't?" She lifted her eyebrows, demanding an answer.

He shifted, then caught her gaze and shook his head.

Lise felt him drift away, disappointed as a heavy silence engulfed them. They finished their meal in silence. Zach filled the void by signaling for the check. He paid for dinner and politely escorted Lise from the dining room. Once outside the hotel, he steered her down Farnam Street. The deserted evening darkness enveloped them.

Zach grasped her hand and hooked it into his arm. "I visited Standing Bear a few days ago," he said. "He's a passionate, intelligent man who doesn't belong where Rufus Christy and the U.S. government want to put him."

Relief warmed Lise. Surprised that he'd admitted his feelings to her, she smiled into the cool spring air. She drew a breath and Zach placed a silencing finger on her mouth.

"It doesn't matter," he said. "The law doesn't care what my opinion is, or yours, or anyone else's for that matter. Justice can't be bent and shaped or changed according to how anyone feels." He pulled her toward a vacant wooden bench outside Goodman's Drugstore.

"Maybe it should be," she said as they sat down.

"Bent?"

"Changed."

He took her hands in his, gripping them tightly. His blue eyes darkened with conviction. "But it's the very consistency of law that makes the system work."

She digested his words, hearing his earnest belief in the system that defined who he was. She softened her argument. "Time changes how we look at things. Events don't always correspond to the circumstances legislation responded to."

"Then the legislation can be changed, statutes altered."

"But doesn't the judicial system need to question the law?"

"Defense attorneys get to question the law. The system applies it."

"Even if the law is no longer appropriate?"

He nodded. "Even then. The system works. Change does happen. With challenges to the law, legislators look at adjusting it."

"And what of 'interpretation'?"

"I don't get to interpret, Lise. It's not my place to question the law."

"Maybe it should be."

He didn't argue. Instead, he pulled her close and framed her face with his hands. "You'd make a damn fine defense attorney," he said, and lowered his mouth to hers.

She melted into the kiss, her heart pounding while panic swelled in one last coherent thought. She definitely was not in control anymore.

CHAPTER SEVEN

Lise turned the tarnished library key, unlocking the weather-worn door at the bottom of the stairs. As she pushed it open, the hinges squealed in familiar protest, piercing the pre-dawn quiet.

"Sounds like they need oil again." The comment came from behind her, and Lise turned toward Thad's youthful voice.

"It seems like I'm oiling them every other week," she responded, offering a wry smile. "You're out and about early."

"You, too. Library don't open for hours yet."

"Doesn't." She picked up the upholstered satchel of books she'd taken home and glanced at the youngster. "I get a lot of work done in the hours before I open to the public. You, however, don't strike me as an early riser."

"I'm a working man. Hired on yesterday. Newsboy. Typesetter said I was to leave one

143

at your door." He dropped a morning edition of the *Omaha Herald* into her open bag, then paused. "You got breakfast in that satchel?" he asked, nostrils quivering.

Lise's glance lingered on the crisp paper peeking out from the satchel. Rufus Christy couldn't possibly have been asking about a job for Thad, could he? The uncomfortable thought that Thad might be a spy jabbed at her. She'd have to find out.

She offered him a smile and inclined her head toward the second floor. "I do. Come on up if you have the time and I'll share. Cinnamon rolls."

"Yes, ma'am." Thad pushed back his hair with such a Zach-like mannerism that Lise's pulse jumped. With his drooping blond hair and eager blue eyes, Thad was a young image of his brother.

She drew a breath and dismissed the impact of Thad's innocent action. Heavens, one dinner with Zach, and the handsome lawyer had gotten under her skin.

She stepped up the narrow stairwell, and the mingled scents of yeast and caramelized brown sugar filled the close space. Behind her, Thad made a small sound of appreciation, and she grinned. It appeared the Spencer brothers were two of a kind. She should have expected it. She unlocked the upper door and they entered the darkened rooms.

"Want me to open the drapes?" Thad asked, his gaze on her satchel.

"Would you? I'll get some napkins. I haven't any milk but there's a jar of brewed tea near the window if you'd like."

He nodded and strode away, intent on his task. Lise gathered the small coal bucket and filled the stove in the center of the room. The scent of leather pervaded the air near the shelves and she drew a deep breath, letting the aroma fill her as she lit the fire and waited for the initial smokiness to diffuse the comforting book smells.

Collecting cups, Lise set them out with the sticky rolls. She sucked the sweet goo from her fingers, doubting Thad would mind her breach of manners. If he was as much like Zach as she suspected, he'd likely appreciate it.

Thad returned to her desk with the jar of tea and sat. Lise poured him a cupful as he picked up his roll. She watched him pull off a messy layer and place it in his mouth, rolling his eyes in pleasure. Definitely two of a kind.

She needed to find out more about Thad's position instead of getting distracted by Zach. Again. "How did you happen to hire on with Tom Tibbles?" she asked.

"I heard I oughtta talk to the typesetter about it. So I did, and he hired me right there on the spot."

Lise knit her brows. "The typesetter? Who told you that?" She'd check Thad's story.

"I just heard it." Thad licked his fingers and stared at her. "Did you really go out to dinner with Zach?"

"I did." She hesitated, wondering what Thad was up to. His vagueness and abrupt shift of topic was unsettling. "But, then, you already know that."

"Yeah. But he's bein' close-mouthed about it. Ma says she's heard more gossip about it at the mercantile than direct reports from Zach."

Zach had mentioned his mother's penchant for gossip, and Lise was well aware of Thad's practice of poking his nose into everything, a habit Zach had said he didn't share.

"It was a very nice dinner," she evaded. "We had a good time."

"What'd you eat?"

She laughed. "Do you two ever think about anything besides food?"

"Aw, I ain't as bad as Zach, not by a long shot." Thad scraped his thumbnail at a glob of hardened caramel. "Betcha he ordered something special," he commented. "Dessert, too."

"We had roast pheasant, brown rice, and candied plums. And apple pie for dessert. We talked about your grandfather."

"Ma thinks Zach is sweet on you."

Lise's breath caught and she struggled to retain a semblance of nonchalance. "Does she? And why would that be?"

" 'Cause Zach punched me when I asked him if he kissed you. And Ma said he was asking her about flowers, whether women like daffodils or tulips or irises, 'cause that's all a body can find in April."

Intrigued, she leaned forward. "And what'd she tell him?"

"She said he ought to —" he paused, guilt crossing his face. "I guess it won't be much of a surprise, now, huh?"

"Tell him I'm partial to yellow." Flowers, hmmm? She glanced at Thad as she cleared the desk. The boy had a way of gleaning information. "Now, was there anything else you wanted to know or have we gossiped enough for one morning?"

Thad's ears pinkened beneath his crop of blond hair. "No, ma'am. I didn't mean to pry, Miss Dupree, and I beg pardon if I was rude. Just seems to me like Zach was keeping it all to himself. Made me curious is all."

She raised her eyebrows at him. "You do recall that curiosity killed the cat?"

"Yes'm," he muttered.

"Do you like the job?" she asked.

Thad nodded. "I learn a lot, that's for sure. Old man Farcus is thinking of selling the mercantile, and Miss Hobart, over at the school, is scared to death of spiders. She was standing on a chair, like it was a mouse, when it was nothin' but a daddy longlegs."

"And you gathered all that on your route?"

"A body just needs to keep his eyes and ears open is all."

Her skin prickled. "And what other news have you gathered?"

"I saw Miss La Flesche drop off an envelope of papers for Mr. Tibbles. 'Course, that ain't really news, though, 'cause everybody already knows she's helping Mr. Tibbles write articles about Standing Bear. Mr. Tibbles isn't making any secret about his sympathies. That's what Ma says."

"I suppose she's right on that." Lise placed their cups in the back room, then returned to Thad. "Do Miss La Flesche and Mr. Tibbles talk about the case?" she asked.

"Oh, they don't talk at all. Miss La Flesche walks the other way every time she sees him." He wiped his hands on his pants. "Guess I'd best get the rest of those papers

148

delivered." He moved toward the door, then paused. "You bring breakfast every day?"

"Only when my landlady makes rolls. I'm afraid you'll need to satisfy your sweet tooth somewhere else, most days."

He shrugged his shoulders and offered a sheepish grin before slipping down the stairs.

Lise scrubbed her desk of the remaining caramel droplets and shook her head. Thad Spencer shared his brother's charm, as well as his sweet tooth. But he also displayed a disconcerting tendency to probe. His curiosity had been amusing when he'd stopped in to borrow books. And it *had* taken him to the Wigwam that day, the day Susette and Joseph had needed to send word of Aunt Rose.

Still, it unsettled her. It shouldn't bother her that Thad was inquisitive about her relationship with his brother. Yet, with all he'd found to gossip about in just one day at the newspaper office, he could become more than just a nuisance, and it could involve far more than her social life. A little bit of digging and the boy would know, and share, volumes about Standing Bear's case. And about Aunt Rose.

Unless, of course, she and Susette made

sure he learned only what they wanted him to know.

Susette stepped into the *Herald*'s front office and glanced around the room. Tom Tibbles leaned over a desk in the rear corner in conversation with an excited reporter in a checked suit. The reporter gestured wildly and Tom shook his head with a vehement release of breath.

Trouble, or at least a sizable difference of opinion.

She hung her wrap on a hook by the door, squared her shoulders, and walked toward her own desk. She suspected she and Tom were going to have their own differences of opinion when they discussed the issues facing them. She'd avoided him for several days, but instinct told her that putting off the inevitable wouldn't work much longer. Today, tomorrow, it would not matter when. She wished she knew whether to wait until he flirted with her again or if she should approach him directly.

Either way, it wasn't something she relished.

Her heels clicked on the wood floor, and Tom looked up at the sound. A hint of a smile crossed his face.

Susette looked away, hurried to the desk,

and slid into the heavy oak chair. She pulled out paper and pen and began to draft her assigned article for tomorrow's morning edition.

The reporter walked to the front of the room, grabbed a dapper black hat from the hat tree, and disappeared out the door. The distant clack of type being set echoed from the back room.

"You're eager to get busy this morning," Tom noted from behind her.

Susette kept her gaze on her notes. She didn't want to lose the tenuous control she'd gained in the past few days. "I should have had the first draft written yesterday."

"Yesterday, I hardly saw you."

She shrugged, evading. "I was busy reviewing my notes from the meeting with Standing Bear. I needed to fill in some details."

"I like that about you. You're very thorough."

"It's important to do things in the order they should be done. It saves doing things twice."

"I can't imagine you needing to do anything more than once."

"I'll have to do this three times if I don't concentrate." She kept her voice light. She didn't want to sound rude, hoping he would let her be.

"Are you angry at me, Susette?" He placed a hand on hers, stilling her pen.

A shiver raced up her arm, and she knew she'd been right to worry. She pulled her hand away and rose from her chair in a mock search of files on a nearby table. "I'm busy," she said.

"You're distant." His tone held concern. "Did I do something?"

She drew a breath and glanced around the room. They were alone. She moved closer, wishing they didn't need to have this conversation, and lowered her voice. "Tom, you're a married man. Distant is how we need to be."

"What are you talking about?"

"I'm talking about the way our eyes met the other day, the way the air grew thick." She held his gaze, and plunged ahead before she lost her nerve. "Don't tell me I imagined that."

He shook his head and glanced away. "No."

"And?"

He swallowed and faced her. "I thought *I* imagined it."

"That is a useful sidestep."

"It's not a sidestep and you know it," he snapped. He exhaled heavily. "It surprised the devil out of me. You want me to tell you I'm not attracted to you?" He paused. "I can't do that. If you felt it as keenly as I did, then you know damn well that I was. I am."

Susette's heart plummeted. She'd expected to feel joy at such a declaration. Irrational anger bubbled. "You're married," she snapped. "Or does that not matter to you?"

Tom ran his hand through his thinning hair. "I didn't set out to feel this way."

Susette bit back the pain. She wanted to believe that it had been spontaneous. "You didn't agree for me to come here for a purpose?"

"Not for that purpose, no." He stared at her. "What do you take me for? Do you honestly think I would ask you to help defend Standing Bear in order to take advantage of you?"

Susette shivered, thinking about the way the deputy had touched her, the leering gleam she'd seen in the eyes of so many white men. "Other men would."

"I'm not other men, Bright Eyes."

She lifted her gaze and looked him in the eyes. "I will not be any man's mistress, Tom."

"I have never broken my marriage vows,

and I don't intend to begin doing so now."

"But when you look at me, will your eyes still grow dark and full of suggestion?" As she said the words, she could feel the heat flare between them.

"I don't know," he told her. He sat down, hard, and looked up at her. "Do you think any of this makes me pleased with myself? It shames me that I think of you this way when I'm honorably married."

He wasn't looking for an answer from her, and any answer she gave would be inadequate. Still, questions nagged at her, ones she wasn't sure she wanted to know the answers to. She shuffled through the file in her hands, set it down.

"Are you happy with her?"

"I thought so. Now, I'm not so sure. We're comfortable."

Susette drew a steadying breath. "Do you love her?"

Silence engulfed them and she watched Tom struggle with his answer. She saw that the corners of his eyes were moist. A deep ache settled in her heart.

"Do you love her?" she asked again.

"I don't know."

Tears pooled in her own eyes.

He caught her hands. "I'm not *in* love with her."

154

She squeezed his hands, then let them go.

"Susette, I have never looked at another woman with adultery in my heart. I don't look at you with that intent. But, I'll be damned if I'll deprive myself of the companionship I feel when I'm working with you. I haven't felt this whole for a long time. I didn't expect to desire you on top of it, but I do. I'll manage that. Somehow."

Adam Foster stood in Abigail Spencer's tidy parlor and savored the steaming tea she'd graciously provided him. The fragile teacup reminded him of the set his late wife had once had, tiny purple violets and vivid green leaves on thin white china. He sipped again as the fragrant vapor wafted to his face.

Abigail and the boy, Thad, were preparing Henry for his visit. It was a shame, the loss of such a fine legal mind. Henry had been his mentor, guiding his political career, just as Adam was now steering young Zach. If fate had smiled differently on him, Abigail would have been his wife. Zach and Thad would have been his sons to raise. But she'd chosen his partner instead. If it hadn't been for Abigail's early widowhood, her husband would have been Henry's favored one. Destiny — and Henry's endorsement — would never have turned his way. Visiting the old man, watching him slump against pillows while spit ran down his chin, was a duty he owed.

"He's ready for you, Adam." Abigail smiled from the doorway, wiping her hands on a neat ruffled apron. She was still a handsome enough woman, despite her age. He had suspected she'd accept his proposal now that he was a senator, but her refusals through the years stung. He'd succeeded without her connections. He didn't need her now.

"Thank you, Abigail. You've been gracious, welcoming me so unexpectedly." He set the teacup on the polished cherrywood table and rose. "Thad, my boy, will you join us?"

Thad drifted back into the room. "Yes, sir. If you want me to."

Adam chuckled at the boy. Of course, he wanted him to. It was the whole damn reason he'd come. "No reason you shouldn't join us. I imagine your grandfather would feel it's time you sat and talked with the men. After all, you're not a kid anymore." He watched Thad's smile broaden and knew he'd greased the wheel well.

He let Thad lead the way into the small back bedroom and steeled himself. It'd choked him up, the first few times, seeing

Henry, pale and wasted. He hoped he went quick when it was his own time. Lingering around for years was a hell of a way to spend a life.

The bedroom stank of stale urine. Adam blanched and tried not to gag. "Henry. You're looking well tonight. You've got a glint in your eye." The old man looked peaked, like a soggy prune. Adam sat in the straight-backed chair Abigail had placed next to the bed and clasped his mentor's hand. It sat loosely in his palm.

From the bed, Henry's jaw struggled and guttural gibberish fell from his lips.

Adam squeezed his palm, then sat back in the chair. "I thought you might enjoy an update on that grandson of yours," he said. "We got a wire from the Stock Growers' Association this afternoon, and they're in our pocket. A pledge of support came in from Union Pacific, and Ed Rosewater's paper is endorsing him. It's all falling into line, just like we planned."

Henry's mouth twitched.

Adam supposed it was as close as the old man was going to get to a real smile. He wondered whether it was too early to turn the conversation to Thad and pick the kid's brain for awhile. It didn't matter. Henry had probably already lost track of how long they'd been talking.

He waited for Thad to finish dabbing at his grandfather's mouth, then beamed at the boy. "And this other grandson of yours, did he tell you he's got himself a job down at Tibbles's place? I hope you don't mind that I pointed him in that direction, despite Abigail's objections. You know how women are when they get something set in their minds. One addled thought and there's no room for any common sense. If the boy wanted a job, then he ought to get it." He leaned back in the chair and crossed his legs, watching Thad mimic his posture on the opposite side of the bed. Just a trio of men.

"What do you think, boy?" he asked. "Will Tibbles endorse your brother?"

Thad shook his head and grinned. "Guess there's about as much chance of that as there is snow in July. I almost feel like I'm betraying Zach by workin' there."

"Nonsense. When you're a working man, you don't let politics get in the way." He gave the kid a worried look. "Did Tibbles say something about Zach?"

"No, but he's got that Indian teacher working there with him, writing stories about Standing Bear so they can win that trial."

It was old news, but he let surprise wash across his features. "The case Zach is working on?"

"Yeah. I think they're working with Standing Bear's lawyers. That Miss La Flesche is gonna be one of the interpreters at the trial. And they were talkin' a lot about the Fourteenth Amendment."

Now that *was* news. If the Indians' case was going to focus on citizenship, Zach had just been dealt a trump card. He could walk his defense all over them. It'd work in well with the savage image Ed Rosewater's paper was creating.

He'd debated whether to set the boy up in the newspaper office, but it looked like Tibbles and the woman weren't paying him any mind. Hell, they were learning something worthwhile anyhow.

"I heard something about the Poncas spending time on Omaha land before they were arrested."

"The Omahas want to give 'em land on the reservation."

"Well, I daresay it's not quite that simple." Adam reached for the blanket over Henry's chest and adjusted it.

Thad propped his stockinged feet on the bed, crossing them at the ankles. "That's what Tibbles said, 'cept in different words.

They asked Miss Dupree to research a bunch of stuff over at the library."

"On the amendment?"

"Uh huh."

"Isn't she that librarian who helped Zach?"

"Well, she's the librarian but I don't think she helped him much. I heard him say she's so distracting he can't get any research done. He spends an awful lot of time complaining about her. At least he did until he took her out to dinner Saturday night."

Adam nodded, digesting the information. "I believe he mentioned something about that." Damn reckless idiot hadn't said a damn word. There wasn't a doubt in his mind that Zach knew he was taking a risk in socializing with the enemy. Not a doubt.

Thad leaned forward, hand on his far hip, looking about as sage as a thirteen-year-old could. "Bought her roast pheasant. And I think he kissed her, too."

Adam choked back a cough of surprise. "That so?"

Between them, Henry stirred and issued more frustrated gurgles.

Thad shifted and managed a quick swipe at the drool on his grandfather's mouth before Henry batted his hand away.

Adam laid a hand on Henry's chest, felt

160

his heart pounding, and offered a comforting pat. "Shhhh. Nothin' to get worked up about. Thad's just postulating."

"I'm guessing I'm right about the kiss, though, because he punched me when I asked him."

Adam chuckled, though he wasn't amused. "Well, perhaps he's trying to butter her up so she'll help him more."

Thad shrugged. "Maybe. But since she's friends with Miss La Flesche, I'd wager two bits she'd side with Standing Bear if you pinned her down. Yesterday, she was carrying around books on Indian treaties in her satchel. I saw 'em when she shared her cinnamon rolls with me. I betcha that ain't to help Zach, not the way she bristles up when folks talk bad about Indians. Zach's a goner when it comes to pretty girls. She'll have him wrapped around her little finger in no time, just you wait and see." He glanced down at his sleeping grandfather, then back at Adam. "You reckon there are any cookies left out on the platter Ma brought your tea on?"

Adam chuckled again and rose from his chair. "Let's go see." It galled him to think the librarian was abetting the Indian case but it didn't surprise him. Now that he'd confirmed it, he'd be damned if he was going to let her milk information from Zach in return for kisses. Women were too good at that sort of thing, and Zach didn't have near the political savvy he needed to realize it.

Having Thad in place as a spy was a greater benefit than he'd anticipated, but something still needed to be done about Miss Dupree. It was better done sooner than later.

CHAPTER EIGHT

"Do you really think Thad's a spy?" Susette asked Lise from across their table in Sorenson's Café.

Lise shrugged her shoulders and sighed. "I don't want to believe it. Maybe I'm just being silly but Thad is such a gossip and his getting a job at the *Herald* at this point in time seems odd. Especially since he evaded my questions." Suspicion had nagged at her like a rash until she could do nothing but scratch it. "I like Thad, but he possesses endless curiosity and a troubling habit of babbling about everything he's observed, even if it's unintentional."

"He has been a friend." Susette lowered her voice. "I can't believe he would tell tales that would put Standing Bear in danger."

"I hope he wouldn't do so on purpose, but he's naive enough to do it without realizing it." Lise sipped her tea and shifted her gaze to the other diners. Susette had

163

convinced her that they'd draw no attention. Located near the Wigwam, Sorenson's often served Indians, and it was now common knowledge that Lise supported Standing Bear's cause. Gossip had made sure of that. It startled Lise a little that no one seemed to care that women of different races were dining together. Tongues would be wagging if they were in Spirit Lake. The citizens of Omaha were more tolerant than she'd given them credit for.

Susette nodded. "I'll tell Tom we must be careful what we say when Thad is present."

Lise leaned forward. "Perhaps we could use Thad to our advantage." She shifted, uncomfortable with the blatant calculation of her words.

"Mislead him?"

"Thad's presence in the newspaper office is too coincidental to ignore. Much as I'd rather think otherwise, we have to consider the possibility. If Zach placed him there on purpose, it would serve him right to have Thad bringing back false information." Anger crept into her voice. She had no right to feel betrayed. It was her own fault, forgetting that Zach was the enemy.

The man made her feel like a clock pendulum. He'd sent her sunny daffodils and brought her a surprise picnic lunch at the library. Yet, she couldn't shake the suspicion that Zach might have purposely asked Thad to gather information. And if he had, she wasn't about to let him get away with it.

"You think this is something Zach would do?"

Lise shifted in her chair. "I don't know." She was lost in a fog when it came to Zach. Against her better judgment, she liked him. But she had to consider Aunt Rose and the Poncas. Trusting Zach made her nervous, suspecting him made her uncomfortable. She sighed. "I think we should err on being safe rather than sorry."

"Do you have a plan?"

Lise glanced around and lowered her voice further. "Poppleton and Webster have decided to focus on the Fourteenth Amendment. No person can be deprived of life, liberty, or the pursuit of happiness without due process of the law. Forcing the Poncas to Indian Territory is in violation of that guarantee."

Susette's mouth tipped downward as she pondered the strategy. "If Judge Dundy agrees with that, wouldn't it mean the end of reservations?"

"In theory, yes. We don't know if Dundy will make that leap. If he does, it will change Indian Law as we know it, and stand the reservation system on its head."

"That will not happen. It's too much."

Susette's words were true. A district judge from Nebraska was hardly going to overturn hundreds of years of legal action. Not when Congress, and Parliament before them, had been unable to reach consensus on how to treat Indians for more than a few decades at a time.

"Poppleton feels the same way. So we need to provide an alternative, a way for Dundy to rule in Standing Bear's favor without having to challenge the whole system. Poppleton and Webster want to create a distinction, to make a case that those in Standing Bear's band are no longer in the same category as Indians in general."

Susette's eyes widened in comprehension. "That's why Tom and I are writing about the clothes they wear and the farms they had."

"Yes, and emphasizing their separation from the rest of the tribe." Lise's thoughts lingered on Susette's recent article about Standing Bear's civilized actions.

"While Ed Rosewater is busy running articles on how savage the Indian is." Susette laughed softly. "He doesn't even realize he's helping our case."

They smiled at each other across the table

as a waitress served their meal. The scent of split pea soup filled the air. Around them, other diners were busy with their meals and conversation. No one looked their way.

Was it only the trial and her role as a sympathetic researcher, Lise wondered, or had she worried too much about the bias of her fellow citizens? No one seemed to think it odd that she was dining with the daughter of the Omaha chief.

She set her spoon in her soup and pulled her thoughts back to their planning. "Poppleton and I spent a lot of time mulling it over last night. We need to watch what we say around Thad. Say nothing more about the Fourteenth Amendment so we don't tip our hand. Instead, let him hear things about treaty law."

Susette looked skeptical.

Lise lifted a spoonful of soup to her mouth and ate, then explained. "If Zach thinks our arguments have to do with the rights of Indians, he'll keep researching that issue. The first time we met, he did nothing but refer to laws that define Indians as less than human. We don't need him digging any further. I've talked about treaties quite a bit. If Thad brings the same information, Zach will be convinced that's our case and he'll focus on that aspect. Treaty law will tie up hours of research and get him nowhere in terms of a defense."

"But isn't the treaty confusion at the heart of it?"

"It is. But Poppleton says there simply isn't enough time to adequately dig into the complications for this case. The trial date is too soon."

Susette nodded, satisfied. "It makes sense, a small difference but one that will be enough?"

"It will be enough. Zach focuses too narrowly for it not to be." Lise told herself the deceit was necessary. After all, wasn't Zach sending his brother to spy?

Lise stood in the front hallway of her boarding house and eyed the wicker creel in Zach's hand. "Fishing?" she asked.

From her landlady's parlor, the other female residents offered speculative glances. Wizened old Miss Moore even winked.

"The weather is gorgeous," Zach announced, oblivious to the stares of the old maids and their curiosity. "It's Sunday, the river's running, the sun's out, wind's nonexistent. You get a spring day like this, you take advantage."

"I haven't fished since I was a little girl." A smile lifted Lise's mouth as she recalled going night crawler hunting with her cousins. They'd chased her around the yard, fat worms in their hands, while she'd shrieked in mock terror.

"You want to go," Zach insisted. "I can see it on your face." He glanced at the women in the parlor and lowered his voice. "Will you join me?"

The invitation beckoned her, urging her to capitulate.

"I'll need a bit of tutoring. Those rods look a lot more complicated than the twigs and twine I used to use."

"You'll get the hang of it in no time. But you'd better change those shoes." He nodded at the sleek black button-shoes poking out beneath her Sunday dress.

"I'll be right back." She left him standing in the front hall, at the mercy of her housemates, and raced up the stairs to her tiny room. Fishing, of all things. But, he was right; it was a gorgeous day. The sun had warmed the air, tempting children to frolic and adults to stroll the parks.

Lise pushed the buttons through their tiny loops as fast as she could and slid the dress shoes from her feet. Shedding her good dress, she put on a woolen plaid, fine for the outdoors, and wiggled her toes before slipping on faded brown boots and tightening the laces. She set her glasses on the bureau, grabbed her shawl, and headed downstairs.

Zach was still standing near the door when she came down the stairs. His blond hair hung over his forehead. He pushed it away in his casual way and Lise's breath caught. Land sakes, the man was attractive.

Keep your guard up, girl. You don't need this complication.

With luck, she might catch enough fish to provide a meal for her housemates. All she needed to do was concentrate on the fish instead of Zach. How hard could that be?

She lifted her gaze and found him staring at her, his blue eyes twinkling. "Ready?" he asked.

Lise drew a breath. Maybe she was making a mountain out of a molehill. Nodding, she donned her shawl and smiled her assent.

He offered the ladies in the parlor a wave of his fingers, then ushered Lise out the door.

"They'll be talking about you all afternoon."

"I figured as much." His face bore an infectious grin as he guided her down the front steps.

Children flooded the streets, their excited

voices overlapping in games of tag and kick the can. Little girls sat in the new green grass, dolls on their laps, playing tea party. Nearby flower beds filled the air with the scent of tulips and daffodils. Sun danced its warmth across Lise's face, and she found her worries slowly melting in the afternoon sun.

They walked down the hill of Dodge Street and turned north, along the riverbank, until they passed the bustle of Lone Tree Landing where the river widened. The sounds of the city gave way to the melody of nesting robins and the chirps of busy sparrows. Along the banks, early wildflowers replaced cultivated gardens. A striped ground squirrel scurried across the grass, rustling through last fall's dried leaves. Lise jumped, then laughed.

"You gotta watch those wild animals, ma'am," Zach teased. "Some of them can be pretty fierce."

Lise punched him lightly on the shoulder. "You're supposed to protect me, you oaf."

"Oaf? I am deeply offended, my good lady. I've put much effort into being a cad and you call me an oaf."

"Oaf, cad, makes no difference. I could have been killed."

"Pshaw."

"Pshaw?" She raised her eyebrows.

He shrugged. "That's what Ma says."

Intrigued by the tenderness in his voice, she mulled this new side of him. "You're close to her, aren't you?"

"She's a peach. Gossipy, but a peach." His tone became more serious. "She did a good job raising two sons. She and Gramps."

"I'll bet Gramps taught you to fish, didn't he?"

"That he did." The bond between them was evident in Zach's expression. "He made sure we did the things boys are supposed to do."

"It sounds as if he loves you a lot."

"He doted on me, took me to the office, taught me to appreciate the law. I've wanted to be like him. In every way."

Lise waited a beat, unsure of how to respond. "I'm sorry you don't have that with him anymore," she finally said.

"Me, too." Zach scooped his blond hair away from his eyes. "How about you? You've never said much about your family."

"There's not much to tell," Lise hedged.

"Sure there is. Where'd you grow up?"

"I was born in Minnesota but mostly raised in St. Louis." She offered him the standard veneer on her life, the truth, nothing more. "My father was a shopkeeper. He

172

passed away a few years back."

"You miss him."

Surprised he'd discerned so much from her limited words, Lise wrangled over how much more to reveal. "He was one of the fairest people I've ever known," she said, her tone conveying her esteem for the man who had allowed her to revere her heritage. She ignored the urge to finger her beaded necklace. "He had a way of looking at every side of an issue."

"And your mother?"

"She still lives in St. Louis."

"Do you see her often?"

"Very little. She's . . . I guess you'd say she's reserved." In truth, Lise's mother wasn't so much reserved as strong. Strong enough to turn her back on her people in order to protect her family. But in doing so, she'd closed off the very part of herself that Lise most wanted to know. On rare occasions, she'd opened the trunk for Lise, but had banned her from telling anyone else. They'd drifted apart in the years since her father's death.

"But you stay in touch?"

"We write. I send her money." Uncomfortable with her churning resentment at her mother's distant behavior, Lise gestured toward the river's edge. "Were we going to fish?"

"You're reserved, too."

Lise stared at him. "Me?"

"You keep a close guard on how much of yourself you share."

"Sometimes." She could tell the answer didn't satisfy him but he let it go, setting the wicker creel on a flat rock beside the shore.

"You've never used a rod and reel?"

She shook her head.

Zach handed her one of the split cane rods. It was lighter than she'd expected given its length. "This catches fish? It looks like it'd break."

"It's a Hardy rod, and it's long so you can cast farther. The Missouri's wide and shallow, and you don't want to get your line tangled up in the weeds along the edge."

"That makes sense."

"It's called a coarse rod, made for catching fish like perch. I've got fly rods, too, to catch trout. They're made to skim the bait over the surface. With this one, you cast it and wait."

"Sounds less complicated. Did you bring bait?"

"There are worms in the creel."

Lise opened the wicker basket and pulled

out a tin filled with dark black dirt. She poked her finger into it and caught hold of a wriggling earthworm. Wrinkling her mouth in distaste, she threaded it onto the hook and ignored the grin on Zach's face. "No fancy lures?" she asked.

"Not for perch." He finished baiting his own hook and glanced at her. "You know how to cast that thing?"

"I haven't a clue. When I was a kid, we just dropped our lines in the water."

He set his own rod on the ground. "Take off the shawl so you can move," he said. Standing beside her, he pointed to the brass reel attached to the rod. "That's called a rotary winch. It lets the line out when you cast. You turn the handle to reel it in when you've got a fish on the line. When you cast, you swing the rod, and the momentum pulls the line out. That's it."

"That's it?"

"Just let the line spin out."

"And I swing the rod how?"

"I'll show you." He stepped away and picked up his own rod, then arced it over his shoulder. The effort tightened his shirt across his chest, defining the muscles under the cotton cloth. Lise smiled in appreciation as he propelled his arm forward and the line flew out above the water. He wedged the rod in a rock cranny and turned to Lise. "Your turn."

Lise stared at the rod for a moment, then swung it back over her head. Twigs fell as it caught in the branches above. Heat creeping up her face, she peered at Zach. He held his laughter but she could see the corners of his mouth twitching.

"Don't you dare," she told him.

"Hard to help it. Just work it loose and take stock of where you are before you swing."

She glanced up, side stepped, and brought the rod up. Swinging it over her head, she waited for the line to arc out over the water. To her dismay, the end with the hook stayed on the shoreline while the line itself snaked out. This time, Zach's laughter poured out, filling the quiet air. Against her will, her own giggles bubbled to the surface.

"Easy, you say?"

He waited while she reeled in the line. "Stand here," he told her when she finished. He moved behind her and wrapped his arm over hers, then grasped her hand. "Loosen up. You're stiff as a board. Put your finger on the line and hold it so it doesn't slip. Then slowly cast out. Release your finger just as the rod clears the top of the arc. Ready?"

She nodded.

"All right. Here we go."

As the pressure of his finger lifted from hers, she removed her finger from the line. Just as he'd promised, the line flew out over the water.

Behind her, his arm still wrapped around hers, Zach drew a breath. "You smell good," he whispered. "Like lemon bars."

"Lemon verbena."

"Nah, lemon bars. Maybe lemon drops. Or lemon pudding." His mouth drew close to her ear, his breath hot, and her head fell back into his chest. He brushed her hair back, his fingertips touching her skin. His lips caressed her neck. "Nope. Definitely lemonade."

Lise relaxed into his nuzzling, wanting more. Her pulse quickened and heat crept through her body. She was tempting fate. She inhaled, then pulled away from him. "Careful, lemonade can be tart."

"I like a little tart mixed in with my sweets."

"Not if it pinches up your mouth."

"Makes me more kissable." He puckered his lips together.

Giggles jumped from Lise's mouth and she shook her head at him. "Makes you look silly. Not to mention you've forgotten all about your line." She tipped her head toward the rapidly spinning reel, unsure whether to be relieved or resentful when he jumped to grab the rod.

He reeled in the fish, oblivious to the turmoil tumbling inside her. His eyes flashed with enjoyment, and his mouth stretched into a satisfied smile that made her breath catch. Good heavens, what was she doing? She was jelly in his hands, ready to melt into the desire he stirred in her. Her knees were weak, for goodness sake.

This was not a good thing, not at all.

Her line tugged and she felt it begin to spin out. Catching the knob on the reel, she turned the winch, reeling the fish in. Fish and small talk, she resolved. From here on out, that'd be it.

Zach pulled in an eight-inch perch and twisted it off the hook. Seconds later, she caught a slightly smaller specimen. After adding it to the stringer Zach had started, they prepared their lines again, and casted out in companionable silence.

The sun made its lazy way across the water, bouncing reflections of the budding trees. Chirping robins chorused in the background with the noisier starlings adding their aggressive presence.

Zach reached for a small flat stone and

skimmed it out across the river upstream of their location. He smiled at the ripples as it hopped its way away from shore. "Lise?"

"Hmmm?" She stretched in the sunlight and looked in his direction.

"How'd you get so interested in Indians?"

A jolt of panic grasped her. "I —"

"And don't try to tell me you're not. You argue about their rights with passion."

She settled down against a sun-warmed rock and searched for an answer that would satisfy him. "My friends, Sarah and Miriam, and I were always campaigning on behalf of something. Indian rights was my contribution to our collection of causes." She shrugged. "There were always Indians in Father's store when I was little, and in St. Louis. I learned a lot about them, respected them." She turned toward him. "I appreciate their culture and their struggle."

"But what makes it so personal?"

She shifted, her eyes back on the river. "Personal?"

Zach sighed. "You're involved. More than just someone who respects a different culture."

"I really don't want to talk about this."

"Because of the trial?" he asked softly.

"Mostly, yes." It was as good an answer as any. Truthful, if not complete.

Zach reeled in his line. "I already know you're biased, Lise. I stopped being fooled by your attempts to mislead me a week ago."

She stared at him, unwilling to admit he'd known. "Mislead you?"

He grinned. "You were too obvious."

"But —"

"You're much smarter than you wanted me to believe and it's hard to hide that, no matter how much you flirt. I just wanted you to know that." He set his rod down, pulled the fish off, and threaded it onto the stringer.

"I . . . I didn't know I was so transparent."

He faced her, the grin gone. "I don't want the trial getting in the way anymore. When I ask you about Indians, it's because I want to know you, not because I'm digging for information about Standing Bear. It's clear you care a great deal about what happens to the Poncas and that Susette is a good friend. I won't ask you to help me on my case."

She met his gaze and offered a tentative smile. "You know I don't agree with your interpretation of the law."

"I know. For what it's worth, I admire that about you. You have firm convictions and you're not afraid to defend them." The blue of his eyes grew smoky. "I hope that makes it easier for you to understand why I have to defend what I believe in."

For a moment, Lise's heart thundered. She swallowed, seeking a way to turn the conversation from the dangerous path it had taken, afraid to tread any further. Her rod jerked in her hand. "My line! I think I caught another one."

"I think you have, too."

"I'm serious. It feels different. Bigger." She turned the small knob, winding the line onto the reel. There was a strong pull as the fish thrashed against the drag.

Zach's jaw dropped. "Holy cow, Lise. You've got more than a perch on there."

"That's what I said. Am I going to break the rod?"

"Reel it in. I'll help." He shoved his rod into a crevice and scrambled to her side. Grabbing the line, he began drawing it in, hand over hand, easing the pressure on her rod. As the fish drew closer, it struggled harder, splashing violently in the murky river. Water flew into the air with each jerk.

Zach hauled the last of the line out of the water and hefted the flopping fish into the air. "Catfish," he told her. "Huge catfish. Must have swallowed the hook. Otherwise, it'd have pulled out."

Lise dropped the rod and hurried to his side. The flat-bottomed whiskered fish flailed about, spraying water everywhere. Clearly, there would be no pulling the hook from this one.

"Can you take it?" Zach asked. "I'll grab my knife and cut the line."

She nodded and took the line in her hand. The weight, when Zach released it, took her by surprise. The fish slipped downward; she grabbed for it with both hands and it slapped against her chest, then flapped out of her grasp. She stumbled after it, chasing it along the shore. Zach's laughter erupted.

Splattering against the rocks, the catfish leapt closer to the river, Lise grabbing the air behind it. As it floundered toward the water, she lunged. She landed with the fish in her arms and her butt in the river, catfish spines poking at her arms and chest as heat crept up her face.

Zach doubled over in hysterical snickers.

Lise rose to her feet, unable to be angry, and slogged her way to him. She stuck out her tongue and tossed the fish at him. It flopped briefly against him before falling to the ground where it eventually stilled. Scratched and dripping, she grinned at Zach, then shoved him.

He toppled, grabbing at her as he fell.

As she landed on his chest, Zach's laughter faded. He grasped her face in his hand and pulled her down, his lips hungry and searching. Her skin heated under his hands and her heart raced as his tongue dove into her mouth and her own tongue responded. His fingers stroked her cheeks, her neck, and brushed against her breast before sliding first one button open, then two.

At the third, his fingertip caught against the leather cord that held her beaded necklace.

Adam Foster drummed his fingers on his desk. Across from him, Thad Spencer slumped in a chair, chugging a bottle of sarsaparilla.

"I appreciate you stopping by like this," he told the kid.

Thad swallowed and straightened. "Oh, no problem, Mr. Foster. I 'preciate the soda."

Adam stilled his fingers and reminded himself to be patient and let the kid enjoy the treat. He'd bought a half-dozen bottles of the sweet swill to have on hand to soften the boy's tongue. "Drink up," he told him. "You've put in a hard morning. Most folks don't stop to think about how hard a kid works making deliveries."

Thad finished off the soda and set the bottle on the floor before leaning forward. "That's for sure. Was there something you needed? I came over as soon as I heard you were looking for me."

"I was over at Sorenson's Café for lunch and they had fresh banana pudding. I had some put up for your granddaddy." He nodded at the jar on his shelf. "Wanted you to take it to him."

Thad beamed, just as Adam had anticipated. "He likes bananas."

"I remember that, used to buy one every chance he got." He let a smile stretch across his face. It was time to get down to business. "How's the job coming along?"

"Like you said, it's a lot of work. But I like it. Mostly, anyhow."

"Good, good." Some days, the kid spouted information like a geyser. Today wasn't one of them. Adam stifled a sigh and probed further. He shuffled a few papers on his desk, feigning half-hearted interest. "Things still busy at the *Herald,* then?"

"Yes, sir."

"Tibbles still running those Indian stories?"

Thad grinned. "Him and Miss La Flesche."

Adam raised his eyebrows and gave the

184

kid a man-to-man nod. "She's a pretty little thing, isn't she?"

"I guess." Thad shrugged. "Mostly, I like her 'cause she treats me like I'm important, like Miss Dupree does. I bet she's a good teacher."

"Could be." Adam filed a few papers in his desk drawer, then glanced at Thad. "She talk much? I've often wondered if Indian ladies are quiet or talkative."

"Her and Tibbles talk about everything under the sun. Last two days, they've talked about Indian treaties and uprisings."

Finally, the meat of things. Adam drew a breath, pleased he'd persisted. This afternoon, he and Zach would talk strategy. It might take a little work, but Zach could pull a case out of treaty law. "Quite a pair of topics," he told the kid.

"Yes, sir. I never knew there was so much involved in all that Indian stuff. I think the lawyers for Standing Bear are gonna make a case on which treaty is valid. There's four of 'em, all for the same land." Thad puffed with prideful knowledge. "Miss La Flesche said the last one was with the Sioux but the Sioux were only there because they got kicked out of Minnesota."

Adam nodded. "I do believe that's true." In fact, the kid's granddaddy had helped

185

make sure of it. He glanced at the boy, sure the kid had never heard any of the details. Abigail Spencer had not been pleased with Henry's involvement in those convictions. He supposed that was why the old man had kept quiet about it all these years.

"Miss Dupree got all hot tempered when they were talking about that," Thad added.

"She did?" Womenfolk were a mushy variety of mankind. Adam stood and casually re-shelved books in the barrister's cabinet behind his desk, letting the kid ramble on at his own pace.

"She said it was the government's fault that there was an uprising, on account of how they mistreated the Sioux. She even cried about it."

He turned and stared at Thad. "She cried?"

"I don't think they knew I was there, else she wouldn't have. I was in the back, gettin' more papers."

"I'm surprised it means so much to her."

"She used to live there, you know. When she was a kid. She saw some of the Indians get hanged. I guess there's some old Indian lady with the Poncas that she knew back then and now she's real upset about it."

Adam settled his pounding heart as he digested the news. "This trial must be very

186

difficult for her then. You must be very careful not to bother her about any of it." He didn't need the kid poking around, stirring things up. He needed time to figure out how to best use the information.

"Oh, no, sir."

He nodded at the bottle on the floor. Time to move the kid along. He had things to do. "Well, son, you finished with that soda?"

"Yes, sir."

"Then I reckon you ought to get that pudding home before your mother makes dessert. Wouldn't want to put her to extra work."

"Thank you, Mr. Foster." The boy stood and retrieved the bottle. "I'll give Ma your best."

"You do that, son."

He watched Thad exit, then settled back into his chair. It never ceased to amaze him how things came together. He'd needed a way to extract Zach from the librarian's web and there it was, wrapped up in female sentimentality.

CHAPTER NINE

Zach stared at the beaded pendant in his palm. He could feel the chill of uncertainty in Lise's stare. She was obviously much closer to her Indian friend than she let on. He swallowed, hating the precarious position he was now in.

He lifted his gaze and stared back at her. "A gift from your friend, Susette?" he asked her.

She hesitated, then nodded.

"Then I guess we need to talk." He stood and offered her his hand. Head down, she accepted his help and rose, then straightened her clothing self-consciously.

"First, though . . . Lise . . . I'm sorry. I overstepped my bounds. I shouldn't have —"

"Don't." She caught his gaze and held it, unblushing. "I'm not a school girl, Zach. If I hadn't wanted you to kiss me, I would have told you."

"But it was far more than a kiss."

"That, too." A smile lit her dark eyes. "The ladies at the rooming house wouldn't approve but I did."

"I did, too." He tossed strewn fishing gear into the basket and gathered up the rods while weighing his next words, then ran a hand through his unruly hair. "I guess that's what makes this so complicated. I'm attracted to you, Lise. In many, many ways. But I'm defending a case that you're close to, that you have more than an intellectual interest in." He shook his head. "And I'm also going to run for senate. That puts me in a delicate position."

Puzzlement etched Lise's features. "You don't strike me as the type of person who can't separate emotions from professional responsibility."

"That's not what I'm worried about."

"Appearances?" Her face clouded.

"Appearances. If it looks like I'm biased, it could affect the outcome of the case."

"And your bid for office."

He nodded. "Being sympathetic to the Indian cause is not something I can afford right now, for both reasons. How close are you and Susette?"

She shifted, a frown creasing her brow, and drew a heavy breath. Zach's gut tightened and he knew he wasn't going to like her answer.

"Close enough that it would be a problem," she finally said.

Zach sighed, resentment chafing him. Right now, he'd much rather be exploring Lise's passion than worrying about the case or how the voting public would perceive their actions. He wasn't fond of complications, and his life seemed damned full of them all of a sudden. And if he wasn't careful, Lise's would be, too.

He caught her gaze and offered what he hoped was an apologetic smile. "Then I'm doubly sorry about the liberties I took."

Lise nodded, her smile gone. "So am I, Zach. So am I."

Midway through Monday morning, Adam Foster entered the library and scanned the room. He was surprised at the orderliness. Shelving filled the space opposite of the door, neat rows of it. He hadn't expected a scatterbrained female to maintain the room that professionally. He'd pictured stacks of books everywhere, maybe frilly curtains and tea services on the tables that were situated under the windows.

He'd have to tread carefully. Miss Dupree

might be a little sharper than he'd anticipated.

As if she heard his thoughts, she appeared from behind a shelf and smiled at him. "May I help you find something in particular?"

"Oh, just browsing. I'm Senator Adam Foster." He approached her and extended his hand. He figured she'd be the type who'd expect a handshake, and he didn't want to set her off, not yet. He had groundwork to lay. "Just taking a peek at the library I've heard so much about."

"Miss Lise Dupree," she said, shaking his hand before she stepped back. "Please let me know if I can help with anything or answer any questions."

Adam waited until she was busy searching the row of books for the proper place to insert the one she held in her hands. Her lips moved, quietly alphabetizing as she scanned the shelf. He could see why Zach was interested in her; she was quite a looker with those big brown eyes. Even behind the wire spectacles, the spark in them was unmistakable. Might be there was more than a little bit of fire in this one. He let his gaze roam as she stretched to place the book on the upper shelf.

Yes, sir, there wasn't a doubt in his mind

what had caught Zach's attention. He cleared his throat and tried to look business-like. "As a matter of fact," he said, "I would like to see the law section. Zach Spencer mentioned that he was impressed by your collection."

She nodded. "It's a good assortment. Most of it was donated by Andrew Popple-ton." She led the way across the room.

Adam followed, choosing his words carefully, laying the groundwork. "Ah, yes, Poppleton. Representing Standing Bear I've heard."

"And Mr. Spencer is representing General Crook."

Surprised at her astute understanding of the intricacies of the case, Adam's gut tensed. Most folks didn't realize Crook was involved — they thought the suit was against the government. There wasn't a doubt in his mind that he needed to get that boy away from this woman. She'd be a thorn in his side all the way through the election. Vo-cal, self-righteous, and clearly opinionated. He figured Zach was a good way under her spell already, no use trying to warn the boy off. She'd ruin Zach's bid for office and Adam's power along with it.

"Quite right, Miss Dupree. I understand you're sympathetic to the Ponca cause."

She took the bait immediately; her chin raised and mouth set. "I feel their removal from their lands was illegal."

He arched his eyebrows and inclined his head, as he would with a constituent who held a bunch of half-baked ideas. "Well, I guess everyone is entitled to an opinion."

As he'd expected, Miss Dupree bristled. A few well-placed comments and she'd be so angry at Zach that she'd never speak to him again.

She drew a breath and calmed. "Is there anything else, Senator?" she asked.

She was a more formidable opponent than he'd anticipated. Adam bit back his agitation and honed his response.

"Oh, no, dear." He patted her hand, knowing the condescension would irk her. She'd be biting her tongue pretty hard before long. "I wanted to thank you for being so helpful to Zach, despite your 'opinions.' I'm afraid his grandfather is no longer able to talk. If he were, I'm sure Zach would have found all the guidance he needed right there at home."

"So I understand."

"Henry was quite the legal mind in his day. Took me under his wing, taught me much of what I know. Taught Zach, too, when he was preparing for practice. Guided him in *every* thought, taught him right from wrong and the sacredness of the law. Good man, Henry. Made his mark on the world back in sixty-two when he served as attorney for the commission that managed to hang thirty-eight of those savages in Minnesota."

The librarian's sharp inhale told Adam he'd hit his target. "He was involved in the Sioux trials?" Her voice wavered and Adam could almost see the wheels in her head trying to measure Zach against what he'd just told her. By God, Thad had sure pinned this one right. The woman had more than a little sympathy for those Sioux.

Adam nodded. "Heavily," he said, then paused for effect. "He'd have sent over three hundred of them to the gallows if Lincoln hadn't stepped in with those last-minute pardons."

Miss Dupree straightened her posture, guarding her emotions. "I see."

"Those folks needed justice and Henry saw to it they got it. He was a rising prosecutor dead set on seeing those renegades get the punishment they deserved. Hung as many as he could and sent the rest of 'em away, made the state safe again."

She blanched, then whirled away. "If you'll excuse me, Senator, I've other things to attend to."

"Oh, by all means. Don't let me disturb you."

Adam let his smile stretch, feeling pleased. He and the kid had both been right. Miss Dupree had very clear sympathies with Indians, and she sure didn't like it that Zach's kin were part of hanging the renegades who caused the Minnesota uprising.

Zach was about to discover a very cold shoulder indeed.

In case his little slip of information hadn't done the trick, he'd mosey over to see Rufus Christy. He'd set the little weasel to work digging up information on the old Indian lady Thad had mentioned. The Indian agent ought to be able to track down the woman's identity, as well as her relationship to Miss Dupree.

After all, one could never have too much information.

Lise stared at Adam Foster's departing form, a hard pit of loathing in her stomach. She wasn't sure if the man had come to the library with the intent to spew his spiteful announcement or if his statements had been coincidence. Either way, she was glad he was gone.

She shivered, the knot in her gut tightening.

Zach's grandfather had hung her uncle along with scores of other Sioux who had rebelled against an unjust system. Dozens of them guilty only by association, either because they were born Sioux or because their names were similar to those who had killed or because a white woman couldn't distinguish one from another.

Zach's beloved Gramps had been the attorney who had worked with the military commission responsible for trying several hundred of the accused. He'd robbed Aunt Rose of her home, sentenced her to a life as a refugee. He'd pronounced her people as savage and unfit for life.

The memory of Zach's touch on her breast, his ardent kisses, flooded her mind. Bile rose in her throat.

How many times had Zach spoken of his grandfather with proud adoration? He'd claimed the man had molded his character, shaped his life decisions, taught him right from wrong and the value of the law.

At the river, he'd claimed he was worried about appearances. She'd believed him but now, knowing what his grandfather had done and how much influence he had in forming Zach . . . she couldn't help doubting his assurances.

He'd fingered her aunt's beaded necklace and maintained a concerned expression, the epitome of a poker-faced lawyer. Letting her think he cared about her. Was he softening her up until she became careless and revealed too much information? Then, he'd swoop in, following his grandfather's example, and use it against the Poncas and Aunt Rose. How could she have fallen for his manipulation?

And Thad? Zach probably *had* set the kid up as a spy. Hadn't she told Susette it didn't feel right?

Well, she'd be damned if she was going to simply sit there and let that man, that self-righteous white man, make a fool of her and hurt those she cared about.

Grabbing her shawl, she stomped to the door, locked it, clattered down the stairs, and flipped the small wooden sign to *closed* before locking the bottom door as well. Her heels clacked against the wooden sidewalk as she stormed up the street to Zach's office. How dare he!

Ignoring the curious stares of townsfolk on the street, Lise remained focused straight ahead. The trickster coyote was not going to fool her.

She jerked open the door to the city offices and stomped up the stairway to the second floor toward Zach's office.

Inside, Zach sat at his desk. He heard her sharp footsteps before she graced the doorway. Wasn't anybody else who made a noise like she did. He smiled and shifted the peppermint stick between his teeth. Despite knowing they shouldn't be seeing each other, he was glad she was there.

She stopped inside the door and slammed it shut.

Zach bit down on the candy and heard it crack. He pulled it out of his mouth and smiled.

"I ought to ram that candy stick down your throat."

Zach swallowed. "What's wrong?"

She marched forward and slammed her knuckles onto his desk. "How long did it take you to plan it out, Zach?" Her chest heaved, much as it had after their kiss yesterday, but it sure as hell wasn't arousal that had her worked up this time.

He set the candy stick on his desk blotter and leaned back in his chair, wondering how to coax her out of whatever had created her foul mood. Then again, it might be better to plunge in and get to the bottom of it. "Plan what, for pity's sake?" he asked.

"Don't play naive with me, Zach." Her

dark eyes flashed.

Irritation prickled and he sat up straight. "Well, I'm not drowning in knowledge here. You care to tell me what you're talking about?"

"You and your twisted motives."

"Now just hold on a minute. Which motives are you talking about?"

She glowered. "The innocent act is tiring."

Zach ran his hand through his hair and stilled his rising temper. "Look, Lise, I have a lot of different motives. They vary, depending on the situation, so you're going to have to tell me what you're talking about."

"All right," she tipped her head. "Let's start with us."

He blinked and drew a breath. On the other side of the desk, Lise's mouth was set in a grim line.

"I thought we'd covered that already," he finally said.

"So did I but it seems I was misguided."

Her anger puzzled him. Hell, her whole demeanor puzzled him. He stood and walked around the desk, her dark, demanding gaze following.

Nearing her, he touched her arm. "I'm not understanding this at all," he said.

She jerked her elbow away and turned on

him. "Did you or did you not pursue me with the goal of using me to extract information about the Standing Bear case?"

"I pursued you because I found you attractive and intelligent, intriguing." Confused, he stared at her. "Wasn't it you who was flirting with me in an effort to distract me from the case?"

"You knew darn well I was working with Susette, Tom Tibbles, and Andrew Poppleton."

He nodded. "Yeah, several days into knowing you."

"So you were using me." She arched her eyebrows.

"I was not using you. Damn it, Lise, I care for you."

"Take me to dinner, soften me up. Teach me to fish. Kiss me, take liberties. Where was it going to end? With me telling you everything about the case?"

"How can you possibly think I'm trying to get information if we aren't even discussing it?"

She twitched, then stared back. "So when did you decide to set Thad up as a spy?"

"What?"

She advanced. "Thad and his little visits to the library for cinnamon rolls, the convenient job at the newspaper office." She jabbed at his chest with her index finger. "How often does he report to you?"

He stared at her finger, unable to form a coherent thought beyond denial. "Thad doesn't report anything to me, and I had nothing to do with getting him that job."

She lifted the finger and began shaking it at him. "I'm not about to swallow that. Not anymore."

He grabbed her hand, stopping her wagging finger. Taking advantage of her surprise, he grasped both arms and held her still. "Lise, what the hell is going on? You storm in here growling about how I've deceived you and I have no idea what you are talking about."

"You can stop playing games with me, Zach. I know all about you and your —"

Pulling her close, Zach lowered his mouth and kissed her. Startled, she offered little resistance as his tongue probed into her mouth. He let the kiss deepen until he heard the shocked catch of realization in her breath. Then he released her.

Lise stood, gasping. Tears welled in her wide open eyes.

"Did that feel like a fake kiss to you? Did it? I don't know what kind of hitch your garters are in but I am not pretending to be attracted to you."

She stiffened. "Did you get in too deep? Is that what happened? You set Thad to spy on me, pursued me, and then couldn't figure a way out? Can't very well be smitten with an Indian-lover, can you?" Her voice wavered. "It isn't appearances, is it? Or politics? Maybe it's just hatred."

He leaned against the desk, half sitting on the corner and dropped his head into his palm. She'd melted into the kiss, met his tongue. He'd felt her breathing quicken. What the hell could make her rebuff him with such force? "I don't know what you're talking about."

"Adam Foster stopped by the library a little while ago." The tears in her eyes pooled. "He told me about your family."

He jerked his head up. What had Foster said to her? "What about my family?"

"How you were raised to hate Indians."

Wary anxiety merged with his confusion. "I don't hate Indians," he said, grasping to comprehend what had occurred.

"You said you wanted to be like your grandfather, to follow his example."

"Yes, but —"

"Hating Indians included."

"I do not hate Indians." He stared at her, at last catching part of what had her so riled. She must have misinterpreted something Foster had said. He needed to clarify, that was all. "I've never thought about Indians, outside what I read in papers or how the law sees them. How can I hate people I don't know?"

He paused, considering. In the past days, since being assigned the case, he guessed he'd formed more of an opinion than he'd realized. His visit to Fort Omaha had left him feeling hollow and uncomfortable, guilty even, though he'd pushed the feelings aside, as he'd been trained to do when his conscience conflicted with the law. Maybe it was time he admitted it.

"If you want to know the truth," he said, "I wish I'd never been assigned to this case. Between Foster using it as part of my campaign, making me out as some sort of crusader, and having to enforce statutes that make me uncomfortable, I would just as soon it was over. Especially since I now have to worry about politics and appearances. It has nothing to do with hating Indians." He held her gaze. "I thought you understood that."

"But your grandfather —"

Comprehension dawned like a brilliant summer day, nearly blinding him. "Did Foster say my grandfather hated Indians?" he ground out. Damn the man for lying. "Is that what this is about?"

Lise stepped back. "He told me about your grandfather's zeal to hang the Sioux in Minnesota, his role in the case, his joy in the convictions, and how he hated that so many 'savages' were pardoned."

"What?" Denial slammed through him. Foster had to have lied . . . except that Gramps had come to Nebraska from Minnesota.

"I lived there, Zach. I knew some of those people. Most of them were starving, victims themselves." Her voice broke, then steadied. "They came into my father's store, begging for food because the government annuities didn't come and they were banned from hunting. When they complained to the Indian agent, he had nothing but contempt for them. Until a handful of young men finally revolted and it spun out of control."

Lise rubbed her arms. "Yes, there were people killed, on both sides. And, yes, there were innocent victims. But justice was never served there. Not when mobs went wild and accused those who had no part in the killings, lynched them just because they were Sioux." She raised her eyes. "I watched them hang, Zach."

Her anger was again palpable, glistening on her skin, and Zach felt his heart drop.

The Sioux Uprising was not an abstract historical event to Lise — it was part of who she was. And she clearly held his grandfather responsible for some of those events.

"My God." He hadn't known. All these years, Gramps had refused to talk about Minnesota. Was this why?

Lise backed away, shaking her head. "Don't you ever touch me again. Don't kiss me. Don't even look at me. People like you disgust me."

He stepped toward her, unable to put his disillusionment into words. How could she believe he'd known?

"Stay away from me," she said, then walked out the door.

Zach sank onto the edge of the desk, his shocked mind in angry denial of the legacy Lise had thrown in his face.

Zach spent the next few hours feeling betrayed and angry. When he wasn't pissed at Foster for crafting such a lie, he was filled with doubt. He didn't want to believe Gramps had been involved in such a sorry chapter of Indian relations. And if he had, it galled Zach that he had idolized him all these years. Any way he looked at it, it pissed him off.

He'd been unable to locate Foster and by

the time he got home and the kitchen door slammed shut behind him, he wanted to stomp into Gramps's bedroom and demand answers.

But Zach knew being confrontational would net him poor results. Direct and dispassionate was more productive. Calming his emotions, he entered the bedroom and stood at the foot of Gramps's bed. "You awake?" he asked.

Gramps opened one eye and peered up at Zach. He nodded slowly, the one head movement he was able to control. The effort taxed him and a thin stream of drool slid down one side of his chin.

Zach settled into the wooden chair next to the bed and drew a breath. "Adam Foster visited the library this morning. He told the librarian you were the driving force behind hanging dozens of Indians after the Minnesota Uprising. Was he lying?"

Gramps arched one eyebrow and gurgled low in his throat, then shifted slightly so that he faced away from Zach.

"Don't turn your back on me, Old Man."

He'd never before spoken to Gramps with such disrespect, and it didn't set well with him, even now, angry as he was. Still, the words were out and couldn't be taken back.

"Gramps, look at me."

He reached over and rolled Gramps's thin frame until his head turned back. His filmy eyes brimmed.

"You never talked about your life before Nebraska, Gramps. I don't know why, but it's long past time I knew about it. For many reasons, not the least of which is that I got blindsided this morning by Lise Dupree."

Gramps shook his head, trembling, and shut his eyes.

"Don't want to talk about it, huh?"

Zach waited, impatient at Gramps's refusal to acknowledge his inquiry. Damn stubborn old man.

"Adam Foster said you worked with the special commission that tried the Sioux. That you were responsible for legal advice that led to the convictions. That true?"

Gramps opened one eye and nodded slowly, then turned away.

Zach drew another breath. "He also said you were proud of what you did."

Gramps turned back, staring with blazing eyes. His jaw trembled and guttural sounds poured forth. He shook, then pounded his fist on the bed.

Zach stared back, unsure what his grandfather was trying to convey. He read the frustration, recognizing the pounding of the fist. But the light in Gramps's eyes was baffling. It bespoke strong feelings but didn't identify any of them.

"You said you were proud of the way you'd applied the law. That you were true to it, in every case you ever represented, that you believed in it with all your heart."

Gramps lay silent, feeding the doubt that was worming its insidious way through Zach's heart.

"Were you proud of what you did there, Old Man? Did you believe justice was done?"

Zach's heart wrenched as silence stretched and betrayal hit home. For the first time in his life, he was ashamed of Gramps and ashamed of himself for believing in him. He stood and looked down.

"All my life, I wanted to be you, to serve your ideals, to follow in your footsteps. No more, Gramps, no more. I despise what you did and I refuse to be like you ever again."

He turned for the door, ignoring the tears on Gramps's face, and choking on his own pain.

CHAPTER TEN

Adam Foster drummed his fingers against the isolated corner table and stared across at Rufus Christy. The Indian agent had demanded they meet over lunch and was still slurping his way through the chicken and noodles he'd ordered. A pile of papers lay near Christy's right arm, haphazardly close. The fool was likely to spill all over them.

He could have done the research himself but Christy'd been a handy errand boy and seemed to know his way around government agencies. No sense tying up his own time and energy.

Adam watched Christy lift the bowl and tip it to his mouth, draining the last of the soup. It was about time. If the train bringing the judge in from Lincoln hadn't been delayed, the Trial of Standing Bear, as the media was now calling it, would be starting. He couldn't be sure how much time he had before Dundy arrived and proceedings started.

"You finished?" he asked, sliding the paperwork further away from Christy.

"Got a half a biscuit left, but I reckon it'll keep."

"Then let's get started. I don't have all day to sit and watch you eat."

"I reckon you got whatever time I take, iff'n you want to know what I learnt." Christy set the soup bowl down with a clatter and leaned back in his chair. "You keep up bein' so pompous, I don't got to tell you nothin'."

"Why, you little weasel. Are you forgetting who you're working for?"

"Seems to me like I didn't get paid near enough."

Adam bit back the retort that formed in the back of his mind. If insulted too deeply, Christy was volatile enough that he'd run to Zach and blab he'd been hired to spy. Adam doubted Zach would take too kindly to manipulation. "I pay you damn well."

Christy peered at his dirty fingernails, then lifted his gaze to meet Foster's. "Seein' as I had to bribe a private over to Fort Omaha to get a copy of the list of who is in Standing Bear's sorry band of scum, my costs rose some."

Adam glanced around the near empty room. "What'd you learn?"

"What's it worth?" Christy shoved a finger into his mouth and picked at his teeth.

Adam sighed, knowing damn well that he needed the information. "That depends."

"The old woman what has the librarian all twisted up ain't even a Ponca."

"I *know* that."

Christy leaned across his soup plate. "She's Sioux," he whispered.

"And?"

"Seems the squaw got sent from Minnesota back in '63 with a bunch of other renegade Sioux."

Adam's temper flared. "Look, you little jackass. I got that much from the records Crook surrendered to Zach Spencer. I'm not going to pay you for something I already know!"

"Then I reckon you ain't wantin' to know about the trip I made up to St. Paul."

Adam eyed the Indian agent, weighing the possible significance of such a trip. He wouldn't put it past the measly little pissant to try to bill him for a pleasure trip. Disgusted, he pushed back his chair and rose. "That wasn't part of our deal," he said, turning toward the door of the restaurant. The greedy little snake could pay for his own damn lunch.

Christy's chair scraped against the wooden floor, and Adam heard him scurrying behind him. "Wait!"

Adam turned and raised an eyebrow. "What?"

Christy thrust out the pile of papers from the table, his butter-greased fingers staining the edges. "I reckon you might want to see what I found out. The old lady's name is Rose. She was married to one of the Sioux that was hung after the uprising," he whispered. "They sent the rest of the family to Dakota Territory. She had a half-sister, a 'breed, what was married to a white man by the name of Dupree. He moved his family to St. Louis. Daughter was named Lise." He rapped his greasy fingers against the papers in a staccato beat. "Worth it?"

Excitement bubbled through Adam and he struggled to contain it as they returned to the table and sat. Lise Dupree was part Sioux. It explained a lot and he could bet the little 'breed was mad as hell over Henry's role in the hangings.

She wasn't likely to forget what he'd told her for a long time — at least long enough to get Zach elected and assure his supporters he had the boy in his back pocket. There would be no further doubts about Zach legislating to keep Indians on the reservations. Their interests, and investments, would be secure. It was a guarantee that might even gain him a bonus. He reached for the papers. "You're sure of this?"

"Sure as shootin'. You gonna pay me?"

"I'll pay you, you little worm. But this goes nowhere. You keep your mouth shut and let me handle it from here on. Understood?"

"Seems fair enough as long as you keep in mind that I was the one what found the information. Might be there's some value in it for me, too. If you ain't gonna use what I found out, I will. Understood?"

Adam stared at the Indian agent and a finger of worry flashed through his mind. "I think we have a deal. My guess is Miss Dupree will want nothing to do with any of Zack's family from this point forward. A careful word here and there and she'll never talk to Zach again."

Christy looked stricken. "You ain't gonna ask her for no hush money?"

"Hell, no. And neither are you. This is my information and it gets used my way. You're not a party to this, Mr. Christy. Stay out of it."

"Seems like a waste of good information."

Adam leaned forward, his voice taut.

"You'll stay out of it if you know what's good for you. Blackmail is not my intent. I'm not a slimeball."

"Well, shit. You sayin' I am?"

"I don't know, Mr. Christy," he asked. "Are you?"

Judge Elmer Dundy entered the crowded courtroom at half-past five and ambled toward the bench. He was late. Most of the spectators had been milling around the courthouse since noon, unwilling to sacrifice their seats despite the delay. And though a portion of the locals had given up and returned to their homes, others had been ready to take their places. Thad's eager face shone, and Lise imagined he would be collecting a good deal of gossip these next few days.

Zach sat at the defense table with General Crook, intent only on his client. Tears rose in Lise's eyes, and she focused on the action of the courtroom instead. The past two days had been difficult, and the circles under her eyes were dark.

She nudged Susette, then shifted her attention to Standing Bear. He sat at one of the front tables, dressed in faded flannel and trousers. Except for his long braids, he looked like most of the local farmers. Stand-

214

ing Bear was wedged between Poppleton and Webster while the official courtroom interpreter sat at the end of the table. Susette, with Lise in the front row, would serve as secondary interpreter. Standing Bear appeared undisturbed by the judge's arrival.

Dundy settled into his seat and shook his nearly bald head at the crowd. In an austere voice, he called the court to order, then scratched at his trim gray beard as if puzzled. "We apologize for our lateness," he said. "We didn't expect to begin tonight, it being nearly the dinner hour. Aren't any of you hungry?"

He scanned the audience, then pulled out a pocket watch and noted the time. "We can begin the case tonight or we can eat, get a good night's rest, and start proceedings tomorrow. We are inclined to the latter. We'll convene in the morning." He struck his gavel against the table, rose, and exited the room.

Lise stared after him. Dundy didn't seem like the type of judge she'd expected for a federal court. His formal manner and use of the royal "we" seemed patronizing, and she wondered about his impartiality.

"What do you think?" she asked Susette.

"About Dundy? He's as self-important as Thomas said he would be. But he has a reputation for justice. I think this is a good thing for Standing Bear. He may be pompous but he will consider the case with care."

The two rose and shuffled after the crowd ahead of them. Outside, the early evening was just shifting to dusk. Lise shivered in the cooling air before spotting Zach Spencer ahead of them. Her step slowed.

"You won't be able to avoid him forever," Susette said.

"I can try."

Susette paused and directed a sharp gaze at her friend. "And be miserable the whole time, too," she said.

"I'm not miserable," Lise lied.

Susette smiled and shook her head. "Then your voice is angry for no reason? And your eyes flash at him one minute and pool up the next because all is well?"

"I'm worried about the case."

"I don't believe you."

Lise shrugged, not trusting herself to comment. The group was thinning, but Poppleton was still engaged in animated conversation with a beady-eyed little man in a plaid jacket. A few feet away, Zach turned, his gaze almost catching hers. Lise strode away, crossing the street.

Susette kept pace, their twin footsteps echoing together as they moved away from the courthouse. "Perhaps it would settle better with you if you talked with him."

"I already did."

"You yelled at him."

The reminder poked at her with its sharp spine of truth. "There's nothing more to say."

"I think perhaps you are not sure."

Lise looked away. Was it that obvious?

"Maybe he didn't know," Susette persisted.

Lise swung her arms and clomped toward the business district. "Of course he knew," she said, unsure whom she was trying to convince. "He told me several times that his grandfather was his role model. Foster said the Minnesota convictions were defining moments, capping Zach's grandfather's belief in the divine essence of the law. It would have been part of what he taught Zach."

Susette marched beside without saying anything. Lise pulled her shawl more tightly around her shoulders and felt a slow ache inch its way across her forehead.

"Did Zach say anything about Minnesota?" Susette finally asked.

"No. But why would he if he intended to manipulate me? He knows I feel strongly about how Indians are treated." She heard the doubt creep into her voice, hating the implication that she'd overreacted. Her temper often ruled her head, and most of the time, it was because she allowed it.

"It seems to me that men who hate are unable to hide that hatred."

Lise paused in defense. "Well, Zach did. Even when he discovered my necklace, he didn't draw away."

"If he hated Indians, he would have. I know how such men act, Lise. I have seen it too many times."

"It all fits. Zach's attention, Thad snooping, the case itself." Even to herself, it sounded like weak reasoning.

Susette's smile stayed firm and her eyebrows lifted a fraction. "Thad is not a boy who hates Indians. A boy doesn't hide such things. He's curious."

They neared Lise's small rooming house in silence. There were no points left to argue.

"Do you really think it might be possible that his grandfather didn't tell him about Minnesota?" The words rushed out, surprising Lise more than Susette.

"Perhaps," Susette responded, "or perhaps he did. You will not know unless you talk to him." She paused, then drew a breath. "And perhaps, you must ask yourself if it even matters."

By the following afternoon, the town was swarming with reporters. All day, a steady stream of newsmen, some from as far away as Chicago and Philadelphia, had paid rapt attention to the proceedings in the courtroom. Since today's adjournment, they'd followed Standing Bear, Susette, the other interpreter, and the witnesses. Lise had been surprised at the interest in the case, as well as by the insistence that every detail of Standing Bear's story be told.

A lone reporter for the *Omaha Daily* stood apart, showing no interest in learning more about what had happened during the Poncas' long weeks of wandering. Other reporters appeared determined to make their readers aware that the group had insisted on living as white men, on forsaking their tribal ways.

What surprised Lise most was the reporters' keen determination to be unbiased, to let Standing Bear's story be told. They were singing the praises of the lonely band of Poncas who had given up most of their tribal ways before being forced to Indian Territory. Reporters eagerly cited testimony of witnesses who had seen the band on its journey with their stories about the willingness of the group to purchase or work for food, their civilized appearance, and their eagerness to separate from the other members of the Ponca nation.

Almost no one called them savages. The Indians attending the trial had been accorded rooms at local hotels and rooming houses and ate their meals in restaurants, just as their white attorneys and the white reporters did. The city council had given Lise free time to attend the trial, allowing her to close the library as other business owners also closed. All over the city, interest in Indians was stirring and a new sense of tolerance seemed to prevail, no doubt due to the flood of news articles.

"Perhaps we should get something to eat," Susette suggested as she neared Lise.

"If you're finished being interviewed like you are Lily Langtree." Lise offered her friend a smile.

Susette grinned. "I didn't know so many newspapers would send reporters."

"I think they're as interested in Bright Eyes as they are in Standing Bear."

"It is all the same. When they speak to me, I tell them about Standing Bear. I think it's only that I'm prettier than Standing Bear and I speak English." Susette's modest appraisal of their awareness was typical of her personality.

"Still, they spend much more time with you than the other interpreter," Lise teased.

"I am prettier than him, also."

Lise laughed. "What do they ask?" She was a little curious. She'd never before seen such regard for native cultures or the fate of Indians, whether singly or as a group. Throughout the city, she'd overheard conversations filled with genuine concern.

"There is much interest in what it is like to be an Indian, how we are treated and how we feel about it. One of the reporters said the public wants to know more because they have been told only about massacres for too many years. They now wish to have a better understanding."

Lise stared at her friend. "And do you believe that's true?" It was a noble statement but reality had always told a different story, one filled with biases and hostile attitude. Surely Susette had experienced much of the same.

"I think, yes. I believe there are many things changing in this world and that people have more open minds now."

Her words shocked Lise. Open minds hadn't existed when hundreds of Sioux were ordered to leave Minnesota because they were Indian. Nor when the Poncas had been forced to leave their homeland. And it wasn't just fear of groups. It had been less than two years since she'd been dismissed from her position as librarian in Spirit Lake because patrons had complained that they didn't want a half-breed Indian influencing their children. "All my life, I have seen whites denigrate Indians."

"And some always will. There is no way to convince those who do not want to change. But I think others are ready. One of the newsmen, from Chicago, wants for Standing Bear to come East and give speeches."

"And people would come to hear an Indian? To hear him rather than gawk?"

"There are many such people, Lise. You need only open your eyes to see them. And perhaps, to open your mind. Changes don't happen when you hide from them."

"I don't hide."

"You hide from who you are and you hide from what you want. I think you are uncomfortable with yourself."

Lise bristled. "I didn't get fired in Spirit Lake because of my discomfort. They dismissed me because I'm Sioux."

"Perhaps in Spirit Lake it was more important." Susette touched Lise's arm. "Spirit Lake had its own uprising, even before Minnesota. Memories are strong.

But look at how people are reacting here. Omaha is not Spirit Lake."

"No, it's not," Lise conceded. "But it's bigoted enough that you and your father were arrested for being here without a pass, that you were manhandled by those two deputies. Being Indian matters, even here."

"Not for all people. Most people here don't fear my tribe. Perhaps it is because the Omaha are a farming tribe whose ways are not so hard to understand. There has been peace here. Only a handful of people are bothered by our visits to town, and it is only the Army making an issue of the passes because they have orders to do so from those who think all tribes are the same. They will think that until they learn differently."

Susette pointed to the crowd. "Look at these reporters, how eager they are to tell Standing Bear's story, to campaign for justice. They will help people understand and learn. And have you listened to the locals? Everyone is saying the Poncas should be left alone, that they should be free to live where they want."

"Because they wish to live as whites."

Susette sighed. "And is that not what you are doing?"

Lise glanced at the crowd, avoiding the

uncomfortable question. She found it difficult to accept Susette's inference that she would be left alone because she had abandoned Indian ways. While she suspected her friend, Sarah, would advise her in much the same way, were she here, her experiences were too hard to dismiss.

"I think you'd find the public has different opinions for different situations," she said. "They don't mind Standing Bear being a farmer but I doubt they'd be content if he were trying to teach their children or open a business." She turned back to her friend. "They don't want an Indian managing their library."

"I think you fail to give the public credit."

Doubt nagged at Lise. "If it doesn't matter so much, why do people like Adam Foster and Zach's grandfather spend their energy keeping Indians under control?"

Susette raised her eyebrows at the sharpness of Lise's tone and grasped her hand, drawing her attention. "Pettiness, perhaps, or fear. I don't know. But if it were me, I would wonder instead why Adam Foster put so much effort into telling you about Zach's grandfather. I don't think it was an accident that he came to the library."

"But, why . . ."

"Zach told you Foster is his campaign

manager?"

"Yes, but why would . . ." Lise caught her breath. "Do you think Foster would really be that concerned about Zach's interest in me?"

"Tom believes Foster would be concerned about anything that would get in the way of controlling Zach. I'm not sure why, but Foster has a much larger interest in Zach being elected than simple friendship."

Her heart racing, Lise stared at her friend. "If that's true, then I think I've made a big mistake." Her eyes widened as she digested the possibility. "Perhaps so big that I won't be able to fix it."

Susette let herself into the darkened front offices of the *Omaha Herald* and closed the door behind her, tucking the key Tom had loaned her back into her pocket. The scent of fresh ink flooded her nostrils and she sneezed.

"Who's there?" Tom's voice called from the back room.

Susette stiffened. She hadn't expected Tom to be there — it was the reason she'd waited so late to stop for the notes she'd forgotten earlier. She stilled her rapidly beating heart and took a deep breath.

"It's me. Susette."

Tom rounded the corner, wiping inky hands on an old cotton cloth, his expression unreadable.

"I forgot my notes."

"Cecil had a problem with the press. We've been knee-deep in parts for a couple hours. Just finished putting her back together and was cleaning up."

"I will be out of your way in just a moment." She worked her way through the front office, toward her desk. There was no need to light a lamp, not with the light that spilled from the other room. Tom watched her from the doorway, leaning against the jamb, and her heart pitter-pattered again.

Fighting the attraction she felt was easier when others were around, when it wasn't dusk, when she wasn't aware of him standing there.

"I sent Cecil home already."

Susette stopped, her hands suspended just above her desk.

"Tom —"

"I had hoped for the chance to talk with you. Alone. I saw your notes there and hoped you'd be back for them. Guess I lingered, waiting for you."

She drew a breath. "You should not have done that."

"I know."

"It's better for us not to be here like this."

"I know that, too, Bright Eyes." His tone was strong. "All the same, I hoped you'd come."

She picked up the papers, turned. Before she lost her resolve. She shouldn't be here. Tom's footfalls sounded behind her and she moved around the desk, eager to retreat to the safety of the front door.

But he was there, waiting as she turned, and her heart raced. His fingers gripped her arms and a molten bolt of passion coursed through her body. She gasped.

"Susette, stop. Listen to me."

"Let me go, Tom. Please let me go."

His hands dropped but he held her gaze. They stood, each breathing hard, staring at one another.

"I need to go," she said.

"In a minute. I have something to say."

She shook her head and stepped to the side.

He countered. "Stand still, Bright Eyes."

She stilled, waiting.

"Do you remember the reporter who suggested Standing Bear tour the East? We met over dinner. The owner of his paper is willing to sponsor a speaking tour."

Susette's desire calmed as Tom's excitement took over the moment. "A tour?"

"All the major cities. He and I would handle all the arrangements, but it would mean a speaking engagement in most of the larger cities. Standing Bear would describe what happened to him, and we'd hold discussions on how to improve Indian rights."

"And you think Standing Bear would do this?"

"He could bring his wife, some tribal members. I will be there."

Susette nodded. Standing Bear was not a fearful man. He would enjoy the adventure of visiting eastern cities, she was sure. And he would enjoy telling his story. "When would you go?" she asked.

"After the trial. Soon."

A small flicker of disappointment tickled at her and she looked away. It did not matter. After the trial, she would return to the Omaha Reservation anyway. And Tom would go on with his life, as if he had never met her. That was how it was meant to be.

"Susette?"

She turned back to Tom.

"He will need an interpreter. I would like you to travel with us."

The following evening, Zach sat in Krug's Brewery, mulling his conflicting thoughts over and over. He couldn't wrap his mind around the difference between what he was doing and the discomfort it was causing him.

He'd strategized last evening with the defense team, making few changes from what they'd envisioned for the past week. Today, his plans to put it all in motion had come to a standstill.

Webster and Poppleton had argued in an entirely unexpected vein, one which had nothing to do with treaties. They'd asserted that Standing Bear and his band of followers had left their Ponca identity behind and, since they'd been living as white men, they deserved all the rights and privileges accorded whites. And, after listening to today's testimony, Zach was damned if he didn't find himself agreeing with them.

The courtroom had been full, most of Omaha's locals in attendance to get a peek at the savage or civilized (depending on what paper they had read) Standing Bear. He'd also recognized a number of attorneys who'd realized the unusual nature of the case. George Crook had sat quietly throughout the day and was now seated across from Zach, patiently enduring the long minutes of silence he'd so far offered.

Zach reached for his beer and offered

Crook a wry smile.

"Mighty big thoughts to keep a man so quiet," Crook noted.

"I didn't notice you being overly conversational, either."

Crook chuckled. "Not much to say that wasn't already said."

"General, I've got to say you're the most disinterested defendant I can imagine." He shook his head. "You isolated yourself from planning your defense, refused to testify on your own behalf, and don't seem to give a lick about getting the writ dismissed."

"Son, I *don't* give a lick. I arrested and detained those people because I was ordered to do so. Told you that before. Told you not to get all twisted up about it. Seems you didn't listen."

Zach stared at the general. He hadn't realized his emotions were that obvious. "Twisted up about it?"

"Well, something's sure as hell bothering you."

Zach eyed him for a moment longer. He hadn't been able to discuss it with anybody else.

"You know, General, I was all ready to begin my defense, arguing treaty law. That's what the case should have come down to. I knew Webster and Poppleton might bring

230

up the Fourteenth Amendment, arguing for equal protection but I didn't think they had a legal leg to stand on. The Dred Scott decision ruled that slaves were a different classification of person. I planned to argue the same of Indians. I didn't expect them to assert that Standing Bear is no longer an Indian."

Crook grinned. "Sticks in your craw a bit, don't it?"

It was true. He'd been bested and he didn't like it. "More than a bit," he admitted. "The only argument I can make is that Indians don't qualify under the protection of the Fourteenth Amendment and that Standing Bear remains an Indian no matter how much he lives as a white."

"I thought the amendment guaranteed equal protection of the law to all persons. Don't recall it says anything about race."

Zach nodded, the cold implication shifting through him. "It doesn't."

"So, what are you going to say, son? Indians aren't people?"

He raised his gaze and stared at Crook, icy reality knotting in his gut. "I think that's the only defense left."

CHAPTER ELEVEN

"Zach?"

Zach stopped at the sound of Lise's voice and peered into the darkness of the hotel hallway.

"Lise? Is that you?"

She stepped out of the shadows, her hands clenched in front of her blueberry-colored dress. "Can we talk? I tried to catch you after court but you were busy. I stopped at your mother's house but she said you'd taken a room here." She looked nervous.

"Have you eaten?" he asked, instantly worried it sounded clumsy.

"Yes, earlier." She unfolded her hands, drew a breath, and stepped closer. "I know it's getting late, but can we discuss what happened in your office?" She paused, then sprang ahead. "I think my anger got the best of me."

"I won't argue about that." His wounded pride warred with his eagerness to resolve the issue. He chose his next words with care. "I think Adam Foster purposefully misled you, and I'd like the chance to clarify, to defend myself."

Regret wrinkled her brow. "I didn't give you a chance to explain, did I?" She glanced around, as if suddenly aware they were standing in the upstairs hallway of a hotel. "Should we go downstairs, in the lobby?"

Zach pointed down the short hall. "There are a couple chairs at the end of the hallway — we could sit there. I think it would be a little less public than the lobby."

"Well . . ." Her gaze followed his. The sitting area was bathed in moonlight.

"Please, Lise," he insisted, hoping she'd understand. "I don't want to air this in front of other people. For several reasons."

"All right."

He directed her toward the chairs, taking care to avoid making her any more uncomfortable than she already was. Once she was seated, he lowered himself into the other chair and asked, "So, where do we start?"

"The beginning?"

"With Gramps, then?"

Lise held his gaze. "Was Foster lying about his involvement in Minnesota?"

Her bluntness took him by surprise. He had been asking himself the same question for days.

"I don't think so," he finally said. "I asked him that day you came to the office. He was evasive but he finally nodded when I asked if he'd been legal counsel for the prosecution."

"You didn't know?"

"He never spoke of it. Never." He wasn't sure if she'd believe him. "I never knew he was part of it or how he felt about his role."

Her features softened, weighing, but not yet ready to accept. "And how *does* he feel?"

Zach shook his head. "He can't form words, and I have no idea what his mind is capable of." He stared at her and lifted his shoulders in a noncommittal shrug. "I asked him if he was proud of it. He didn't answer, but got agitated, angry."

"So, there's no way of knowing . . ."

"Not unless I talk to him again, ask him more direct questions."

"Foster implied that it was common knowledge in your household. Common knowledge and common pride."

"Foster lied," he insisted, unable to control the raw emotion any longer. "Lise, I yelled at Gramps. I stood there and berated him because I hated it that he didn't tell me and that he was even involved. I'm not familiar with many of the details about the Sioux Uprising — it was a very small part of my law study — but I do know many of the convictions were shams. I'm ashamed he was involved. And when you marched into my office throwing accusations, I was so shocked that I barely figured out what you were saying before you stormed out. It hurt that you thought I could be proud of something like that."

Lise's eyes darkened. "You've said many times that you wanted to emulate your grandfather in everything, that he had taught you everything. It stood to reason that he would have told you about something that significant."

Zach knew the subtle anger in her voice was rooted in his own words to her. He *had* told her that, and with a great deal of pride. Now he was contradicting himself.

"But he didn't."

Lise's lips tightened as the pause grew. "Foster lied on purpose then?" she said.

"Foster thinks I should have nothing to do with you." A spark ignited in her eyes, but he plunged ahead anyway. "He thinks you're using our relationship to learn what you can about the defense, then taking the information back to Poppleton."

"That I'm spying?"

Zach winced at her volume, but responded in kind. "Is that so hard to believe?"

"He thinks that I'm cozying up to you just to learn about the case? That would make me nothing but a strumpet." She stood with the liquidity of a cat, her hands on her hips. "How could you believe such a thing?"

A door down the hall from the alcove opened and a haggard, unsmiling man peered out at them.

"I didn't say I believed him," Zach whispered, and the door closed.

"It sounded like you did."

He stood, instantly toe to toe with her. "What are you so fired up about?" he demanded. "You didn't think it was unfair when you were accusing me of the same thing."

"What was I supposed to believe?"

The picture near the haggard man's door shook as someone pounded against the wall, and a muffled "shut up" sounded from inside one of the other rooms.

Lise smoothed her dress, her head lowered. "Maybe we should settle this tomorrow."

"Not when we're just getting this sorted out. Let's finish what we've got to say."

"We've already been told to quiet down twice."

"We could go to the parlor of your rooming house . . . or into my room?"

Lise offered a wry smile. "I'm not sure either of those is a good solution."

"Well, I don't think my mother is going to allow me into her parlor. Not after the way I left things with Gramps. Come on." He led the way back down the short hall, and stopped to unlock his door. Opening it, he entered, turned up the gaslight, and waited for Lise to follow him in.

She entered slowly, giving the room a quick appraisal, and took the sole straight-back chair. Zach settled onto the edge of the bed.

"What did you mean," she asked, "about your mother?"

"I'm not staying in a hotel to be close to the courthouse, Lise. My mother threw me out."

"Threw you out?"

"Gramps got upset after I raged at him. Ma was more than a little angry, said she didn't want me in the house until I apologized and could behave myself."

She chewed at her bottom lip, then raised her gaze to meet his, her shoulders relaxing as her tension drained. "If you're not spying and I'm not spying, why is Foster trying to make us believe otherwise?"

"Part of me thinks he really believes it himself. He seems to hold a pretty dim view of women. I don't think he credits you with enough intelligence to have any other interest in the case."

She shook her head. "But why the deception about your grandfather?"

He would prefer not to believe it, but Adam Foster was obviously determined to run Zach's campaign his way. "He thinks I'll do better in the senate race if I take a hard line against Indians. It looks bad to be involved with you because of your closeness to Susette and Standing Bear."

"So we're back to politics?" The question brought a sharp image of their day at the river to his mind. He'd referred to politics then, right after he'd let his hands drift into her bodice. "*That's* what all this is?"

He nodded, it had to be at the root of everything Foster had told Lise. "It would seem so."

"And you agree with this?"

He didn't have to think about his answer. "I'm uncomfortable as hell about it and more than a little mad at Foster for setting it all into motion." He shifted, resenting that he'd been forced into this situation. "I don't want to be seen as a crusader against Indians, and I sure as hell don't want to have Foster dictate whom I can and can't spend time with, especially when he manipulates people behind my back."

Lise leaned forward in the chair, sureness filling her pose. "So why don't you tell him to stay out of your business?"

The smile that stretched its way across his face was as much a surprise to him as the resolve that came with it. "I'm thinking I will," he said. "Until now, I thought he was looking out for my best interests, sharing the knowledge of his own experience. He's an old family friend and I trusted him. Now, I'm not so sure."

"Does he have anything to gain from you winning the senate race?"

"I thought he was helping me because he was a friend of Gramps."

"Maybe it's time to look for his real reasons."

The uneasiness that had lodged in Zach for the past few days stirred. "I don't like being involved in this trial, either. The more I talk to Crook and learn the details, the more I think Standing Bear is right."

"He is, Zach."

Zach stood and paced the small room. It wasn't often that his emotions warred with his commitment to the sanctity of the law, and he didn't much care for it. He felt

239

boxed in.

"The law says he isn't, though," he finally said, wincing at the lack of conviction in his voice. He strode to the lone window, pulled back the heavy brocade drape, and leaned against the top of the windowpane. Below, the city was still busy, as patrons entered and exited the varied cafes and saloons that lined the street.

Lise touched his shoulder, her hand warm and gentle. "And what makes the law correct?"

"The fact that it's the law." He'd believed it all his life, and the lack of certainty in his tone prickled at him.

She moved her hand up and down his arm, stroking him with a reassurance he hadn't realized he needed. "Maybe the law needs to change," she said, an echo of the doubts that were slithering around his confidence.

Her hands moved to his neck, and he melted into her massaging touch. "Susette told me earlier today that people can change. Maybe the law can, too."

His neck became putty under the strong strokes of her fingers, and his head dropped forward. "But until it does, I have to respect what it says. My job is to apply the law, not to change it."

"You don't sound happy about it."

"I'm not."

"Then, maybe you need to make your own changes."

He straightened and turned to face her. "What do you mean?"

"If you weren't a district attorney, if you were a defense lawyer, wouldn't you see the law differently?"

The idea was foreign, opaque as window glass after an ice storm. "I suppose." He shivered at the thought, not sure exactly what it was that bothered him most about it. "But this is what I do, who I am."

"Is it?"

Zach's gaze wavered but he said no more, and Lise wondered if she'd prodded too much. She suspected Foster was using Zach as some sort of a puppet but she sensed he'd need time to figure it out on his own. Much as he presented a carefree front, she had learned that he mulled things over before reaching a decision.

She dropped her hands to her skirt, suddenly nervous. "I . . . uh . . . I guess I should get home."

"Stay awhile?" he asked in a soft tone.

She looked at him, rooted to the spot, knowing she *should* leave.

"We've wasted a lot of time being misled

and feeling angry with each other. I'd like the chance to make up for it."

Still, she couldn't bring herself to move. "Zach —"

"Kiss me, Lise?"

Warmth crept through her body, intensifying as she recalled the touch of his lips on hers, the insistence of his tongue seeking hers. The heat coiled at her center, and she damned the propriety that nagged at her. "And what do I tell the ladies at the boarding house?" she asked.

Invitation lifted one corner of his mouth. "Why tell them anything? They don't wait up for you, do they?"

"No. They don't. But I wouldn't put it past them to lie awake listening for my return."

"They're sound asleep by now," he said, his tone caressing her.

Lise reached for her watch, conscious of Zach's hooded gaze as she touched the small timepiece and pulled it away from the broach on her breast. "Nine o'clock." She let the tension pull the tiny chain back to the broach, her fingers still on the watch.

"Does your landlady leave the door unlocked?"

"She does."

"Then stay. For a little while, at least."

Zach moved toward her, his blue eyes vulnerable. Lise swallowed, unsure of how to respond to a Zach that was neither confident nor teasing. Her fingers drifted from her bodice, waiting. He stood before her, took her face in his hand, and slowly lowered his lips to hers.

His mouth was warm, and gentle in a way she hadn't before experienced. Her mouth parted open, soft and welcoming. Savoring.

"I missed you," he said.

"I missed you, too." They spoke between light kisses, the hungry demands of their past encounters not guiding this one.

"I know Foster was right about the trial. If we're seen together now, the door will be wide open for an appeal." His lips moved to her neck, tickling it with soft butterfly kisses that made her tremble. He pulled back, catching her gaze until their eyes locked. "As for the politics, if I can't win on my own, I sure don't want to win on the basis of misrepresenting myself or my views. Adam Foster can be damned. I want you in my life."

Lise shivered. "He won't be very happy about it."

"I don't care how he feels." He lowered his mouth to hers, and she felt the heat of his kiss pour through her, simmering a trail

243

downward to her belly. Then he lifted his lips and leaned his forehead against hers. "Should we get you home?" he asked, his words ragged.

Under his hot breath, her face warmed and her lips remained parted. She panted, recognizing the desire to stay with him, to chase the moment. It wasn't proper, it wasn't chaste, and it wasn't what he was asking.

But it was real and urgent and insistent.

She leaned against him, her longing fighting reason as his fingers stroked her back with the lightness of feathers. Tomorrow would take them back to the trial and forced distance. And after that, they would face politics again, whether they wanted to or not. A candidate for the senate stood no chance of winning if he was involved with a 'breed.

Her heart clenched as that reality settled itself in her mind. If Zach was to have any future in politics, she wouldn't, couldn't, be a part of it.

"In a little while," she heard herself say.

Zach groaned and pulled further from her. "In a little while, I'll have my hands all over you."

If tonight was all she'd ever have of him . . .

She stepped back, her heart pounding with the realization that she might never face a decision like this again. She wanted Zach, maybe she even loved him, and closing the door on this moment might be shutting out love forever. With a sureness she had never before known, she knew she couldn't deny what they were feeling, or where it would take them. It might not be proper, but it was *right.*

She stared into his eyes and fought to keep her knees from buckling. "Maybe I'd like that."

A slow, anticipatory grin crept across Zach's face. "I think maybe you would."

He lowered his mouth to her neck, slowly inching the moist heat of his tongue downward from her jawline, then nibbling at her ears. She shuddered as the tickle became molten hot. Her hands plunged into his heavy blond hair, caressing as they shaped his head and pulled him closer.

His fingertips moved across her bare skin with the lightness of a gentle breeze, each tiny movement making her crave more. He skimmed across her breasts, cupping them, thumbs circling until her nipples tightened against his palms.

"Lise . . ."

"Don't stop."

His hands stilled, forcing both of them to stare at each other. "Are you sure?"

She nodded. Though her mother would be mortified, Aunt Rose would not. Tonight, she felt the pull of Aunt Rose's people and she hoped Zach would understand. "Sometimes, I think there's something to be learned from native cultures."

He lifted one curious eyebrow. "Such as?"

Stories Aunt Rose had told her about her Sioux girlhood whirled in Lise's mind, stories that had once made her giggle. Tonight, as the warmth engulfed her, she understood, and offered her heritage its rein. "The Sioux have a custom," she explained. "When young people are exploring a relationship, they may meet under a blanket."

His smoky blue eyes narrowed. "In private?"

"Well, no. Outside the door to her lodge."

"I don't think this is quite the same."

"No, not quite." She felt a chuckle bubble in her mouth before she could catch it. She let it escape, then sobered, afraid to let the moment get away from them. "What I mean is that everyone accepts there will be kissing and touching. It's not a great evil." She searched his gaze, suddenly unsure. "You think me forward."

"Not forward, no. Exceptional, yes." His fingers continued their lazy circles. "And will that be all, then, Lise? Kissing and touching?"

She exhaled and met his gaze. "Yes."

His teeth nipped at her neck and she shuddered amid the heavy breaths she couldn't stop. She moved further into his embrace, drawn, unable to resist the heavy closeness of his body, until she felt his hardness between them.

Her head tipped back and she stared at him, her mouth open.

His hooded eyes stared back. "And all that it may imply?" he asked in a tight whisper.

Lise melted into him, her arms under his, her hands pulling his upper body to her. She kissed him, hard. "I would like that, yes," she told him, then kissed him again.

He groaned against her mouth and somehow formed words. "Ah, Lise."

His lips sought her neck, caressing her just below her ear. His soft breath sent a shiver down her spine, and she leaned into the kiss. His lips brushed her skin, barely making contact, just hints of his moist tongue, tickling against her throat. Her head tipped back. The small, butterfly-like kisses, so completely different from the intense hunger he'd displayed at the river, were devastating. Lise's legs melted beneath her and her breath labored.

His fingernail etched a line from her ear, down her neck, to the vee of her bodice. Like his tongue, it barely made contact with her body. She shivered again, and her eyes drifted shut. Feathery strokes continued beneath the fabric of her dress, delicate sweeps of contact, light between her breasts, then moving back up to her throat.

His warm breath was at her ear again, then his tongue, moist against her skin, and his teeth nipped at her earlobe.

"Like spun sugar," he whispered.

"Hmmm?"

"You taste like spun sugar. Delicate and light as air. My tongue tingles with the taste of you."

Lise tingled as well, but the sensations consumed her entire body. She grasped his head and pulled his mouth to hers.

He kissed her, a gentle endearment where her mouth demanded more. Then he moved his mouth away and licked her throat. She arched and her nipples tightened.

He caressed her with the tip of his finger, first one breast, then the other. He stroked the outside of each, teasing her through the fabric of her dress. He brushed her nipples as she watched him through heavy eyes, his touch just enough that they hardened and grew taut beneath his thumbs.

He watched her, too, his blue eyes a smoky gray, a smile playing at his lips.

"And what do Sioux customs say about clothing?"

"They don't."

"So we may make up our own rules?" He slid her top button from its buttonhole. "I think it would be very easy to slip one's hands under a doeskin tunic while huddled under a blanket, or even to loosen its laces and let it drop to the waist."

"I don't think anyone would notice."

"I think I like this blanket custom." His fingers slid the second, third, and fourth buttons from their holes and parted the fabric. "Ah, Lise."

His fingers pushed aside her beaded necklace on its stiff new cord then loosened the ties of her chemise. He touched the bare skin of her breasts above her corset, then began to push the corset hooks from their eyes. Lise struggled to keep her own hands still, to avoid grasping at the corset and pulling the hooks all open at once. Her body strained for his touch.

She touched the buttons on his shirt tentatively, afraid of being too wanton, then damned the fear and opened it wide.

Zach gasped and his nipples hardened, amazing Lise with the intensity of his physical reaction. His chest muscles rippled, lean and hard under her hand. She let out a breath, hearing a fractured sigh leave her mouth at the same time.

He spread her garments open. His firm hand molded itself around her waist, caressing as his thumb traced the creases on her skin left by her corset. Her legs trembled and he eased her onto the bed, lowering her to the quilt. His tongue traced the lines his thumbs had awakened just seconds before, stopping at the waistband of her skirt. Raising his head, he watched her.

She stretched, languid under the steam of his gaze, wanting his hands on her. She peered down her body, drawn to his gaze. His uneven breath was hot against her stomach, his mouth open slightly. Then, his tongue flicked out, marking her again, then withdrew. She quivered.

He lifted his head and moved his face closer to hers. "Lise . . ."

She reached between them and slid her index finger down his abdomen, relishing the sharp shudders of his body. At the top of his trousers, she paused, then followed her instincts and cupped him in her hand.

"My God . . . Lise."

Her grip loosened.

"Don't . . . do you know what you're doing to me?"

"The same thing you're doing to me?"

"I haven't begun to touch you, sweetheart. I want to savor every inch of you, taste every subtle flavor of your skin, your moistness. I want to make you quiver so hard you think you can't stand it a second more. But if you touch me that way —"

"Then you'll quiver so hard *you* will think you can't stand it a second more."

Comprehension widened his eyes, crept down his face, and landed in a slow, innuendo-filled smile. He shook his head and the smile stretched. His lips touched her skin again, laved its way between her breasts, around her pendant. Lise shivered, her nipples puckering in the cool air.

He kissed first one, then the other, washing her areola with his tongue in a slow, delicate waltz. His fingers traced their way upward from the roundness at the side of each breast, urging her nipples to quicken even more.

"Ah, Lise . . ."

She distantly heard herself respond, a soft unexpected mew of pleasure.

He nipped at her nipple with his teeth and she arched into his mouth. Heat rushed

251

inward, downward, coiling into a tight spring deep in her belly, and she gasped.

His fingers flitted over the skin of her abdomen to her waist. She felt him open the hooks of her waistband, then his hand glided lower, his palm beneath her skirts. Heat filled her body and she arched again, feeling the heat of his hand against her. She pushed into it, feeling, needing. He cupped her tighter and she mewed again.

She felt his fingers move, dancing over her, into her, until she thrashed beneath him. Still, he pushed deeper while his thumb caressed her. She fought to breathe and her vision clouded, then shattered into a kaleidoscope of brightness as her body convulsed around his hand.

Gulping for air, Lise opened her eyes and stared at Zach. That same suggestive smile filled his face. Her panting slowed and satisfied warmth pulsated through her sated body.

"Just touches, sweetheart."

She closed her eyes, her inner body remembering, twitching, and shuddered again.

He drew her into his embrace, pillowing her head on his chest. Her eyes pooled with tears. She'd fallen in love with a man whose career, whose goals, would be shattered if anyone discovered who she really was.

CHAPTER TWELVE

Lise treaded down the last few steps of the library stairwell and flipped the window sign to *closed*. Her mind had been wandering all day, filled with thoughts of Zach, and business had been non-existent during the few hours she'd kept the library open with most of the town still in attendance at the trial. There was no sense staying open any longer, especially since the city council had given her leave to adjust the library's hours as she saw fit. She glanced at her watch. If she hurried, she could catch part of the afternoon session. Provided she could find a seat.

She pulled the door open and slipped into the warm spring sun.

"Whoa there. You ain't lockin' up already are you?"

Lise stared into the scruffy face of Rufus Christy and shivered.

"Did you need something, Mr. Christy?"

"Let's go back up." He nodded at the stairway. "What I need won't take more than a minute or two."

Lise's toe tapped the wooden stoop. Christy frowned, and she stilled her foot. "I've already closed the draperies and put things away."

"It ain't like I need the sun comin' in the windows. Just need to check on somethin'." His gaze moved up and down her body until goose bumps formed on her arms. "I didn't figure you'd be shirkin' your duties and closin' up early." He paused. "The city council know you're doin' that?"

She sighed, unwilling to argue, and tried to shake the feeling of ill-boding that came with Christy. Impatience, that was all, and she *was* closing early. "Come on up, then," she said.

He pushed past her and trod up the stairs, mumbling.

Lise rolled her eyes, then closed the door, leaving the *closed* sign in the window to discourage any other patrons, and followed him. Rufus Christy had never struck her as a man who would have a pressing need to obtain information from a library. Christy waited for her to reopen the top library door and entered the main room. He sauntered over to her desk and turned, waiting.

Lise's brow knit. What in heaven's name did he want? "Is there a particular volume you'd like me to get for you?" she asked. "I can likely find it fairly quickly."

"Nope. No book. Don't need nothin' like that. Just wanted a few words with you is all."

She shifted under his scrutiny. "A few words? With me?"

"You got a problem with that?"

"I'm not sure I understand, Mr. Christy. I was under the impression that you needed something from the library."

"Never said that now did I?"

"No-oo." Wariness crept over her.

"You seem like you're in a mighty hurry to close up today. Headed over to the courthouse maybe?"

"As a matter of fact, I was. Not that it's any business of yours."

He grinned. "Well, see, that's where you're wrong. It is my business."

"I don't see how —"

"There's lots I make it my business to know, Miss Dupree." He strutted back and forth. "You missed my testimony this morning. I told 'em all about the treaties signin' away the land that Injun says belongs to the Ponca. Told 'em how it happened, how the government put me in charge of relocatin' 'em all to Indian Territory. You wouldn't believe how damned fussy that man tried to be, sayin' he refused what was offered to him. Ornery cuss."

"Mr. Christy, I think —"

He stepped forward, slapping his fist into his palm. "Had to keep draggin' 'em back down there 'cause they had the nerve to go back to Dakota Territory on their own. Told the court about the government orders and how that Ponca bunch violated all of 'em."

Lise moved behind her desk, her goose bumps gone but the uneasiness deepening. "This has nothing to do with me, Mr. Christy." She motioned toward the door. "Now if you don't mind, I think we should go."

"I do mind, little missy." He slammed his hands onto the desk and leaned over it. "And it has lots to do with you. See, them treaties say the land up there is Sioux land. Sioux've been livin' there now over thirteen years. 'Course you know that, seein' how they're your relatives."

Lise backed up, staring at the Indian agent. Her stomach churned at his words, and she swallowed, hard.

"Ain't got nothin' to say about that, now, have ya?"

"I . . . I don't know where you heard that."

"Don't matter none where I heard it. I got my ways and I got the records provin' it." He stood and patted his jacket pocket.

Lise's heart pounded and she fought to keep her voice even. "I don't know what you think you know but I can assure you —"

"And I can assure you that it don't make no difference how much you deny it. You're still a 'breed, ain't ya? Bet the good folks of Omaha would like to know that, huh?"

She stared at him, digesting the implication. For months, she'd been afraid of this very thing. She'd be brought before the city council, scrutinized as they confronted her, then asked to vacate her position. Then, the stares and whispers would begin on the street and she'd be asked to leave town, taking her shattered dreams with her. Once again, failure would find her.

Refusing to let Christy take away all she'd worked for, she strode to the door and opened it wide. "I think it's time to go."

Christy shook his head, a predatory expression filling his face. "How long you think you're gonna stay librarian when it comes out you're nothin' but a 'breed?"

"That's . . . that's ludicrous."

"Is it?" He raised his eyebrows.

Lise drew a breath and inclined her head

258

toward the doorway. Her only hope lay in calling his bluff. "You need to leave, Mr. Christy."

With unexpected speed, Christy crossed the space between them, slammed the door, and leaned against it, panting. "Ain't goin' nowhere, yet, not when we still got talkin' to do. I seen you, out with Zach Spencer. Seems like an odd mix, you ask me. Attorney fightin' to keep Injuns on the reservation is sparkin' with his own little squaw?"

Lise closed her mouth and stared. Zach. Last night's realization that she might lose him squeezed around her, choking her confidence.

Christy's eyes filled with excitement, mocking her. Then they narrowed with comprehension, and he exhaled an audible, wavering breath. "Hooo-oo-oo! So that's the way the wind blows, is it? He don't know, does he? Didn't think he did. Man like that would have more sense, him runnin' for senate."

She shook her head, terror crowding her thoughts as she realized her emotions were no longer controlled. She had to stay calm. For Zach. "I don't know what you think you've discovered, but you're wrong."

"I ain't wrong, girlie, and you know it." He grinned. "You're ma is Sioux, sure as her sister, Rose, is, the one over at Fort Omaha. She was listed on the Lower Sioux Reservation rolls when she was a tyke. You're listed too, on the Minnesota census, right there in black and white, as 'part Sioux.' Kinda hard to deny."

"I — want — you — out."

"No, you don't. You don't want me goin' nowhere, tellin' the town fathers who you are. Tellin' your beau Spencer. Would sort of put a damper on your love life, now, won't it?"

Hostility burned through her like fire in a livery stable. "You'd do that? You hate Indians that much that you'd destroy my life?"

"I ain't fond of 'em, that's for sure, seein' how they killed off my family. 'Course, I *am* a man of reason, too."

"You're a —"

He put his finger to her lips. "Careful, there, missy. Don't go sayin' something you'll regret. After all, I'm agreeable to workin' something out, if it's worth my while."

Lise struggled to control her panic, drawing even breaths as she sorted out his meaning. "Are you blackmailing me?"

" 'Less of course you want me tellin' Spencer who you are?" He opened his arms in a gesture of helplessness.

She kept her voice steady, even, needing to convince him. "I can't pay you, Christy. I don't have anything to pay you with."

"Then you'll find a way." He winked at her.

"I don't have a way," she shouted, the panic crawling up her throat. She battled it, shaking. Deep down, she'd known she'd lose Zach. She'd known it last night. Just as she'd always known she'd be forced to leave Omaha. "You do what you need to do." She sighed. "I've relocated before; I'll do it again."

"And Spencer?"

Lise shook her head. "There isn't any future there, anyway."

"No future for the two of ya or no future for him?" The taunting edge to his voice caught her attention.

Another finger of panic clawed at her. "What do you mean?"

"Seems to me you're makin' decisions here for the both of ya. You don't mind tossin' him away, fine. But what's he gonna say about you tossin' away the senate for him?"

"This has nothing to do with him."

"I'd say it does, seein' as you're in need of a little more motivation."

"I can't pay you!"

Christy laughed. "Spencer can. Him and that fat little turd, Adam Foster. Foster and his cronies got so much money backin' Spencer, they can't afford for a squaw to ruin it. Seems to me you got more of a way than you figured you did. Foster won't want no one to know what I know."

"Get out." She reached for the doorknob only to have Christy put his hand over hers. She jumped, shudders flooding her body.

"Here's what I'll do," he whispered. "You and me are gonna take a walk over to the bank, and you're gonna make a withdrawal. Whatever you got in your account will do fine for today. We'll call it a down payment, how's that? I'll give you three days to get more or I go to the papers."

She nodded, unable to do anything else. If Christy followed through with his threat, Zach's dreams would be finished and he would hate her forever.

In the courtroom, Zach shifted in his seat next to General Crook and glared at John Webster. Webster and Poppleton had managed a solid case, creating more pressure on him to denigrate Standing Bear's character. It was one of the things he hated most about being a prosecuting attorney. And, though

262

he was technically defending Crook in the case, it still felt like prosecution.

Or persecution.

A soft rustle caught his attention and he glanced back at the front row. Lise had returned, sitting with Susette, her face etched with tenseness.

Zach's breath hitched and he hoped she wasn't regretting last night.

He was more than ready for the trial to be over. But, unless he wanted to hand an appeal to Webster, he had no choice but to wait it out. Just as soon as this mess was over, though, he was going to pursue her. And he'd be damned if he was going to let Foster and the campaign keep him from doing so.

Images, tastes, filled his mind.

He'd never met anyone like her. Innocent and proper, teasing and yielding. She was an enigma. Last night, she'd been all of that and more. And he couldn't get enough of her.

He pulled at his collar. God, it was hot for the beginning of May.

He glanced at Lise again, tempted like a kid at a candy store.

She filled his thoughts. Concentrating on the trial was a nightmare. Concentrating on anything but her honeyed skin, those chocolate eyes, and the taste of her.

Her easy understanding of the legal system, her keen intelligence, her perception — on so many levels — were qualities he'd never found in the women he'd known.

What other woman would suggest a native custom with such eager modesty? With anyone else, he would have found the idea too common, too forward, too carnal. But Lise's offer had come from somewhere else. And their pleasure had been so much more than satisfaction of lust.

He knew without a doubt that she hadn't offered herself to him on a whim.

And his actions?

He'd worshiped her. Touched and smelled and tasted and adored her.

When in God's name had he ever worshiped a woman?

His gut clenched as it hit him.

Worship.

Love.

He turned abruptly and stared at her, swallowing hard.

Her face was a mask, her gaze moving around the room but never to him.

His heartbeat caught, the intensity of desire and discovery shifting to anxiety. He drew a breath, praying he hadn't misread her responses, hoping she didn't regret what they'd shared.

The pounding of Dundy's gavel drew his attention. Zach closed his eyes and drew a breath. Damn this trial. He wanted nothing more than to pull Lise into his arms and reassure her. To tell her what he'd neglected to say last night.

He loved her.

It was nearly 1:30 when Lise slipped into the courtroom for the following day's afternoon session. Dundy had indicated this would be the final day of the trial, and once again the room was full of curious spectators. At the front, her usual spot on Susette's bench was already occupied by several Ponca tribal members who had come for the final arguments. Susette had been summoned to interpret.

She glanced at Zach's empty chair, her heart pounding. She wanted him to gather her in his arms, but she knew it would be better if she sat in the back, away from the temptation to approach him.

She'd avoided him after yesterday's session, refusing to come out of her room at the boarding house when he called on her. Her eyes stung from the tears she'd shed, but she knew she had no choice. Zach's fate was in her hands. She sighed. Her choices were to pay or run or confess to Zach.

Lise searched the room, seeking an empty seat.

Halfway back, Thad Spencer eagerly waved his hand at her and slid to one side, opening a small spot. "Over here, Miss Dupree," he called. "You can sit with Ma and me."

Lise made her way into the row, inching past a portly businessman and two whispering young women who seemed more intent on what others were wearing than the trial itself. She squeezed in next to Thad and offered him a wary smile.

"This is my ma," he announced. "Ma, this is Miss Dupree."

"Abigail Spencer," the thin woman said. "My sons have had a great deal to say about you. I'm pleased to finally meet you."

Lise's cheeks grew hot. Between Thad and Abigail, Zach would know every detail of her demeanor today. She fought to broaden her smile and nodded to the woman. "And I you," she said. "Please call me Lise."

"I don't think my boys have ever spent so much time at the library as they have these past few weeks."

"I think Zach's found it helpful to have a law library in town." Lise avoided Abigail's penetrating gaze as she skirted the implication of the statement. "Tell me what's happened so far today."

Thad's face lit as he summarized the morning session. "Webster's been talking the whole time about how Standing Bear and the rest of the Poncas don't even want to be Indians no more."

"My gracious, I could hardly believe the injustices those people have endured," Abigail added. "They moved them to Indian Territory without so much as any consent whatsoever. I can't believe the appalling conditions they've been exposed to."

Lise nodded, wondering if Abigail had known about her father's role in the Minnesota hangings or if she'd been left in the dark as well. Though Lise found it hard to believe she wouldn't have known, she also couldn't reconcile the sympathetic Abigail with someone who would hide such a thing from her family.

Of course, she knew from experience that there were many reasons for keeping information hidden.

Christy's threat to derail Zach's campaign left her with no choice but to continue hiding her own secret.

The side door of the courtroom opened and the attorneys entered. Zach strode forward with General Crook and two of the officials sent from Washington.

Lise's heart hammered as she watched his lean body settle into his chair. Her skin tingled with phantom caresses and she could taste his kisses. Her throat tightened. If she fled, she'd never again know Zach's touches. If she left, Christy would go directly to Zach with his blackmail scheme and her sacrifice would be for naught. She would lose her job, her dream, and Zach . . . all for nothing.

She'd go to Foster tomorrow, swallowing her pride and hatred every inch of the way.

The side door creaked open again and silence sliced through the courtroom. Beside Lise, Thad drew a sharp breath and pointed to the front of the room.

Standing Bear had entered in full tribal regalia. His costume was rich and full, accented by a red Indian blanket. He wore moccasins, a bear-claw necklace, and a breastplate. An eagle feather graced his hair, and beaded earrings hung from his earlobes. His manner was regal, a chief.

A tenseness filled the air as the full implication hit the spectators.

"He sure don't look like someone who don't want to be Indian anymore," Thad whispered.

Lise stared at the chief, feeling the awe

surround her. This was a man who was proud of who he was, of where he came from. This was a man who did not want to relinquish his Indian heritage.

This was a man who had just lost the case.

Susette sat in the crowded courtroom, fighting fatigue. It was nearly 9:30 p.m. Around her, people stifled yawns and sighed. Due to another pending case, Dundy had insisted they finish arguments today. Evening had turned to dusk, and still the lawyers droned uselessly on.

Uselessly because in a single moment, when Standing Bear had entered in his full tribal dress, the case had been decided. And with it, so many other outcomes.

Susette stretched her toes while she watched Tom from the corner of her eye. She'd spent half of last night mulling Tom's idea, unsure if it appealed to her because she wanted to advance Indian rights, to be in the limelight, or to be with Tom. Now, it no longer mattered. Standing Bear would be sent back to Indian Territory, and there would be no eastern tour. She would return to the Omaha Reservation and once again teach the children. There would be no more newspaper articles and no more time with Tom Tibbles.

Lise's future would change, too. Susette glanced behind her. Lise was still there, drawn and distracted. During the last break, she'd tearfully confided her renewed worries about her Aunt Rose. If the Poncas were sent back to Indian Territory, Lise would need to care for Rose herself.

Susette hadn't had the time to reassure her. Besides, how could she tell her friend Rose would be all right when Standing Bear was sitting there in full tribal regalia, a sharp contrast to the case Webster and Poppleton had spent their time creating.

His appearance was defying the assertion that the Ponca band no longer considered themselves Indians. Susette fought the tears of compassion that threatened behind her eyes. She knew how it was to battle pride, but she hated thinking about what would happen to the Poncas now.

His eyes weary and his shoulders slumping, Webster had surrendered the floor to Zach Spencer mid-afternoon. To Susette's surprise, Spencer failed to seize on the opportunity Standing Bear had created. Instead of emphasizing that the man still considered himself Indian, Spencer had stuck to his original premise, questioning the legality of the writ in the first place and claiming Indians were non-citizens who lacked the right to file such actions. He'd cited treaties that confined the Poncas to defined areas and which excluded them from the Omaha Reservation before surrendering the floor to Poppleton.

She glanced up. Poppleton's rebuttal finally seemed to be winding down. His voice had changed, signaling a major argument point.

"I do not believe it is possible to view the Ponca as wild beasts. They are human beings, with as much right to the protection of the courts as anyone else. Unless the defense can cite a law that excludes 'people' from the benefits of *habeas corpus*, it must uphold the writ. Unless the defense can cite a credible source that requires a petitioner to be a 'citizen,' it must uphold the writ. Unless the court is prepared to find that these Ponca are not 'human beings,' it must uphold the writ."

It was a good argument — one that might have won the case but for Standing Bear's appearance. Susette watched Poppleton return to his chair and sit. On the other side of the room, Zach Spencer expelled a breath and shook his head. Dundy lifted his gavel and adjourned the case.

It was over. A surge of dread filled her and she looked to Tom. Dundy had promised

Standing Bear would have a chance to speak on his own behalf. Tom winked at her, then motioned to Dundy. Dundy nodded. He was going to follow through after all.

Susette's breath caught. Perhaps . . . just perhaps . . . there would be a chance after all.

"Standing Bear has asked to speak to address this audience. He may now do so," Dundy announced.

Susette waited for Standing Bear to rise, then moved forward to interpret; the other interpreter had been sent back to the Omaha Reservation yesterday.

As Standing Bear stepped to the front of the room, the audience quieted. He wore the red blanket draped around his shoulders as if it were a king's robe, the feather in his hair as if it were a crown. His bear-claw necklace clacked in the silence as he moved. His moccasins whispered in the expectant air. Once again, a sense of awe filled the courtroom.

This was a man who took pride in his heritage, who was a leader. A man who was not willing to sacrifice his identity.

At the judge's solemn nod, Standing Bear began to speak. "I see a great many of you here," he began, pausing for Susette to translate. He continued, sentence by sen-

272

tence, relating his experiences, his forced removal from Dakota, his desire to return. Then, he recounted two incidents, telling the courtroom how he had found nearly frozen white men and how he had taken them in and cared for them.

Susette watched the audience's eyes fill with sympathy, and she adjusted her tone so that it conveyed Standing Bear's mix of pride and humbleness. She hedged a glance at Dundy and her heart pounded as she recognized his willingness to hear the story.

"If I had been a wild, savage Indian, would I have done this?" Standing Bear asked. "I guess not; I would have been more likely to cut off his head and take his scalp." The room was eerily quiet as Susette relayed his words. Then, he continued, relating how he had also farmed and lived in a house and raised crops on his forty acres of land. He told them of his increasing self-sufficiency, until the day Christy arrived and took the Poncas away from their life.

"I asked him what his orders were to remove me. He said he had none. I sent word to the Great Father about it. He said they didn't know anything about it." He waited as Susette translated, his gaze roaming over the audience. "Perhaps you don't believe this, but it is true. That is all I have to say to you."

He nodded once, then returned to his seat.

Susette followed, tears in her eyes, while the courtroom sat hushed and spellbound.

CHAPTER THIRTEEN

The following morning, Adam Foster sat at his desk, impatient to get on with his day. He was more than a little displeased with Zach's weak response in court and the extra campaigning now necessary to counter the damage to his image. He had things to do, campaign speeches to arrange for Zach, now that the trial was in recess. Speeches back in Lincoln, or elsewhere in the state, away from the temptation of that damned librarian. He drummed his fingers on the desk and glared at Rufus Christy. "What the hell do you mean you fixed things?" he demanded. He should have known better than to let himself get involved with the slimy little bastard.

"Just what I said." Christy grinned. "I had a little talk with the librarian."

Adam forced back the alarm that was rising in his throat and slammed the open desk drawer shut. "I told you I would handle things."

"Yeah, you did say that."

He stared at the Indian agent, not wanting to believe the man's stupidity. He had to get him under control. "I don't need you messing things up, Christy. Stay out of this."

Christy leaned back in his chair, arrogance almost steaming off him. "Seems to me that would leave me out in the cold. I done a lot of diggin' for you and you paid me next to nothin' for it. You and your pompous orders, treating me like a minion." He paused, his beady eyes catching the flinch Adam couldn't hide. He smirked at it. "That's right, a minion. You didn't think I knew what that meant, did you?"

Adam's fists balled, his panic tasting like bile. "Mr. Christy —"

"All this time you thought I was stupid." Christy stood and looked down at Adam, his finger wagging in his face. "Well, I got news for you, Senator. I ain't stupid. I ain't fancy, don't got much education, but I ain't stupid."

Adam stood, catching Christy's finger in his hand. "Well, you aren't exactly smart, either." He squeezed, watching as Christy winced. When he was sure Christy got the message, he let go. They stood, staring at one another, while Christy's cockiness shrank.

"She been to see you yet?"

Adam rolled his eyes, desperately feigning indifference. "Who?"

"The 'breed. Miss Dupree?"

He sighed. "And exactly why would she come to see me?"

"I told you I had a little talk with her." Christy's voice was almost whiny.

Adam shook his head. "I already took care of her. You didn't need to interfere." He nodded to the door and settled back into his chair, dismissing him.

Christy's eyes narrowed at the slight. "Oh, I wasn't interfering. Just furtherin' my interests."

"What the hell are you about, Christy?" Adam fought for calm. Clearly, he'd made a tactical error in trying to dismiss the man.

"Bet you don't know what I know."

"You are a worm, Mr. Christy. I really do think it would be best if we severed our relationship."

"You might want to rethink that."

"Will you stop with the damn riddles!" Adam pounded his fist on the desk.

"I was gonna wait, let her come here herself and do this, but she ain't yet so I guess it's time for me to take things in hand myself, specially since I got more information."

Adam sprang up, his patience shredded, and strode around the desk. "I'm going to wring your neck." Damn the man for a babbling idiot.

"No, you ain't." Christy grinned again, toe to toe with Adam.

"Spit it out," Adam demanded.

"How much you think it's worth to keep it quiet-like that Lise Dupree is a 'breed?"

Adam stilled as Christy's meaning finally emerged. "I thought I told you we weren't going to blackmail her. It's too risky. I handled it my way."

"First off, *we* aren't blackmailing her. Second, I don't think you handled it quite so good as you think you did."

Adam stilled. "What?"

"I figure you don't want it out in the open neither."

Christy's full intent hit Adam. He stared at the Indian agent. "You're blackmailing me?"

"Let's just say I think you got a real interest in keeping this quiet."

Adam slowed his breathing and re-evaluated Christy. This was no imbecile puppet. He'd need to tread carefully. "Mr. Christy," he began, "do you know who my friends are? I know powerful people. People who squash bugs like you and don't think twice about it."

Christy nodded. "Let's see . . . there's bankers, and there's railroad men, and there's businessmen, and there's cattlemen. Lots of folks with money. Lots of folks who like politicians in their pocket, who've invested already to make sure of it and who've promised to keep paying in the future. Those folks don't want to mess with backing politicians whose sympathies are in doubt, who could lose elections if certain facts were made public, now do they?"

Adam swallowed. He'd vastly underestimated Christy. The slimy little bastard wasn't stupid at all. Astute as hell, that's what he was. And if he wasn't careful, Christy would have him backed into a corner. "What are you implying?"

"Oldest game in the world, Foster. They've been paying you for years while you back the bills that favor them. They're looking for the same in Spencer and the kid don't even know it, does he? You'll just keep collectin' on his behalf."

"Hogwash," Adam bluffed.

"I told you I ain't stupid."

"You don't have anything worth paying for. So the librarian's an Indian? She broke it off with Zach." Adam smiled and shrugged his shoulders. He had everything under control after all.

"There's a lot you don't know, ain't there?" Something in Christy's eye glinted, and Adam's smile wavered.

"They haven't seen each other since I told her the old man hung her uncle."

Christy waggled his fingers and the glint in his eye deepened. "It pays to know folks in lower places, too, Senator. For instance, I got friends at the hotel where I'm stayin'. One of 'em heard somethin' the other night. Seems Spencer and the 'breed were arguin' in the hallway outside his room, woke him up." The glint had become a full-fledged gleam.

Adam shrugged off a knot of foreboding. "So they argued. Seems to diffuse your threat a bit."

"Oh, it ain't that so much. It's the other sounds. The ones comin' from inside Spencer's room. Ain't no doubt what was goin' on."

"I'm sure Spencer has many acquaintances," Adam said, dread rising in his gut.

"Might be. But the only one leavin' the room afterwards was Lise Dupree and the kiss he seen 'em share in the hallway at one in the mornin' weren't exactly chaste."

Christy paced, letting the words soak in, then turned and stared at Adam, his eyes so bright with greed that Adam's dread tightened into a hard ball of fear.

"I'm thinkin'," Christy said, "that you'll be wantin' to talk to those folks you know."

Zach strode down Dodge Street, worry picking at him. The trial had recessed late last night, and he needed to see Lise. But the library was locked up tight and Lise was nowhere to be found. He kicked at a pebble on the wooden sidewalk, sending it flying into the street, and headed for Lise's boarding house.

He had less than an hour before the afternoon train left for Lincoln — the train he should have been on early this morning. He'd already received two angry telegrams from the district court judge in Lincoln who had been forced to delay proceedings because of Zach's absence. He didn't dare test the judge's wrath by waiting until tomorrow's train.

Lise had disappeared immediately after Standing Bear's speech. Zach had shoved his papers into his leather case and turned around only to find her seat empty. Her worried face haunted him all night. Ever since she'd come to his hotel, she'd avoided him. His gut clenched with the need to see her, to make sure she was all right. He approached the boarding house and climbed the threadbare front stoop. The landlady opened the door before he could knock.

"Look who's back," the woman said. "Would you like to come in?"

"I'd like to see Miss Dupree, if I may."

"Well, now, I don't know if she's available. The poor thing didn't come down to breakfast again." She fluttered her thinning eyelashes at Zach and guided him toward the parlor. "Why don't you step in and I'll see if I can rouse her."

Zach turned into the room and stalled. A cloying combination of floral scents assaulted him, and the chairs were filled with a gaggle of blushing spinsters, most of whom were either beaming at him or slyly glancing in his direction. He stifled a groan and took the nearest empty seat. One or two of the women tittered quietly and someone uttered a quiet "oh."

He nodded to them, then let his glance settle on the hallway.

"I don't think she'll come," one of the women said. Zach turned and caught the gaze of a plump lady dressed in varying shades of purple. "If you ask me, she's giving you the cold shoulder," the woman said.

"Nonsense, Violet. She's ill. Pure and simple, she's ill."

A third woman, this one thin as a bone, sniffed as though affronted. "Cold shoulder, indeed. Have you looked at the man?"

"We've all looked at him, Winifred. A real heartbreaker."

The group tittered as a whole as they continued to speculate about him as if he weren't there. He'd forgotten about Lise's odd assortment of housemates.

He shifted in his chair and loosened his collar. The grandfather clock in the hallway continued to tick the minutes away, and Zach fought the urge to rise and check the time. Worry that Lise might be sick warred with concern that she was refusing to see him out of regret over the evening they'd spent together. She wouldn't have closed the library unless she were physically ill.

Footsteps sounded in the hallway and the landlady emerged into the parlor, shaking her head. "She won't come down."

Behind Zach, several of the old maids made tsking sounds.

Zach's heart plummeted. "Did she say why?" he finally asked.

"Only that she couldn't see anyone right now."

"Didn't look sick to me," the purple clad

woman said.

"Hush now," the yellow lady said. "Don't you remember how she looked yesterday? The poor girl was pale as a ghost."

He caught the landlady's gaze. "I don't suppose I could speak to her through her door?"

The collective gasp in the parlor told him the answer even before the landlady's vehement headshake. "Oh, dear. No, I can't allow that."

Zach's shoulders slumped and he stood.

"You could leave a note," one of the ladies prompted.

"Oh, yes, a note. I'll deliver it," Violet volunteered.

"I'll deliver it," another offered.

"I should be the one," Violet insisted. "After all, it was my idea."

A chorus of voices chimed in, each vying for the honor of delivering the note. Zach winced. He glanced at the landlady and sighed.

"Do you have notepaper and a pen?"

"I do, indeed." She rummaged through a secretary, waved a sheet of stationery at him, then positioned it on the drop-leaf table.

Zach made his way to the desk, scrunched his face at the rose scent lingering in the air, and removed the stopper from the ink jar. It would have to do — there was no way he could postpone leaving any longer.

He completed the note, frowning at the words left unsaid. He had no doubts that the ladies would read the message the moment he left, and he wanted to protect Lise's reputation. He hoped she'd be able to read between the lines.

Waiting for the ink to dry, Zach folded the note and asked for an envelope. He sealed the message inside, aware that behind him the ladies were still arguing over who should take the note upstairs. Unease drifted through him as he imagined them steaming open the envelope and the note drifting from one to another of them, never making it into Lise's hands.

He pulled out his watch and glanced at it. If he hurried, he had enough time to catch Thad before he had to be at the depot. He'd ask the kid to deliver the note.

Somehow, it seemed less of a risk.

Susette glanced around the newspaper office. It was early afternoon and the May sun still lit the front windows, reminding her how far spring had advanced since she'd come to Omaha. It was time to return to the reservation. With her duties at the trial

285

over, she knew her brother would arrive soon to take her back.

Tom entered from the press room and paused, his gaze on her.

Susette's skin tingled, and she choked back a sigh. When he looked at her like that, her resolutions were for naught.

"Did you read the article?" he asked.

Her hand drifted to the draft of Tom's article on her table. He'd applied his usual flair with words, paraphrasing aptly, subtly persuading. She pushed the article across the table.

"It's good. You've captured the spirit of Standing Bear's words well."

"It's not too flowery?"

Susette shook her head. "Forceful, perhaps. And descriptive. But not flowery. Will you wait with it until the verdict comes back?" It had been several tense days since Dundy had recessed. The *Herald* had already run her stories about Standing Bear's comments. Tom's article summarized the speech differently — as if emphasizing the Poncas' validity. It lacked only a lead-in to direct the reader. With the appropriate introduction, it could be used to either celebrate or denounce the decision.

Tom nodded. "I'd intended to, yes. I want to be ready so I can slip in a few paragraphs at the beginning and the end. Knowing Dundy, he could send the verdict in the middle of the night."

"Do you think he'll rule in our favor?"

"Our favor, Bright Eyes?"

She blushed. She'd thought of the case as theirs for so long that she seldom referred to it as Standing Bear's case anymore, except in print.

Tom set his hand on her arm, a brief touch that set her on fire, then walked toward his desk with the article.

Susette pulled her arm close and followed Tom with her gaze. She couldn't tell if he'd noticed her reaction, couldn't read his feelings anymore. He kept his gaze shrouded, even when looking directly at her. The uncertainty she felt as a result was almost worse than knowing he wanted her as much as she wanted him.

"If any judge has the guts to rule for Standing Bear, it will be Elmer Dundy," Tom said. "He's one of the fairest men I know. It boils down to whether or not he's prepared to overturn Dred Scott."

"Ruling that an Indian or a Negro is the same as a white man is too big a step." Susette straightened the remaining items on the table, putting off telling Tom she would be returning to the reservation. "Dundy might be a very fair man but it is a step he might not be ready to take."

"Time is ripe for change. The world is waiting."

She glanced up. "Waiting for what?"

"To experience the truth. To make changes. To become familiar with the plight of the downtrodden and the forgotten."

She laughed at the excitement in his voice and studied his face. "Your eyes have that sparkle, Tom. It is as if gears are spinning. Next thing, you will begin ticking like a clock."

"I think we need to go to Washington as soon as the verdict comes in."

"What?" Her hands stilled. She'd pushed the idea of the tour from her mind, dismissed it as something that might never occur. "So soon?"

"I think Standing Bear needs to visit the White House and the Capitol. He needs to shake hands with men of power and remind them we are all human beings with the same needs, entitled to the same rights."

She shook her head. "It will not work. It is too much."

He strode to the desk and grasped her hands. "It's not. I got a telegram this morning. One of the newspapers in Boston already has backers to finance it. Crowds would pay to see him, Bright Eyes. People want to shake his hand. We'll go to Washington. Just think, if we could gain enough publicity, we could force politicians to take legislative action to pass new laws." His eyes danced at the prospect. "Say you'll come with us."

She shook her head, quelling her desire to make the journey, to put Standing Bear's words into the right context, to be with Tom in faraway places.

"I'm needed here. I have a school to run, children who need me."

"You sister can continue teaching them. You said yourself she's done well while you've been here in Omaha." His fingertips stroked the back of her hands.

Heat flowed up her arms and Susette struggled to keep her own hands still, to avoid turning them to grasp Tom's. "My sister did not agree to take the job permanently."

He pulled her hands up, melting the resistance she'd urged upon her muscles, and kissed each hand once. "But she would, you know she would."

Susette raised her gaze. The raw desire in Tom's eyes slammed through her, landing in the very core of her being. She shivered and pulled away, willing herself to stay resolute. "And what would your wife say to you traveling across the country with me?" she asked him.

Tom swallowed, watching her hands, then sighed. "We'd take a chaperone. Your brother Frank could come. He'd protect your virtue. Amelia would not argue with that. You know how much she believes as I do."

Susette shook her head. If she were Tom's wife, no amount of belief in their cause would prevent her from arguing against such an idea.

"She believes in you, Tom. There is no room for me here." Susette turned away, gathered her things, and walked out of the office as Tom watched, silent.

Dusk was settling when Adam Foster finally made it to the Spencer house. He was about to knock on the front door when it sprang open before him. Thad stood on the other side, poised to exit.

"Whoa, boy. What's got you all in a dither?" The kid was wired up about something.

"Hey, Senator Foster. I got an errand to run. Are you here to see Gramps?"

Adam nodded out of obligation. He really had little desire to sit and watch the old man drool, but he knew Abigail would expect it. Besides, the kid spilled more gossip when they were visiting in Henry's bedroom than any other time.

"Aren't you going to join us?" he asked, hating to waste a visit.

"Can't. Gotta deliver this note to Miss Dupree."

Adam started, then stared at the boy. "It's pretty late in the day, son." He placed his hand on Thad's shoulder and steered him back into the house. "I'm not sure she'd appreciate a call so close to bedtime. She must rise pretty early to get that library prepared for opening."

Thad frowned as Adam closed the door behind them. "But Ma already made me wait 'til supper was done. I was s'posed to deliver it right away."

"And I told you it wasn't polite to interrupt at mealtime." Abigail emerged from the kitchen, wiping her hands on a flowered apron. "And like it or not, Adam's got a point."

"But, Ma."

"It can wait 'til morning just as easily. You can give it to her along with the morning paper. You've got chores that need attending to here." She shifted her attention to Adam. "Father's asleep already. Do you want to sit a spell?"

Adam glanced at Abigail, then shook his head. He'd heard that she'd had a rift with Zach. The odds of her having much information were pretty slim. "No, I should be on my way. I was just passing by and thought I'd poke my head in."

Thad stood, shifting from one foot to the other.

"What is it, Thad?" Abigail asked. "Those chores are waiting."

"It's just that I promised Zach."

"Oh, for heaven's sake. I'm sure there's nothing in that note that can't wait until morning."

Adam offered a benevolent smile to the boy and raised his palms in a gesture of innocence. "I could drop it off on my way back to the hotel . . . just in case she's still up."

"I'm s'posed to give it to her myself," Thad insisted.

"Thad!"

"It's all right, Abigail. I appreciate his commitment to his responsibility." He squeezed Thad's shoulder. "I'm sure Zach will understand that you couldn't get the note delivered until morning."

Thad swallowed and Adam felt the familiar rush of victory in his pulse. The boy glanced at him and sighed. "I reckon it'd be best if the note got there tonight." He reached into his pocket and withdrew a folded envelope, then handed it to Adam.

Adam nodded reassurance as he pocketed the note. "Don't you worry, son. I'll make sure this is taken care of."

CHAPTER FOURTEEN

The following afternoon, Adam Foster stormed into Zach's Lincoln office and slammed the door so hard the hand-stitched sampler Abigail Spencer had made fell to the floor. Foster didn't even glance at it.

"What do you want?" Zach demanded. He wasn't in a particularly good mood himself, and Adam Foster was the last person he wanted to see at the moment. His mood had gone from bad to worse with each bout of speculation over Lise's reasons for refusing to see him. He resented having been forced to leave a note instead of speaking to her in person.

The fact that Foster had been nowhere to be found for the past few days had fueled Zach's anger even further. He'd wanted to deal with the man on his own terms. He sure as hell didn't have the time or patience to deal with him now. Zach raised his head and glared at him.

Foster strode across the room and plopped into the wooden chair across from Zach. "We've got something to discuss."

Zach bit the inside of his cheek. As far as he was concerned, there was damn little left to discuss with Foster. His interference had almost cost Zach Lise's affection. Then Foster had disappeared. Zach stared at his mentor, knowing that confronting him would endanger the rest of his campaign. Foster had enough power to persuade major donors to support other candidates. It was not a conversation Zach wanted right now — not while he was this angry.

He drew a breath and reined in his emotions. Foster was glaring back at him, obviously as upset as he was. He suspected Foster's concerns would be as petty as usual.

"Adam, I don't have time to speculate on what Dundy is going to decide or when he'll deign to do so. If you've come to nag me about it again, you can turn around and leave. I told you before the trial started, I'm not going to contact the man. Dundy will construe it as interference, which it is, and reprimand me."

"It's not about Dundy." Foster leaned forward, anxious. "We've got a problem, Zach. A big problem."

"Yeah. I imagine we do," he finally said. "Can it wait? I've got a court appearance in an hour."

"No, boy, it can't wait."

Zach lifted an eyebrow at his haughty tone. "I thought I told you to stay away from Lise Dupree."

The tightly wound knot in Zach's gut unrolled, and the fury coursed through him. The time had come, then. He pushed back his chair and rose.

"And you told Lise my grandfather took pride in hanging people who might have been innocent — people she knew." The words came out in a rush of bitter hot rage. Zach squared his shoulders and stepped around the desk until he stood over Foster. "What's your stake in this, Adam? Telling a woman something like that is cruel. Implying I knew about it and felt the same way is worse than cruel. You put words in my mouth that were a lie. We don't have anything to discuss."

Foster's lips tightened into a shrewd, thin line. "Oh, but we do," he said.

Zach stared at him again. "Why the hell do you care so much whether or not I like Lise Dupree?"

"It's a damn conflict of interest. The papers would have a heyday. The public won't elect a man who can't be trusted to conduct his personal life with integrity."

"Oh, for Pete's sake, Adam." Zach paced the room, running his hand through his hair. Much as he hated it, he recognized the reality of what Foster was saying. Still, there had to be a better way around it. "She's friends with an Indian and she thinks the writ was legal. How does that impinge upon my integrity? And how does it give you the right to interfere?"

"I support you, for God's sake." Foster stood, his voice no longer restrained. "Me. *My* power. *My* money. *My* influence. *My* backers. Without them, you're nothing."

Zach waited until Foster's red face returned to its normal pale shade. He felt none of the disappointment he knew he should at the senator's berating. He didn't feel chastised. Only used. "So you threatened her?" he asked.

"You weren't listening to my advice. And you've sure as hell made a mess of things now."

Zach stared, unable to comprehend how Foster could think any of this was his fault. "What are you talking about?"

"Did you have that woman in your hotel room?" Foster demanded.

"Did I — ?" How could Foster know?

Fury bubbled again. Foster had no right, no right, to ask about his personal life. And he sure as hell didn't have the right to spy on him. "I refuse to answer that, Adam. It's none of your business."

"It sure as hell is when we're being blackmailed because of it."

Zach sank into the nearest chair, disbelief rocking him. "Blackmailed?"

Foster cracked his knuckles. "The men who pledged their money and power to support you have certain expectations. One of which is that you get elected. The second that you support their interests once in office. Right now, because of your careless behavior, both of those are in doubt."

Zach still didn't understand. "Lise is a threat to their interests? To me getting elected?" He shook his head. "How so, Adam? How so?"

"She's a goddamn Indian," Foster yelled as he slapped his palm on the desk. "An Indian. You've just finished fighting a case in which you maintained that Indians aren't entitled to basic rights. The papers have touted you as anti-Indian, a desirable thing to be when most of the state feels the same way and half your major supporters are vying for tribal lands. Now you've slept with her and it's going to cost me a fortune to

298

bury it."

Zach's breath stilled and his heart pounded in his chest. Lise was Indian. All these weeks, she'd never told him. It made sense — her necklace, her outrage and interest in Standing Bear, her knowledge of Sioux customs. Why hadn't she told him?

"I can't ask them for money," Foster continued. "They'll pull support from us the minute they hear a hint of scandal. They're not going to take the risk of damaging innuendos coming out before the election. There's still time for them to groom another candidate. Don't think they won't."

"So let them," he said, his mind on Lise. What she must think of him, all his comments in the courtroom about Indians not being people. Cold sweat broke out on his skin.

"She's a quarter Sioux! One of the old women with the Ponca group is her mother's half-sister. She's been turning on the charms to discredit you all along, just like I warned you she was doing. Except now somebody knows."

"She's Sioux?" He glanced at Adam, finally digesting the implication. She hadn't told him because she knew damn well what it would mean. Even if he didn't give a damn, the public would. There was a hell of a difference between courting an Indian sympathizer and courting an Indian.

His mind began to filter the knowledge, toe to toe with his tumbling heart. She *should* have told him, she should have trusted him. He could have laid groundwork to prepare for what might happen if someone discovered the truth. Now, if that truth got out, his political career would be over. He glanced back to Foster.

"Our only chance is you ending whatever it is you have going with her. I can pay him off, once. But he's going to ask for more. They always do." Foster drew a breath. "If you end it now, it'll be in the past and he won't be able to prove anything. It might get messy, and we'll have some fixing to do, but if you stop things now, there's still a chance."

Zach felt dazed, like he'd just been hit by a falling tree. "A chance?"

Foster nodded. "You still want to be senator, don't you?"

Lise reined in the horse she'd rented at the livery and sighed. It was late in the day, she was bone tired, and right now, nothing had ever looked so welcoming as the bare wooden cabin standing in front of her on the Omaha Reservation.

The door flew open and Susette ran down the stoop and across the yard. "Lise," she called.

Lise eased down from the horse, her muscles screaming. The sixty-mile journey from Omaha had been far rougher than she'd expected, even with stops to rest the horse and an overnight in Bellevue.

"What are you doing here?" Susette asked.

"I needed to talk." In truth, Lise was more confused than she'd ever been. Her housemates had told her Zach had left town without leaving the note he'd written her, and she'd been unable to locate Foster to discuss paying off Christy. She prayed Susette would listen without censure.

"And you rode all the way here?" Susette's eyes were still wide with surprise, but her voice hinted of an eagerness to converse. "This must be a very large need."

"It is." Lise glanced at the house, the doorway filled with Susette's chattering siblings. Like Susette, they wore white man's clothing but several displayed beaded decorations and traditional hairstyles.

Susette smiled at the clamor of voices and shook her head. "We'll walk to the schoolhouse, where there are not so many ears." Her gaze stalled on Lise, and doubt crept across her face. "We'll walk slowly."

In spite of her aching body, Lise laughed.

"Frank?" Susette called, and another dark head poked out of the doorway. "Will you care for the horse?"

Frank wormed his way between his brothers and sisters and strode across the yard. "He will be in good hands." He took the reins from Lise and led the horse around the house.

Lise exhaled in relief, glad she didn't need to spend the extra energy removing tack and currying the animal. Susette tugged at her arm and Lise turned, willing her legs to move with her friend.

She knew it had been impulsive to rent the horse and undertake the long trip to the Omaha Agency but she needed to confide in her friend. Thank goodness, the city council had accepted her explanation of a family emergency with few questions.

Susette's own sudden departure had also worried her, especially when Tom Tibbles had become evasive. The extra apprehension had folded into the anger and confusion she'd already been feeling so that Lise's thoughts were so jumbled she could hardly sort them out. It was good to see Susette's dancing eyes again and at least know *she* was all right.

It was one less thing for Lise to worry

about. With Christy's threats looming over her and her uncertainty about Zach's feelings, she needed all her wits. She needed to make the right decision, for her and for Zach.

They turned the corner of a building and Susette approached its door, beaming with pride.

"Your school?"

"My school." She opened the door and waited for Lise to enter. Inside, the bare wooden floor, neat rows of benches, and tidy piles of slates looked like any other schoolroom. But in the front of the room, bright examples of beadwork and native implements hung on the wall next to the bookcase of primers and geography books. Math problems filled one side of the blackboard while Omaha and English sentences coexisted on the other.

"Two cultures," Susette confirmed. "So that they may survive in the white world but not forget who they are."

Envy stabbed at Lise. "You make it look so easy. You move in the white world with such confidence, and such acceptance, but you never shed your identity. How do you do that?"

"I expect nothing less than to be accepted."

Lise stared at her friend. "How?"

"My father is a wise man, Lise. He sees the world as it is. From the time he became a leader, he set a pattern. To survive, we must adapt." Susette settled onto a bench at the side of the room and pulled Lise down beside her. "The Omaha have learned how to live as whites, to have farms and schools and churches. The children learn English and white man's history lessons. But in our homes, we keep the memories of the old ways. I have grown up in both worlds, and I have been taught to be proud of both of them."

Lise knit her brows. "But how do you 'expect' acceptance."

"I do not throw my Omaha-ness in the face of whites." Susette paused. "But neither do I hide it away."

"Yet you are not accepted enough to avoid being thrown into jail for not having a pass, and you would not be hired to teach at a white man's school or run one of their libraries." Lise recognized the bitterness that tinged her words and lowered her gaze.

Susette cupped a hand over Lise's and squeezed. "I do not need to do those things," she said softly. "I am making changes at this place. I am teaching my people to live in two worlds. As to passes and jail, it's the law and I disobeyed it. The Omaha have laws, too. And how do we know they wouldn't let me run a library? I haven't asked them."

Lise sighed. "You do this so easily. And Standing Bear walked into that courtroom, unafraid to be fully Ponca while claiming to be on the same footing as whites."

"Ah, but there is the difference. He did not claim to be white. It is not about being white or being Ponca or Omaha or Sioux. He did not ask for that, even if his lawyers did. He asked instead for the world to see the commonalities, to change how we define ourselves."

"Maybe it's easier for the Omaha and the Ponca."

"Because our culture already practiced farming? Because we are smaller tribes, with more agreement among us? Because fighting is not so much a part of our culture? Because our white agents did not cheat us of our annuities?" She shrugged. "Perhaps all this did make it easier."

"I wish it were that easy for me." She left her hand in Susette's, letting the silence buoy them until she felt her body relax. The chill of the empty room embraced her, calming her further, and her breaths evened into a pattern of peace.

Her white acquaintances would rush to fill the silence with words, destroying the bond being created within the stillness. Susette let it build until Lise squeezed her hand and absorbed the strength of the moment.

"What has led you to these thoughts, my friend?" Susette finally asked. "You did not ride all these miles to look at my school and ask me about the Omaha."

Lise drew a breath and drew in more strength. "Rufus Christy is blackmailing me."

"About your heritage?"

"Yes."

Susette nodded in understanding. "So you must decide if you will pay or take a chance."

"The last time people found out I was part Sioux, I was dismissed from my job and asked to leave town." It was a story she'd told her friend before but one that threatened to reoccur, this time destroying more dreams than before.

"And you are sure this will happen again?"

"Yes."

Susette let the silence build again, offering Lise time to compare the past and the present. Was she sure? There were differences, certainly. But differences had never mattered. In the end, she'd twice lost everything she cared about. She shuddered.

"Perhaps it is time to change how you think." She patted Lise's hand. "When this happened the last time, it was in Spirit Lake?"

"Yes."

"Doesn't that explain much? Over thirty people there were killed by Sioux."

"But it was twenty-two years ago." Lise's anger roiled. Sioux in Minnesota, her family among them, had been held responsible for that massacre, though it had been committed by an outlawed Sioux and a small band of renegades. As punishment, annuities were withheld from the reservations, beginning a pattern of hunger that would erupt into more violence five years later.

"People do not forget such things," Susette said. "You have not forgotten what happened to your people, have you?" She paused. "You saw the anger of the whites in Minnesota. Do you think it was any less for the people in Spirit Lake? An uprising leaves scars for everyone. Sorrow and anger and revenge."

"But I had nothing to do with it. I am more white than Sioux — my mother made sure of it."

"Your mother taught you to hide. Instead

307

of choosing well when you took that job, you hid, with full knowledge that a Sioux would not be tolerated there. Of course they dismissed you. Now you are in another place, a place that has no history of violence. Are you so sure of what will happen?"

Lise shook her head, denying the small grain of doubt Susette had created. "It always happens. They burned my father's store because he was married to an Indian half-breed. My mother had to hide who she was every day. They fired me."

"Yes, all those things happened." Susette squeezed Lise's hand. "But what happened to Standing Bear in court when he refused to hide in white man's trousers and a flannel shirt?"

"N . . . nothing." Lise stared at her friend as the doubt continued to nibble at her certainty.

"Not nothing. You were there. What happened?"

There was only one word to describe what she had witnessed. "Awe."

"And inside you? Did you feel inside you the same thing I felt?"

Her shell of denial cracked a little further. "Pride," she said, recalling her emotions.

"Awe and pride. Perhaps these people are ready to accept changes. Do you see how you must look at things differently?"

Lise nodded. Perhaps this time, the public would not insist her post be terminated. Perhaps this time, no one would care that her mother had been a half-breed. If only it were that simple. The public might not care that the librarian had mixed blood, but Zach's political rivals would seize on it.

Her eyes pooled with tears. "I'm not the only person involved," she said. "Oh, Susette. I don't know what to do."

"I think there is much that you've not told me."

"I went to talk with Zach, after we spoke, to ask him about his grandfather. I . . . we . . . he didn't know until I yelled at him and he was angry. But he didn't know and the picture Foster painted of him isn't true." She was rambling, her thoughts jumping.

"And?" Susette prompted.

"And one thing led to another. I went to his room with him. I let him kiss me, touch me."

Susette digested this, then asked, "Are you ashamed of this?"

"No," Lise said, vivid memories of the night etched into her mind. Warmth flooded her heart, and she knew the truth. "I would have given myself to him, all of me, if he hadn't respected me enough to stop when he did. I love him."

"In spite of everything we thought about him?"

"It was Foster." The certainty of that burned into her. "I believe in Zach."

"You would live your life with him?"

"I would. But I can't. He's running for senate."

A frown crossed Susette's face. "He has discarded you because you are Sioux?"

"He doesn't know."

"You didn't tell him." It was a statement, not a question, and Susette's quiet knowledge pricked at Lise.

"I was afraid." The simple admission clarified much of the confusion she'd felt. Fear. She'd let fear rule her life and made Zach vulnerable because of it. "Now, if I don't pay Christy, it will be in the papers and Zach will lose the senate race. And I will lose him."

"Perhaps. You do not think you should let him decide?"

"He's already told me how important it is to him to win the senate. He's dreamed of it for years." Lise's heart pounded. "It doesn't matter whether he cares that I'm Sioux or not. Even if he accepts my heritage, if he loses the senate race because of it, he will hate me forever."

Susette drew a breath. "So you will pay Christy?"

"I can't." A small sob escaped and Lise felt hot tears stream down her cheeks. Susette drew her close, letting her cry until she was able to continue. "I already gave him everything I have. He wants more money and I don't have anything left to give him unless I go to Adam Foster and ask him to pay it for me."

"And you think Foster would do that?"

"I think he would. He won't like it, but I think he would do it. He's been trying to keep Zach away from me since we met. That's why he told me about Zach's grandfather — so I would hate Zach."

"And this is what you want to do?"

Anger surged and Lise stood, her fists balled in frustration. "No it's not what I want to do!" she shouted. "I don't want any of the choices open to me. I don't want to lose what I could have with Zach, I don't want to pay, I don't want to run."

"If you pay, Christy will ask you to pay more and it will not stop. And Foster will demand you stop seeing Zach. You know this."

"I know, I know. And Zach came to the boarding house several times. But he didn't leave the note he wrote and I have no idea

311

how he feels. If he cares, I'll have to make him believe I don't want to see him and I don't know if I can do that. Not unless I leave town." She paused, shrugging. "Maybe that would end the blackmail, too. No one knows what happened between us. It will only be speculation. And if I am not here to fuel it, it will die."

Susette stood and grasped Lise's hands. "Are you certain of how you are viewing this? That you know how people will respond?"

"I'm sure."

"Are you? Truly?" She pushed Lise gently down onto the bench and stared at her, her bright eyes dark and probing. "And are you certain it is impossible to change the outcome?"

Susette left Lise in the schoolhouse, reflecting in the silence. Her friend had much to think about.

She meandered away from the building, not yet wanting to return to the cabin and confront her noisy siblings. When Lise had arrived, her heart had jumped, eager for the chance to tell Lise about Tom's increased pressure over the trip East.

It would be good to discuss the temptation to introduce Standing Bear, to bring his story to others. In truth, she had basked in the attention she'd received as his interpreter. She had never known this about herself, that she enjoyed attention, that she could command it.

And it would be good to discuss the other temptations as well. She hadn't realized how desperately she needed to examine her feelings for Tom until she'd seen Lise.

Resentment stabbed at her and she tamped it down. Today was not the day for Susette's concerns. They paled in the light of Lise's problems.

Susette kicked at a stone and watched it roll through the new grass sprouting in the schoolyard. She continued to kick at it, sending it bouncing across the playground until she reached the swing, a bare board suspended on worn ropes from a tree branch. She sat, pushing the ground until she'd started an easy sway.

Perhaps it was time she thought about what she really wanted, as she had advised Lise to do. Did she really want to stay on the reservation forever?

She glanced at the schoolhouse, and warm pride crept through her. She'd wanted to teach, set out to accomplish it, and was good at it. The children loved her as much as she loved them, even her sometimes annoying siblings. She wrinkled her nose, appreciating their boisterousness.

She'd wanted to teach, but she had never yearned for it as she did the idea of traveling East as a spokesperson for Indian rights. Teaching paled in comparison to the glow she felt when holding reporters' attentions. The satisfaction of being quoted in papers as an expert filled her so deeply that she knew teaching math and English grammar for the rest of her life would never fulfill her in the same way.

Emptiness was not what she wanted from life.

The desire that flowed through her when she was in Tom's presence was also unparalleled in her quiet life on the reservation. Despite knowing neither of them would allow it to follow its natural course, denying it entirely would leave her forever empty in so many other ways.

Perhaps nature was simply awakening urges that she'd been unaware of. She knew every man on the reservation. None of them made her skin tingle. None made her body ache deep inside or made her feel excited and scared at the same time. If she stayed here, she might never experience such sweet discomfort again.

Susette pushed her toe against the ground,

and the swing drifted back and forth. There was much in the world that she didn't know about. If she left the reservation, doors would open for her in many ways.

She glanced at the schoolhouse again. She'd just told her friend to confront her fears.

Could she refuse to open the doors of opportunity that stood before her simply because *she* was afraid?

CHAPTER FIFTEEN

Zach tapped his fingers on the wooden trim of the seat in front of him. The damn train seemed to be moving at the rate of a snail.

He shifted, seeking a new position.

The week in Lincoln had been filled with court during the day and political meetings every evening. He was tired of smiling pleasantly while sipping brandies, and he was exhausted from maintaining a curt politeness with Adam Foster as he fought to keep his campaign alive.

And then there was the worry over Lise. He ached to reassure her about his feelings, to ask her why she hadn't told him who she was, about the blackmail and the strategy they'd now need to follow.

It all made sense now that he knew she was part Indian. That's why he hadn't been surprised at the revelation. Chances were half of Omaha probably realized it as well. Her defense of native cultures and her interest in Standing Bear's case were common knowledge. Then, there was the necklace, the blanket custom, her lack of prudish restraint. He smiled, aware that no one in Omaha knew everything he was privy to.

He ran his hand through his hair and sighed. They didn't know, and they couldn't know. Not until he was safely elected and sworn in as senator.

Lise sat on the hard courtroom bench, alone in the busy hum of activity around her, and bit at her fingernails. As soon as Judge Dundy walked in and delivered his verdict, she'd have no choice but to face Zach. She knew it as surely as she knew her life was a tumbled mess. And had been for over a week.

Every day, her heart had died a little bit. Rufus Christy had seen to that. He'd stepped into the middle of what she had hoped would be a temporary delay in her relationship with Zach. No longer could they wait until the trial was over. She would have to set Zach free in order to salvage his campaign. She would lose both Zach and the life she'd created for herself.

Today, as soon as Dundy announced his decision, she would tell Zach it had all been a sham. An attempt to gain information, just as Foster had warned. Worst of all, if Christy hadn't upped the stakes, she might have taken the chance. She might have told Zach the truth, with the same pride Standing Bear had displayed, and left it up to him to decide. Now, there was too much at risk and no choices left.

Christy would make things public and everyone would know. She couldn't pay him and that was that. But no one had to know Zach was involved. She'd let him believe she was scum because the rest of Omaha would believe it, too. It would be easy to convince a cynical public that she'd seen him socially to gain information. She'd let them think he'd been the one to call off the relationship as soon as he found out her secret.

Christy could not prove otherwise.

And when the public outcries began, whether over her being a 'breed or over her actions, she'd pack up her things and leave town. She tore off a sliver of nail and winced. She couldn't see any other way.

The courtroom stilled. Dundy had entered and was ambling his way to the bench.

Lise straightened on the bench and sat on her hand. Susette sat at the wooden table with Standing Bear, his wife, and the two attorneys, ready to convey the decision.

Poppleton had sent for Susette at Standing Bear's request the moment Dundy had telegraphed when he would reconvene. Everyone looked tense.

Dundy settled into his chair and peered at the packed courtroom. "I see you all came back," he said, unusually blunt, and called the court to order.

Standing Bear's group was solemn as they sat. Across the aisle, Zach and General Crook appeared equally apprehensive. Dundy had deliberated a long time.

"We've been a judge for fifteen years," Dundy said, his formal tone returning, "and we've never been called upon to decide a case that appealed to our sympathies as much as this one."

Zach swallowed, his attention focused on Dundy, and the audience waited, almost silently. Lise drew a breath.

Dundy continued, reviewing the situation in his concise way, displaying clear sympathy for the Poncas and sarcastic censure of the U.S. Government and Rufus Christy's blatant cruelty. "But, this country is regulated by law, and this case must be decided on the principles of that law." He paused and let the comment stand.

Zach's expression altered, just slightly, and Lise saw the suggestion of relief before he shifted in his chair, turning toward the front. She watched from behind, trying without success to read his emotions in the set of his shoulders.

Beside Lise, Tom Tibbles paused his scribbling and waited.

"The district attorney has questioned whether this court had the jurisdiction to issue the writ of *habeas corpus* and to hear this case. He has argued well, citing English common law that only free citizens have such rights." Dundy paused and pinned his gaze on Zach. "This country's founders looked at things differently — they were concerned that every person have certain rights. Therefore, we rule that Standing Bear was entitled to sue for a writ and that it was properly executed."

Lise felt the suppressed excitement shift its way through the room. Zach had straightened, Tibbles was furiously recording notes, Susette was explaining the decision to Standing Bear, and Poppleton was smiling broadly. Satisfaction tugged at the corners of her own mouth as the implication settled itself in her mind. Though short of establishing citizenship for Standing Bear, Dundy had just pronounced Indians as persons, entitled to the same rights under the Constitution as all other people.

320

Dundy cleared his throat, and attention returned to the bench. In his characteristic direct manner, he outlined the rest of the decision. He had found no law preventing Indians from separating themselves from their tribe, and, therefore, Standing Bear and his followers were entitled to the same protections under the law as any other free non-citizen and could not be forced to any reservation. Though General Crook, as an agent of the government, had had the right to arrest the Poncas for being on the Omaha Reservation without permission, it had been illegal to detain them at Fort Omaha. Because they should have been turned over to civil authorities, this portion of the case was being dismissed, and the Indians were to be released immediately.

A number of persons in the audience responded with applause and audible agreement. Dundy frowned but allowed the chatter. Standing Bear's shoulders straightened with pride, and his attorneys clasped hands. Tibbles rushed out of the room, notes in hand and a grin on his face. Most of the other reporters followed, scurrying to telegraph the news to their eastern employers.

Lise's mind scrambled to sort it all out. Dundy had just upended years of Indian policy. He'd given Indians rights they'd never before had and had redefined their position in the eyes of the law. He'd changed the law.

The realization punched at her. Zach.

He stood, still at the defense table, half-turned. His eyes blinked, and he looked stunned.

Lise stood and spoke his name.

He turned, his gaze finding hers. Surprised comprehension slowly filled his expression. Surprise, but not anger. He smiled, then the smile thinned and his breath slowed. His eyes darkened, hungry, and fastened on her.

Lise's heart skipped a beat, and heat overtook her.

Every second of their night together played through her mind, and she shivered despite the sweat forming at her pulse points. She wanted him. He wanted her.

She sank onto the bench, suddenly weak.

Rufus Christy wouldn't give a damn that she was now a person, but she would have the right to take legal action against him for his blackmail efforts. If she dared endanger Zach's future.

Had Dundy wrought enough change for her to risk it?

Susette walked into the *Omaha Herald* of-

322

fices and closed the door behind her. Typesetters clicked type into place in the back room, preparing a special edition.

The front room was deserted, reporters having long ago finished their stories about the trial. Darkness was already creeping into the early evening. A single gas lamp lit the room, and the curtains were pulled across the front windows.

"Susette!" Tom called from the curtained doorway. "I thought you'd come earlier. I missed you."

She knew he referred to her sojourn back to the reservation. "I was busy with Standing Bear, interpreting interviews. I'll write my own up if there's still space."

Tom nodded. "There is. I knew you'd have something. Do you want me to have a typesetter stay?"

"I should have the article written up in about an hour."

"That would be fine." His tone was lighthearted. "Was it wild?"

She knew he'd missed much of what happened after the trial in his haste to get the paper to press and scoured her mind for the things he would most be interested in. "It was like a circus, Tom. You couldn't see from where you were but there was shock on Zach Spencer's face. And General Crook looked pleased. He wouldn't answer any questions afterward, but he was pleased."

"I knew he wouldn't agree to an interview. Politics."

She watched him scuttle around the room, his energy still seeking outlets. In minutes, she had paper and pen and was seated at her desk preparing her own article. The words flowed easily, and she handed the pages off to Tom in record time. He skimmed them, nodded his approval, and disappeared into the back room to find the typesetter.

Susette stood, her own nervous energy abounding. The day's events had caught her up in a tornado of attention, swirling her emotions from apprehension to giddiness at times, eliminating any doubts in her mind.

This was what she wanted to do with her life.

She glanced at Tom as he returned to the room and turned down the gaslight. Her heart pounded.

"Do you truly think this will change things?" she asked, surprised at the tremor in her voice.

He turned and stared at her, curiosity in his gaze. "It can," he said, approaching. "Whether or not it will depends on what we do with it. We can let it sit there or we can keep it alive and make people aware of it, so they don't forget it, so they talk to their senators and congressmen. That's how you translate it into real change."

Susette nodded and drew a breath. "So you are still planning to tour the East?"

"I am. If Standing Bear will go."

"He'll go."

Tom searched her face. "How do you —"

"We spoke about it. After the trial. He was very concerned with the reporters, all the questions, that his answers be conveyed correctly." Knowing she would play a vital role in assuring this made her feel invaluable, complete.

"He's been concerned about that for days. It's why he asked that you interpret his closing speech."

Susette nodded and reached for Tom's hand. "I know. He told me."

"But he said he'd go?" Excitement crept into Tom's voice, and his eyes searched hers. "Last week, he wasn't sure."

"He will go," Susette said, then let a moment of silence linger. Steady clatter filled the void. "If I go."

"And have you decided?" Tom's voice was so soft she barely heard it over the beating of her own heart.

"I will go. I will go because it is important

that we take these changes further, that we make things happen. You are right. It depends on how we use what Dundy has given us. And I will go because it is what my heart wants."

Tom opened his mouth and she silenced him with a finger to her lips. "But there are matters between us that we must talk about before we do this." She caught his darkened gaze and met it with her own. "I've already told you I will not become your mistress. Is this something you can accept?"

He swallowed, then nodded. "I will not betray Amelia."

"No matter how much your eyes linger on me or your breath catches?" Even as she said the words, she recognized his answer would provide little assurance in moments like this one. Moments she knew would come.

"My breath will always catch when I look at you. But I will not act on it." His tone was solemn, the words sincere.

"Then I will come and we will pursue change. And if there is ever a day that you are free, I will be there, ready to embrace what we must delay until then."

He held her gaze, his eyes dark and heavy with promise. "It will happen, you know. Everything we want, all the changes, they will happen."

Her heart jumped and she nodded. "I know, Tom. In time, all things happen."

CHAPTER SIXTEEN

Zach stuck a peppermint stick into his mouth and clamped his teeth down on it. Hard. The end of the stick broke off and he tasted the sharp flavor of mint. Seconds later, it lodged in the back of his mouth. He jerked forward as the candy flew into his throat and coughed until both pieces fell out on his desk and peppermint scent filled the air.

Damn.

He stared at the broken sticks of candy and fought to catch his breath. Running a hand through his unruly hair, he sat back in his chair and closed his eyes.

His life was a mess.

He'd managed to lose a case that would be discussed for years. As would his performance, or lack thereof. Despite Dundy's assertion that the district attorney's arguments had been well prepared and logical, he doubted many folks would view it that way. They'd see what it had really been, a desperate attempt to find something, anything, to argue with in a case that shouldn't even have been tried.

Asserting Standing Bear and the other Poncas weren't entitled to the same rights as people, that they indeed weren't persons, had been ridiculous. Shameful.

But the law hadn't left room for any other action.

He coughed again, the taste of the candy suddenly bitter.

Or was it the aftertaste of what he'd done in the name of the *Law*?

He'd spent his whole life in awe of the Law and the way it worked, and Standing Bear had stood up and shattered that awe in one simple plea to be seen as a person.

What else in his life was a shallow façade, a misdirection?

Dundy had praised his efforts enough that, if he worked hard, he could still pull it together and emerge unscathed. Yes, people would discuss him. They'd talk about how illogical his case had been. But they'd remember he argued with passion, and they'd see that he'd used every tool he had to fit Standing Bear into the law.

Dundy had decided to change the law, that was all. He'd flouted English common law, the basis of the American legal system, and replaced it with his own interpretation of the Constitution.

It happened. It was the way the system was designed.

So, he'd pick up and carry on. The campaign would suffer a few days, maybe a couple weeks, of upheaval, then gossip would settle down as fresh news occurred.

Zach would still be the favored candidate. His backers would still be there.

Less one.

As soon as he could, he intended to sever his relationship with Adam Foster.

It went against his upbringing to reject the guidance and support of a family friend — a man that often seemed to be courting his mother's favor — but he thought she would see it his way. Yet Adam Foster had his own motives, and he wasn't as magnanimous as he pretended to be.

His machinations behind the scenes angered Zach, and he no longer believed Foster had his best interests in mind. Zach suspected Foster was looking out for himself. Aside from currying the favor and money of wealthy businessmen, Foster had done little to really benefit Zach.

Surely, there were the supporters Adam had secured. He'd need to find them. He'd talk to each of them, assure them their support was well founded, create personal relationships independent of Foster.

His stomach soured.

Adam had pretty much told him it wasn't him they liked; it was his potential of granting them political favors.

It was politics not honor. Not ability. Not fair and ethical representation. Money and politics and power.

Shit.

Had that been part of Gramps's life as well? Was it all a façade?

That kind of life would not accommodate a relationship with Lise.

His heart pounded in his chest.

He'd hoped they would get through the case, avoid any chance of a mistrial. Then, he'd convinced himself he could get through the election without anyone finding out the truth. Foster would fix the blackmail problem. He'd place his relationship with Lise on the back burner until he was safely elected.

But sure as he'd shattered that peppermint stick, he realized it wasn't going to end there. He couldn't shut off his feelings, set her aside, pretend he'd never touched that silky skin or kissed her curves or taken her to heights she'd never imagined.

He'd known it yesterday, when he'd looked across the courtroom and caught her gaze. He'd known it surely enough to turn tail and leave courthouse as soon as he could do so. Her chocolate eyes had been filled with such unexpected hope that he knew he'd never be able to turn his back on her.

And that meant he'd have to walk away from everything else.

Damn. Damn, damn, damn.

It was all a smoke screen anyway. All of it. The honor, the service. Even the Law.

He'd be expected to file an appeal. No doubt the government was even now preparing an appeal. He'd likely get a telegram tomorrow, outlining every action he was supposed to take to assure statutes were not broken and the Indians were relegated to their lawful places.

His mind revolted when he tried to imagine Lise as less than a person.

He pictured her in her beaded necklace, the faded design flush against her naked ruddy skin. She'd molded herself into a proper white woman, fighting to improve life for her people while struggling to hide the reasons for her passion. Suppressing the pride she had in her past, the influence of the culture she claimed was not hers.

They were both fakes. Both of them.

And he hated it with a fierceness he'd never known.

Adam Foster, the greedy businessmen, Gramps and his expectations could all go to hell. It was time Zach Spencer discovered who he really was and forged his own path.

It was late in the day by the time Zach reined in his horse at Fort Omaha. The sentries, recognizing him, waved him through to the general's quarters. Within a few minutes, he was tying the horse to the rail in front of the big yellow house.

Crook himself opened the door, moccasins on his feet and a pipe in his mouth. "Figured you were going to show up."

Zach stepped inside. "Taken up fortune telling, have you, General?" He followed Crook into the parlor and waited while he cleared a stack of papers from the horsehair sofa.

"Watched you wound up tight as a spring through that trial. Day before yesterday, soon as the verdict came in, all the spring went out of you. All in a whoosh." Crook motioned for Zach to sit, laid the papers on a side table, and plopped into a rose-upholstered chair. "Nobody else you can talk to about it. Am I right?"

"How'd you come to all that?"

"Son, you were focused on trying to make Dundy see your way. Someone so intent on proving himself isn't going to handle defeat easily." He lifted his feet onto a small floral-embroidered stool. "I can't see you talking to your man Foster about it. Man doesn't know the meaning of defeat. You, you're looking for a new definition."

Zach shifted and the horsehair rustled beneath him. Crook's insight was uncanny, and Zach wasn't sure he was comfortable with it, now that he was here. "I came to talk about the appeal," he said.

Crook nodded. "Sure you did."

"You know the Army will send new orders for you."

"Already did." He pointed to the pile of papers he'd moved earlier. "I'm to release the Poncas and locate them on federal land near the Omaha Reservation. Near but not on."

Zach glanced at him in surprise. "The government is giving them land?"

"Not if that bald-headed fool Commissioner of Indian Affairs has anything to do with it. Hoyt issued a statement that the decision would be appealed." Crook's brows knit. "Where you been, son?"

"Holed up in my office." He didn't say

334

anything further. Crook would gather enough information from those few words.

"Then we got some catching up to do." Crook passed over the pile of papers and waited while Zach scanned them. The forms verified what the general had said.

He looked up, saw apprehension on Crook's face. "I've missed more?"

"You missed a bunch. You walked out of that courtroom too soon. There was deeper meaning to what Dundy said. Poppleton understood it, took Standing Bear aside and warned him." He leaned forward, serious. "Once those folks are released, they can't go near the Omaha Reservation. Any reservation, without permission. They've severed tribal ties."

Zach stared at him, disbelief stunning him. "They can't go home?"

"The Niobrara is officially on the Santee Sioux Reservation. The Poncas set foot on it, they'll be arrested for trespass. Despite what those damn attorneys told him."

"Poppleton?"

"No, the others . . . the ones the government sent to sit at *our* table and look pompous." He set his pipe down on the table and shook his head. "They were here yesterday, visited with Standing Bear, told him it was 'perfectly safe' to return to the Niobrara.

Damn idiots. I wouldn't have known about it except the private escorting them kept an ear out."

Zach digested the implications. "What a mess."

"You gonna file the appeal?"

"I won't have a choice, will I? Once Hoyt sends a directive to me."

Crook sat back in his chair and stared at Zach. After a few moments, he cracked his knuckles. "There's always a choice."

Zach rose to his feet, his fists balled at his side. "Damn it, General. I don't want to do this." He ran his hand through his hair and paced the room. "I didn't want to do it in the first place. How can it be right and lawful to keep insisting Standing Bear is not a person?"

"Then don't do it."

Zach stopped. "Don't do it?"

"Refuse."

"I'll lose my job." He stared at Crook, his mind rapidly scrambling through the scenarios that would result from a refusal. They all ended the same way.

Crook picked up his pipe again, as casually as if they were discussing dinner, and patted his shirt pockets until he located his pouch of tobacco. He filled the pipe, stuck it in his mouth, and lit it with a wooden match. "Can't tell me you like it so well right now, anyhow. Can you?"

Zach's heart thudded. "If I'm fired, I might as well give up the senate race as well."

"Seems to me if you don't like this case, you're not going to like much about being a senator." Crook's words were so similar to the thoughts that had plagued Zach all day that he swallowed in surprise.

Crook blew a smoke ring and nodded. "Shit just gets deeper, son, the higher your office. Seems like it'd be the other way around, don't it? It ain't."

The sound of a scuffle in the hallway caught their attention. Crook's aide entered the room and handed Crook a folded sheet of paper.

Crook opened it and scowled.

"Damnation," he yelled. "Soldiers just discovered Standing Bear left for the Niobrara. Late yesterday."

CHAPTER SEVENTEEN

Zach rode hard, arriving back in Omaha less than an hour after Crook had received the news. He found the *Herald* office dark, as he'd expected, and debated whether to head for Tibbles's house or to track down one of the attorneys.

Legally, he should notify Poppleton and Webster first, but Crook had said to find Tibbles. He turned his horse up Davenport Street, toward Tom's place.

A single lamp glowed in a side window.

Zach dismounted near the door closest to the lit room, and knocked.

The curtain fluttered and Tom Tibbles's questioning face peered out. Tom opened the door and stared at him.

"Crook sent me," Zach said as Tom motioned him into the kitchen. "I was at the fort when he got word that Standing Bear had left."

Tom shut the door and joined Zach. "He

does have that right, according to Dundy."

"He was headed toward the Niobrara."

"He's free to do that, too." The matter of fact tone of Tom's voice suggested he distrusted Zach. Either that, or he was unaware of the implications Crook had mentioned. Most likely, both.

"In theory," Zach said, "but there's a catch. Poppleton told Standing Bear the ruling means he can't go on any other tribe's reservation without written approval from Indian Affairs. His old reservation is officially Sioux land, according to the last of the four treaties involved."

Tom wandered to the cookstove and poured himself a cup of coffee. He sighed and turned back to Zach without offering a cup to him, an indication that he didn't especially like the enemy dropping by his house. "So he'll be arrested again?"

"Yes. Couple of fellows from Indian Affairs visited him after the trial." Zach paused. "Told him it was safe to return."

Tom set his coffee cup on the table with enough force that the steaming brew sloshed over the rim. "They did what?"

"They set Standing Bear up, told him Poppleton made a mistake. He's on his way up there, and Rufus Christy will have men waiting."

Tom stared at him, measuring the news, measuring him. "How long ago did he leave?" he asked.

"Late yesterday."

He swore under his breath. "And they just noticed now?"

Zach shrugged. He'd initially thought the same thing until Crook had explained fort procedures had been eased at his order. "They haven't exactly been treating him like a prisoner. No one had been by his lodge."

"Then we've got to catch up." Tom gulped the hot coffee, urgency filling his movement. "I'll head north to the Omaha Agency, find someone to interpret, and continue on to the Niobrara. We'll ride spare, make better time. Standing Bear'll be in no hurry. We should be able to overtake him." He stopped and let his gaze linger, again measuring. "You fill Poppleton in, let him decide what to do here?"

"Will do," Zach promised.

"Spencer?"

"Yeah."

"Thanks. I know you didn't have to do this."

Zach swallowed. "Yeah, I did, Tibbles. I did."

The day was still early when Lise heard the

squeaking hinges at the bottom of the stairs announce the library's first customer. She'd missed the library, interacting with avid readers, listening to the rustle of pages, breathing in the familiar smells of leather bindings and old ink. Between the trial and the trip to see Susette, she'd been away too long. A satisfied hum played through her mind as she sorted the books on her desk into neat piles for re-shelving and waited for the customer to ascend the stairway.

Moments later the door opened, and Zach entered the room.

Lise's breath hitched, and she could almost hear her heart pounding in the silent room. Zach. When he'd abruptly left after the trial, she'd almost convinced herself she wouldn't have to face him, wouldn't have to say the things that needed saying.

"Are you all right?" he asked.

She nodded and drew a breath. She was not all right. She could feel the heavy weight of the moment pressing on her heart. The time had come for her to tell Zach everything, and she was afraid. She almost wished she'd fled, leaving Zach to continue his life without the complications she was about to throw at him. But there was too much at stake. The complications wouldn't have left with her, and she couldn't leave

341

Zach to face them alone. He needed to know about Christy. About her.

"Lise?"

By the time she looked up at him, her face was calm, smiling. "I'm fine. How are you?"

"Fine." He frowned at her. "Why wouldn't you see me?"

She swallowed.

"For God's sake, Lise, I've been aching to talk with you, to make sure you're all right. You wouldn't see me after . . . after I shared your blanket." He blushed. "Then, I had a trial in Lincoln, and I had to leave. Did you get my note?"

"What note? My housemates said you wrote one but didn't leave it."

"They were so all atwitter that I thought it would get lost. I asked Thad to deliver it. Damn. I didn't just leave town." He reached for her and stroked the back of her hand with his thumb. She jumped with unexpected desire. "I don't want you to think what happened didn't matter to me."

"Thank you," she whispered. "I'm sure Thad tried. I left to see Susette on the Omaha Reservation. Maybe he couldn't find me."

"Why wouldn't you see me?" he repeated.

She moved away, memories of Christy's visit still vivid enough to make her shudder, to feed her fear. Once she told Zach about her heritage, he'd want nothing more to do with her. Her eyes stung as she transferred the books onto the wheeled cart next to the desk.

Zach's gaze was on her, and her skin tingled. She'd tell him in a minute.

"Washington wants me to appeal," he said.

Lise nodded. "I expected as much. Are you going to?"

"When they make it official, I won't have any choice. Just like this trial. I was assigned. The appeal will be part of my job. If I want to continue as district attorney, I'll file it."

"Oh." Bitterness stabbed at her. They'd once again be on opposite sides of the issue. It was just one more indicator of how mismatched they were.

"That means more legal action I don't agree with." He stepped closer, stopping behind her. His hands touched her shoulders, and she shivered. "More pressure to avoid conflict of interest. I'm sick of both." He turned her to face him. "Do you have any idea how much I wanted to just walk away from this? How I hated trying to prove Standing Bear wasn't entitled to be treated like a human being? How much I've hated keeping my distance from you?"

Her eyes pooled at the pleading tone of his voice. "Yet you did," she said, needing to anchor herself to reality.

Zach continued to hold her gaze. "Yes, damn it. I did." He swallowed. "And I'm sorry I did."

"You had no choice. You knew it. I knew it. It's why we fought the attraction. We accepted that."

"Well, I'm not accepting it anymore."

Lise shook her head, resigned. "You said you'd have no choice if they ask you to appeal."

"Not necessarily."

Christy's leering face intruded into Lise's thoughts, squashing the tiny hope Zach's words had lit. "You'll file the appeal." She moved away from him, pushing the cart toward the shelves. "It's better that way."

"It's not better. It's not what I want."

"And your career?"

"I don't think I want this career anymore, Lise. I've had a bitter taste in my mouth, and I don't like it."

She stopped and turned back. "And what about the senate race? Are you going to give that up, too?"

"That seems to taste worse than the Law right now." Zach's face filled with anguish.

Lise's heart fluttered, hope flickering, battling her desire for Zach to follow his dreams. "You're just going to walk away from all that? Everything you've always worked for? Everything you've always wanted to be? I don't want to be a part of you abandoning your dreams."

"What I've always wanted to be was an honorable man who stood up for what was right." He leaned his butt against the desk and ran his hand through his hair, sighing. "Instead, I'm being bought by Adam and his influential friends. I'm quoting the law instead of serving justice and humanity. This has got to be the least honorable mess I've ever been in."

She grasped the cart, anchoring herself as she searched for the strength to tell him the truth. "Then *make* it honorable. Follow your dreams, Zach, but forge an honorable path doing so."

He shook his head. "I don't know if there is one. Foster isn't who I thought he was. My grandfather isn't who I thought he was. Hell, the *Law* isn't what I thought, and I'm not who I thought I was."

Guilt flooded her and Lise knew the moment had come. If Zach was going to make this decision, he needed to do so with all the information available. "Zach . . . I need to tell you something."

"Do you think I'm wrong?"

"I'm not who you think I am, either."

"I know who you are, Lise. You're transparent. You know what you believe in and why you feel that way."

She crossed the room and stopped two feet in front of him. "I lied to you." When he simply stared at her, she drew another breath. "I'm part Sioux."

The corners of Zach's mouth curled upward. "So?"

Lise stared at him in the quiet morning sun. "But I lied to you," she said. "I risked your integrity. I risked your case. I risked your campaign."

He shook his head. "No, you didn't."

"But —"

"I risked those things, not you." He straightened and moved closer to her, his blue eyes steady. "I've wondered for a long time. Foster confirmed it a few days ago."

"Rufus Christy knows. He'll take it to the papers if I don't pay him. I'll be fired. You'll lose the senate race." Her words spilled, uncontrolled.

Zach raised a finger to her lips. "I'm withdrawing from the damn senate race."

Her heart surged.

"I don't want to be a politician. I only wanted it because Gramps had been a senator, and I thought I wanted to be like him."

Lise stared at him. "And now?"

"I don't want to be an Indian hater or a corrupt politician. I don't want to apply law that isn't just." He stroked her cheek. "I'm resigning. From all of it."

"But your dreams —"

"Dreams change." He pulled her close, nestling her head against his chest, and she heard the pounding of his heart. "Damn it, Lise. I don't care if you're full-blooded Sioux. It doesn't matter. I don't care what Christy does — he's blackmailing Foster, too. Let Foster pay him off. Or not, I don't care."

She raised her face and found him close. His lips met hers. Desire throbbed. In her heart, in her deepest core, in all the places he had touched and kissed her. Her arms encircled his neck, and she pulled herself against him.

They kissed, their hands playing across each other's backs until Lise remembered they were in the middle of an unlocked library. She stepped back, breaking the moment, and they gazed at one another.

"Do you think Poppleton and Webster would allow an ex-district attorney to help Standing Bear fight that inevitable appeal?" he asked.

The prospect filled her with joy. It wasn't his original dream, but it was one with honor. "They might."

"Good. Because I have a hunch Standing Bear is in a bunch of trouble, and he can use all the help he can get."

Lise entered the tepee and squinted in the dim light.

Naomi sat next to Aunt Rose at the back of the circle. Though the day was warm, a low fire burned, and the scent of sage hung in the air. Seeing Lise, Naomi rose and shuffled forward. Worry lines filled her aging face.

"How is she?" Lise asked.

"Her body has grown stronger, but her mind has not returned."

"Will she know me?"

"Come. We will see."

Lise followed as the older woman shuffled to the seating area. A small log collapsed into the fire, sparks snapping. Lise coughed at the rush of smoke. Behind the fire, Aunt Rose sat on a folded gray army blanket moving trade beads from one basket to another.

"Hello, Aunt Rose." Lise approached, eager to talk now that Rose appeared to be recovering.

Rose continued moving the beads, one by one, intent on her task.

Lise touched her lightly on the arm.

The old woman looked up. A swift bolt of happiness crossed her features. "Anna," she rasped.

Disappointment shifted through Lise. "No, Aunt Rose," she said. "It's Lise. Anna's daughter."

Rose cackled, bobbing with mirth. "She would need a suitor first." Her shoulders shook as she continued to laugh.

Lise's memory stretched, recalling the stories of her mother refusing the Sioux boys who had tried to woo her. She'd preferred white beaux. She'd eventually fled the reservation to take a room in town.

"Aunt Rose, do you remember me? It's Lise."

"Lise?" she paused, her face lined with concentration. "Sit down, child. I will teach you to bead." She gathered a handful of the trade beads and let them shift through her fingers. "Do you want a pea? See?" She held up one of the baskets, beaming. "Gooseberries! I picked them myself." She extended one hand to Lise and moved the other toward her mouth.

Before Rose could pop the bead into her mouth, Naomi caught her hand. "You must not eat them, sister."

"Oh," Rose said. "Did you see my toes? I can't find my toes."

Lise's heart dipped, and she glanced at Naomi. The other woman patted her hand and motioned for Lise to sit. They settled, one on each side of Rose, and let the silence bring peace.

"Each day, it is like this. She is no longer ill, but she will never be the same."

Lise watched her aunt's aimless bead-sorting and tried to listen to the wisdom of the Great Spirit. She heard nothing. Nothing but the protests in the back of her own mind. She looked at Naomi. "Perhaps if a doctor looked at her, he could tell us something."

Sorrow graced the old woman's eyes. "The post surgeon has seen her. He can do nothing. Her mind boiled with the fever, and now she is a child again."

Lise nodded, her soul accepting what was. "Do you think she knows me at all?"

"For a moment, yes."

They sat, the three of them, in silence, their energies mingling with the sage and the smoke and the air itself until they were one.

Naomi's tired voice asked, "Do you know where we will go, child?"

The hide shifted at the door, and Albert ducked into the lodge. "It is a good question, Grandmother," he said. He followed the circle, approaching Lise. "In a few days, the Army will release us. We can no longer stay here. We cannot stay with the Omaha without permission. Your friend General Crook says the government officials will not allow that." He sat next to Lise. "The men from Washington, who came to the trial, visited us and told us we can return to the Niobrara, but General Crook says we cannot do that. Crook said they are lying to us, and we will be arrested. Do you know how this can be?"

"General Crook is right," Lise said, her heart miserable at the truth. She tried to explain what she had learned from Zach. "The judge said you don't have to be Ponca anymore. You don't have to live in Indian Territory with the other Poncas unless you choose to do so. But because you're not Omaha, you can't stay on the Omaha Reservation. And because the Niobrara was given to the Sioux, you can't live there."

Albert stared at her, confusion filling his features. "So what did Standing Bear win in this court?"

Lise pondered the question. The victory was a legal one, one that left the Poncas with no tangible improvement in their present situation. In fact, it left them with less than they'd had for they could no longer petition to stay with the Omahas.

"All Indians are now considered people who can decide if they want to remain with their tribe on the reservation or live on their own."

Albert nodded, digesting the meaning. "But where are we to live?"

"As a group, there is nowhere. Each family is on their own, like white families."

"But we are not white families," Albert said. "Who will sell us a farm? Who will sell us a house in a town? I do not think Standing Bear won anything in this court." He shook his head and stared into the fire.

Naomi grunted her opinion, then rose to tend the fire. She glanced at Albert, then Lise. "What will happen to Standing Bear when he gets back to the Niobrara?"

"He will be arrested," Lise said.

"But the government men told him he could return safely."

Albert stood, anger storming in his dark eyes. "They lied, Grandmother. They are waiting to arrest him already."

Naomi looked to Lise for confirmation and Lise nodded. "That is why Tom Tibbles and Bright Eyes and their friends went after him."

"And what will he do then? Where will he go? Where will any of us go?"

Zach ran his hand through his hair and exhaled. Across the library table, Lise propped her head on her elbow. Tom Tibbles rubbed his eyes, yawning. Susette had fallen asleep a half-hour earlier, sprawled over a map of the western United States. Her breath came in tiny spurts. A finger of envy inched its way into Zach's tired mind as he watched her doze.

"Are we any closer?" he asked, already sure of the answer.

No one answered. They were all acutely aware of the lack of progress. The pile of law books near Lise had grown steadily throughout the night. Still, they hadn't found a loophole in any of the treaties. Standing Bear was safely back at Fort Omaha, but he had yet to find a home. Crook would be forced to release the band soon.

Tom slid his chair away from the table. "I've had enough," he said. "Research isn't my forte, especially after thirty-six hours in the saddle."

Zach glanced at his new friend, relieved

they were on the same side. "At least you caught them," he said.

"A lot of good it did. The man doesn't understand why he can't go home. Hell, I don't understand it. Dundy had to have foreseen this. He should have declared them citizens and been done with it." Tom scowled, his expression voicing what they all felt.

"I think Dundy made the most progressive decision he could." Lise removed her glasses and set them on the table. "Had he declared them citizens, it would have been too big a step."

Though he understood Tom's frustration, Zach nodded in agreement. "You're right. I would have easily been able to appeal, and it would have been with the Supreme Court in no time. And they would have overturned the decision. As it is, Dundy has kept the door closed. An appeal will change nothing."

"Then what good was it?" Tom mumbled.

"It laid the groundwork," Zach explained. "If Indians are legally recognized as people, then the next step up to being citizens won't be so big when it comes. That's the nature of legal change — step by step."

"And in the meantime, these people have nowhere to go." Tom stood and stretched.

"I need to get a few hours sleep. In the morning, Bright Eyes and I will start working on a public campaign. We're better at that anyway."

He touched Susette on the arm and she stirred, blinking.

"Let's get you to the hotel. I booked you a room."

Susette nodded, then rose slowly. "I'm sorry. I wanted to be more helpful."

Zach shook his head. "I didn't expect much. You two haven't slept in days. Lise and I will keep working on this, maybe get some sleep ourselves and start fresh in the morning. It's past midnight."

"Somewhere, there must be an answer," Lise said, determined optimism lingering in her voice.

"We'll get an article ready for Monday's paper, maybe write a few letters. You'll find us at the office." Tom guided Susette out the door, leaving Zach and Lise in the silence of the darkened library.

Lise stretched, then followed after them. "I'll go down and lock up."

Zach watched her move through the dim light, her backside swaying, and quick warmth spread through him. She didn't have a clue what she did to him, just with a few steps across the room. Keeping his mind on the search for legal remedies would be difficult now that Tibbles and Bright Eyes had gone.

He'd meant what he'd said to her, though he'd be damned if he could remember when his mind had accepted her heritage. Hell, before the trial, he would have avoided any woman with mixed blood. He would have accepted it wasn't good for politics or his career and never thought any more of it. His lips curved upward. Whatever she'd done to him, he was damn glad she had.

When she reappeared in the dim lamplight, his heart skipped a few beats. Her dark hair was coiled tightly at the back of her head, a respectable white-woman style, but he itched to have it loose in his hands, her sweet-tea skin bare of plaid woolen dresses and her chocolate eyes urging him forward.

"Zach?" she questioned.

"Hmmm?"

"You were staring."

"I can't help it." His gaze met hers. "You're worth staring at."

In the dimness, he couldn't be sure whether she blushed or not but her lips curled into a knowing smile. She crossed the room, entering the lamplight, and stood at the opposite side of the table. "I suppose we should put these maps away and get some sleep ourselves."

"I'll roll them up if you want to sort out those law books." He stood up and reached for the maps as Lise began stacking the tomes. Behind her glasses, her tired eyes held defeat.

"I wish we'd found a way," he said. The words failed to convey how much he wanted them to have succeeded.

She nodded. "My Aunt Rose is with them."

"I know. Foster told me." He stood, helping her gather the research materials.

The thud of the thick law books filled the silence, musty puffs of air rising with the release of each new volume Lise added to the stack. When they were piled four high, she paused.

"She'll never live on her own again. She could go back to the Niobrara, if it weren't for that." Her voice was forlorn, her dark eyes teary. "For years, the government forced the Ponca to share their homeland with the Sioux. Then Rufus Christy made an issue of nothing, and now the Poncas have no rights there, after fifteen years of believing the Sioux to be the interloper."

She circled the table, nearing Zach, and rested her head on his shoulder. He pulled her close and let her draw on his strength.

Her dark hair smelled like fresh rainwater and lemon, and he remembered the day they'd gone fishing. She'd smelled of lemons, then, too.

He loosened her hair and let it sift through his fingers. She shivered as the air touched the bare skin on her neck, and his groin tightened.

Drawing a breath, she shifted in his arms until she was facing the table, her gaze on the reservation map. "Aunt Rose finally has a home of her own and she can't live there because the Ponca who have become her family are no longer welcome." Her finger traced the line of the river. "She used to write about how beautiful it was there, how the Niobrara could get so full that it shifted course. Those were the years the gooseberries were plentiful. She loved gooseberries."

Zach held her, allowing her tense body to fall back against him. He envisioned Lise there. She would have been glorious in a doeskin dress, her long hair blowing in the breeze, feeding him currant-colored berries, sweetly sour on his tongue. He stroked her hair, almost tasting the tartness of the berries as his mind captured the picture.

She relaxed into him and sighed, then suddenly leaned forward. "The river," she said. Her tired eyes held a glimmer of excitement. "The river shifted." She grabbed her glasses and rummaged through the pile of maps, her movements almost frantic.

The river had shifted. Comprehension dawned on him with the force of a hurtled brick. He brushed her hands away and sorted through the maps. Those they needed lay at the bottom of the pile. They'd ignored the maps of the reservation along the Niobrara, searching for other options, not even considering the answer lay right where the problem was.

"Here," he said, sliding the detailed reservation drawings out and plunking them on top of the stack.

Lise's fingertips traced the river marking the boundary of the first reservation. "Where's the next one?"

He moved the paper to the side, revealing a drawing related to the second treaty. Pulling the third and fourth maps out, he arranged them in a large square.

Lise bent over them, comparing the river channel, then straightened and looked at him. Her eyes danced as if a handful of crushed golden butterscotch had been tossed into the liquid chocolate depths. "The river channel is different," she announced.

Zach leaned forward, comparing the

maps. Sometime between the original 1858 treaty map and the erroneous 1868 extension of Sioux lands, the river channel had indeed shifted. Near the southern boundary of the extended Sioux lands, just before it joined the Missouri, the Niobrara had split to create several small islands. They had not been included as part of the Sioux lands.

The islands were bigger than the shifting sandbars often found in rivers. One of them appeared large enough to support several families.

Zach looked up, victory flooding through him. "It looks like you've just found your Aunt Rose somewhere to call home."

Lise's heart raced at his confirmation. Could it really have been that easy? She stared again at the map, double-checking. The islands were there, just beyond the border of the Santee Sioux Reservation, yet within the borders of the original Ponca Reservation.

She exhaled, relief gusting from her, then threw her arms around Zach and kissed him hard.

The suddenness of the kiss surprised him — she could see it in the widening of his eyes as she pulled back to digest the action herself. And a moment later, when the surprise relaxed into appreciation, his eyes darkened and she knew she was lost.

One corner of his lips lifted in a lopsided smile, urging her own to respond.

He touched her face, a soft caress along her cheek, the smallest of brushes, and she shivered before leaning into his hand. His palm lingered on her face, then he encircled her neck with his hand and pulled her close.

He nibbled at her bottom lip and she opened to him. Their lips played at one another, tongues exploring, tempting. Then his mouth was on her, owning her, and his kiss spread through her.

She shuddered, feeling the heat spark as her breasts swelled and the fever filled her center until she clutched at him, pulling him to her as she pressed against him, wanting him closer still. Wanting him.

Zach's feather touch moved down her neck and inside her collar. He slid his fingers beneath the cord of her necklace and followed it to the front, then slid open the buttons of her bodice with agonizing slowness.

She waited, anticipating, as he slid each button open. Her chest heaved until finally he reached the bottom of the garment and parted it. He loosened the ties on her chemise and opened it. She shivered as the air touched her bare breasts and another bolt of white-hot desire raced through her. Zach's fingers traced her skin around the beaded pendant, under it, with an ethereal touch.

"From Aunt Rose?" he whispered, fingering the faded amulet and its leather cord.

"Yes."

"I'd like to meet her."

"She won't understand who you are."

"It doesn't matter. I'll understand who she is. And who you are, because of her." His words sent a second warmth through her, this one separate from desire.

"Are you sure? That my background doesn't matter." She hated the catch in her voice but needed to hear him say it.

He lifted her glasses from her nose and kissed her gently. "You're all that matters to me."

Lise's breath hitched as he gazed into her eyes. "Whichever world you're in. Bespectacled librarian, beaded Indian, in plaid woolen flannel, or under a blanket." He traced searing lines on her cheeks, then his hand drifted lower, around the pendant, and cupped her breast.

She swallowed. "There's no blanket tonight," she whispered back, knowing he would understand her meaning. "Only us."

She slipped the buttons of his shirt open

and touched him, marveling at the hiss of his breath as she made contact with his hot skin. Her palms brushed across his nipples. Like hers, they tightened, becoming hard and erect. She traced her thumbs across them until Zach moaned.

He pleasured her, his fingers trailing feathery circles around her breasts. She shivered and her breath deepened. With each circle, he moved closer to her nipples, and her breasts grew heavier, aching for more. He bent and suckled them, then nipped until her back arched and an ache wound its way to her core.

His mouth left her and her nipples puckered as the cold air whispered across the moist circles left by his tongue. She shivered.

Hunger filled Zach's eyes, deepening the pale blue to a smoky haze. "I want you," he whispered.

"And I you." She trailed her hands down his torso, across his tight stomach, to his trousers. She slipped one lone finger beneath them. He gasped, his stomach flattening further, and she slid the buttons open until her hand eased downward. "I want to do to you what you do to me."

"Here?" he breathed. "Now?"

"Here and now."

He drew her close, one arm pulling her close to his chest, the other cupping her bottom. Her fingers sought him, through soft curls of hair. He moved slightly and she drew him out until his hardness lay between them.

She encircled him, marveling at the satin texture of his skin and the hard ridges beneath it. Her fingers explored him, moving from base to head, light touches as he had given her, with circling pauses when he gasped. She stroked him, her fingertips dancing just under his head, until he groaned and grasped her hand.

"My turn. If you keep that up any longer, I won't last."

Easing her hand from him, Zach trailed the lightest of kisses between her breasts, leaving moist dots of tingling pleasure as his mouth dipped lower. At the top of her skirt, he slid his fingers to the back and slipped the rear hook free and untied her petticoats. The skirts puddled at her feet.

A slow hungry smile graced Zach's lips and she shivered under his gaze. Groaning, he stroked her with fingertips, caressing her as he slid off her remaining garments.

Then he lifted her. Lise clung to him, her arms around his neck, her legs encircling his waist. He moved, carried her to an empty table, hot and rigid, he brushed against her with each movement. The motion sent pulses of pleasure through her and her hips undulated against him, seeking more. Laying her on her back, he parted her legs. As if they were liquid, they opened for him, her thighs quivering in anticipation as he stood before her.

"My God, Lise, what you do to me."

He kissed her stomach, then moved his lips lower.

As his tongue touched her, she arched. He opened her with his fingers, then moved his tongue across the inner folds between her legs, licking her, tickling her, teasing her. She writhed beneath his hot mouth, unable to think. His tongue flicked out, stroking her until she shook. Over and over, his tongue danced.

She shuddered, wanting more yet unable to get close enough to his wondrous mouth.

Then, he nipped at her. Colors exploded behind her closed eyelids as spasms racked her body, plunging her into a chasm of pleasure. She fought to catch her breath, then opened her eyes.

Zach stared down at her, his eyes smoldering.

He kissed her gently on the mouth and pulled her into his arms.

"Let me love you," he said. "All of you."

She moved beneath him, feeling him still hard against her core, and parted her legs further.

He pulled her to the edge of the table and rested against her. He slid a finger into her and her body jerked, shudders overwhelming her again. He continued stroking until her hips moved in tandem with his hand. She moaned, needing more.

"Please," she whispered and lay back on the table before him. He removed his finger and pulled her to him. Hot desire washed over her as she recognized the shape her fingers had explored earlier. She ground against him, wanton need overtaking her. He pressed inward until she gasped at the sudden pain.

Zach stilled. "Shhh . . . breathe, sweetheart. Relax." He waited until her breath slowed and she again opened herself. Then he was thrusting into her, his ridges pressing her inner walls, blinding her with pleasure. Her legs grasped him, pulling him inward until she exploded again and again, tightening around him until he groaned.

Warmth flooded her, her limbs melting as he encircled her with his arms and pulled her upward into a hug. He cradled her there, tight against his chest until the air

grew cold around them and Aunt Rose's
beaded pendant slid from her neck.

CHAPTER EIGHTEEN

Fatigue clawed at Zach as he strode toward his mother's house. The white paint was thinning, leaving gray boards exposed. He supposed he'd need to paint within the next few months.

He and Lise had fallen asleep in one of the leather chairs until dawn, sated and cuddled. Snaking fingers of sunlight had wakened their bodies enough to rouse the latent desire coursing through their blood. They'd made love once more before Lise had realized that last night they'd copulated on a library table. With barely enough time to clean up and prepare the library for the day, she'd sent him on his way with a blush and a kiss and promises to meet for dinner.

Now, after several hours at the office, the mellowness was turning to fatigue.

He'd made notes about their Niobrara discovery and prepared his letter of resignation, finding the latter both easier and far more difficult than he'd anticipated.

Leaving his position, the job itself, was a surprising release. He hadn't felt so unencumbered for years. It left him wondering if he hadn't made a mistake years ago, when he decided to become a prosecutor. All that time, he'd sworn the Law was the most important guidepost in his life. Yet, he felt no regret in abandoning it.

His regret lay elsewhere.

Somewhere along the line, he'd lost the bitterness that had stabbed at him when he'd learned of Gramps's role in the Sioux hangings. The emotion had turned to pity, and he regretted that as much as he did the severed relationship itself.

Both needed to be faced.

He drew a deep breath, opened the front gate, and approached the house.

Abigail Spencer met him at the door. "You aim to be civil?" she asked, her tone brooking no nonsense.

"I'll be civil." Zach bent to kiss her forehead, then slipped past her into the front hall. "How is he?"

"Weak and listless, like he has been ever since you had words with him." She closed the door, her shoulders lifting in a silent shrug. "He needs to see you as much as you need to see him."

"Is it that evident?"

"I learned a long time ago to see through that façade lawyers think they invented. You're my son. Of course, it's evident. You make sure you don't rile him up again."

"Yes, ma'am."

He walked toward the back bedroom, leaving her to her worries. Gramps looked small in the narrow bed, shrunken under a worn patchwork quilt. Even his breath seemed shallow. The room was stale, with traces of urine hanging in the air despite Abigail's rigid cleanliness.

God, how Gramps must hate such helplessness.

He'd always been a strong man, as competent with hunting and fishing and maintaining the house as he had been with his profession. Zach's heart constricted. There must be a ton of frustration keeping Gramps company in that sickbed.

As if he could sense Zach's presence, Gramps opened first one milky eye, then the other. The second eyelid drooped, leaving that side of his face in a perpetual squint.

"Hello, Gramps."

Gramps gurgled and moved his good hand up until it rested on Zach's arm. A tear slid down his cheek, dampening the pillow.

Wetness formed in the corner of Zach's eye, as well, and he covered Gramps's gnarled hand with his own.

"I had no right to say those things. I'm sorry."

Gramps nodded slowly. His fingers wriggled under Zach's hand, a soft pat.

The pat became insistent, forcing Zach to release his grasp. Gramps raised the released hand and pointed a shaking finger across the room. A scratched maple dresser faced the bed, next to it, a battered wooden trunk.

"The dresser?" Zach asked.

Gramps's face scrunched slightly as he tilted his chin downward. He pointed again.

"The trunk?"

Gramps's finger twitched.

Zach crossed the room and opened the worn lid of the trunk. Inside, yellowing papers crowded together. He had no idea what Gramps wanted him to retrieve.

"There's something here you want me to see?"

From the bed, the old man grunted in encouragement.

Shaking his head at the volume of the task, Zach looked at Gramps. "What do you need? Do you need me to bring the papers there? So you can look at them?"

Gramps waved his hand, a vague, uncontrolled gesture, pointed again, his grunting more urgent.

Zach turned back to the trunk and began shifting through its contents. There were threadbare envelopes of correspondence and stained sheets of paper in Gramps's handwriting. Zach set the envelopes aside and scanned the pages of notes, seeking something that seemed important enough to prompt Gramps's urgency.

Two-thirds of the way down, beneath financial documents and real estate papers, he found a packet bound with twine. When he lifted it from the trunk, Gramps's slow grunts became agitated.

Zach turned and held the packet up. "Is this what you wanted?"

Gramps patted the bed and gurgled.

Zach looked at the mess. Ma would have a fit if she came in. But he left it on the floor and went to Gramps's side, the papers in hand, and sat on the bed.

Loosening the twine, Zach surveyed the papers. The first appeared to be letters, dated from September 1862, advising Henry that he had been appointed to serve as a civilian advisor to a five-man military commission to try those Sioux Indians accused of participation in the uprising that had occurred the month before.

Zach glanced at Gramps, discomfort coursing through him. He swallowed against the bitterness that was raising its head. Gramps grunted and waved his boney finger at the packet.

Under the letter of appointment, Zach discovered further correspondence, letters from Gramps to his superiors requesting to be excused from the appointment. It was clear from the replies that Gramps had been given little choice in the matter, not if he wanted to retain his position. In the end, Gramps had reluctantly accepted, his response indicating his intent to bring a balance to the commission. Transcripts of the trials followed, interspersed with correspondence.

Zach read through them, a heavy layer of remorse building in his conscience. Throughout, Gramps had urged restraint and justice, frequently citing lack of evidence only to be overruled by the other members of the commission.

The last letter in the pile was a copy of a resignation letter, advising Gramps's superiors that he was leaving the state.

Zach's hand trembled and tears slid down his face as he digested his own guilt and belief that Gramps had chosen to be a part of the commission.

He looked at Gramps. Henry gave a slight one-sided nod and motioned for Zach to turn the page.

On the back, Gramps's once elegant handwriting defended the Law he cherished and revealed his distaste for the travesty enacted by the commission and its dismissal of justice in the face of expediency, confusion, and public pressure.

Zach set the letter down and took his grandfather's hand. He blinked to clear his eyes, swallowed, and drew Gramps's weakened body into his arms and held him.

"I'm sorry, Gramps. I believed the worst, didn't give you the chance to explain."

Gramps gurgled and patted Zach with his good hand.

Zach drew back, his gaze intent. "Does Adam Foster know about this?"

Gramps offered a slight nod, then grew rigid as a violent spasm wracked his body.

Zach held him, waiting for the shaking to quiet and his body to relax.

"Gramps?"

Henry gurgled as he struggled to form words.

"Adam was the only one who knew," Abigail said from the doorway.

"Som . . . bit," Gramps uttered and fell back against the pillows exhausted.

"He needs his rest, Zach."

"I know, Ma. But he needs to hear my news, and so do you. I've resigned as district attorney, and I'm withdrawing from the senate race. I'm through being Foster's puppet."

"His puppet?" Abigail entered the room. "Whatever do you mean?"

"Adam Foster has been setting me up. He's promoted me as tough on Indians, using that platform to increase contributions from businessmen who see them as a threat against acquiring tribal lands. And he lied about Gramps's involvement in the Sioux commission to drive a wedge between me and Lise Dupree."

"The librarian?"

"She's part Sioux. Her aunt is with Standing Bear." He turned and met Gramps's gaze. "Her uncle was hung at Mankato."

Less than an hour later, Zach barged into Adam Foster's office and slammed the door shut. "I've had enough."

Foster jumped, staring at Zach from behind his large polished oak desk. "Heavens, boy, whatever has gotten into you?"

"What's the matter, Foster?" Zach crossed the room, standing before the desk so that Foster had to look up. "You don't like me

375

thinking for myself?"

A brief expression of discomfort flitted across Foster's face before annoyance registered. "Sit down, Zach. What seems to be the problem?"

"Sit down so you can lecture me?"

"Lecture you? When have I ever presumed to lecture you? Is that how you're seeing my offers of wisdom now?"

Zach recognized the condescension in Foster's tone, thinly disguised as concern. He raised an eyebrow. "Your wisdom?"

Foster offered a smile and gestured in the air. "These questions are hardly productive, boy."

"You're right. I'd prefer to take a swing at you right now." Zach drew one of the heavy captain's chairs closer to the desk, angled it, and sat. He propped his feet on the desk corner.

Foster's brow creased and his jaw tightened. "All right, son . . ."

"Let's get one thing straight. I'm not your 'son,' and I'd prefer we drop the charade of you caring one way or the other what I feel."

"You wound me."

Zach shook his head. "Bullshit. You'd only be wounded if you had feelings."

Foster leaned forward and pounded his hand on his desk hard enough to shift the papers. "That's enough." He stared at Zach, a distasteful scowl on his face. "You're still upset about that librarian, aren't you? You need to start thinking with the right head, son."

Zach pushed back so that the front legs of his chair lifted off the floor, a projection of indifference he knew would nettle the senator. "I'm thinking for the first time in years, Adam," he said. "This is about a hell of a lot more than Lise Dupree, as if that alone weren't enough."

Foster's jaw twitched. "We talked about this some days ago, Zach. You can't win this election if you remain involved with her."

He crossed his arms behind his head and leaned back. "Then maybe I shouldn't be running?"

"Good God," Foster's voice broke, anger seething. "You're in up to your chin, aren't you?"

Zach let the chair legs hit the floor with a thud and leaned forward so fast that Foster backed away. "You've been manipulating me." Dead seriousness replaced his earlier mocking nonchalance. "Took me a while to see it, but when you involve family —"

"Look, I didn't mean any harm with the boy. Since I found him the job, we might as well utilize the advantages that come with it. It's not every day we get an inside view on what the opposition is planning."

Zach stared at him. "Thad? You set Thad up, too?"

"I didn't set anybody up."

Zach shot up out of his chair. "You lying son-of-a-bitch. That's all you've done. Me, Gramps, Thad, Lise. Was it so important that you had to control everything?"

"Someone had to be in control, son. You weren't." Foster leaned forward. "Not from the first minute you laid eyes on the little squaw."

Hot rage filled Zach's veins and his fists balled. "You watch your tongue, you bastard," he said and punched Foster's face.

Foster's head snapped back, and blood gushed from his nose. "You hit me. You goddamn little twerp. After all I've done for you." He patted his vest, located his handkerchief, and gingerly covered his face.

"For me?" Zach shook his hand and stepped back. "It wasn't for me and you know it. It was about you. You lining up my supporters so they'd invest in my campaign. How much extra did they invest with you to make sure I'd be in their pockets? No wonder you were so damned worried about me straying off the platform. It was their platform from the beginning, and they paid you to make sure it became mine, too."

Foster held his head back and sniffled, eyeing Zach as he weighed his options. He squared his shoulders and lowered the handkerchief.

"I think you'll discover your own profit. It's amazing how campaign contributions continue to funnel in, long after the campaign officially ends."

"The campaign is over. Now. I'm withdrawing my candidacy."

"You can't do that," he stated. "I've made promises."

Zach shrugged. "Then unmake them, I don't care. They weren't my promises."

Foster's expression was edged with smugness. "I'm afraid some folks won't see it that way. Most will assume the money went into your pockets." The control faded, and only the threat remained in his eyes.

"Not if they know you, they won't."

"I can make things very difficult for you."

"You've already made things difficult. Setting yourself up as Gramps's devoted partner, stepping into my father's place after he passed on. Nurturing me all these years as if you were doing me a favor when it was your own gain you had in mind. Twisting facts to suit your greed and nearly ruining several lives in the process." Zach held

Foster's gaze briefly before he turned toward the door.

"Politics is not easy," Foster said. "Never. There's a future out there, Zach. All you have to do is reach for it and put aside this fascination you have with that librarian. She's not worth it, you know."

Zach glanced over his shoulder, his hand on the doorknob. "Go to hell, Foster. I don't want you near my mother again. I don't want you 'befriending' Thad. I don't want you visiting Gramps or managing my campaign."

"They'll be wanting their money back, boy." Any effort of friendly persuasion had left his voice. Only intimidation remained.

Zach drew a breath and met the threat straight on. "Then you'd best have it ready for them because I'm wiring them all that you managed the finances. Or mismanaged, if you will. Any moneys due will come from you."

"They won't believe you. I've known them for years."

"That's exactly why they won't have any question believing my banker's statement that none of the funds made it to my account. He'll have it ready tomorrow." Zach shook his head. "If you raked in as much as I think you did, you're gonna be in a hell of a mess."

"You'd best be careful, boy." Foster's tone hardened into rock-solid evil. "You don't have a clue whom you're playing with here. You or that whore of yours."

Cold night air blew down the length of the alley. A tinny piano in the saloon next door played a bar tune, and muted laughter punctuated the otherwise quiet evening.

Adam Foster loitered near the back of the alley, checking his pocket watch while his foot tapped an impatient staccato rhythm on the dried mud. The place reeked like rotten meat. Good God, he was hunkered down in an alley of all places, like a common criminal.

He heard a shuffled footstep and focused on the shadowy figure approaching from the street. Rufus Christy in all his rundown glory.

Christy neared, his breath leaving clouds in the coolness. "Sorry I'm late. Bunch of little tykes playing kick-the-can. Got caught up watchin' 'em."

Foster tucked his watch back into his vest pocket and snorted in disbelief. "You left me waiting while you stopped to watch a bunch of snot-nosed kids?"

"They ain't snot-nosed." Enjoyment lit

the Indian agent's face. "Kids is a joy."

Adam wanted to gag. Kids is a joy, indeed.

"Listen, Christy. I'm not here to chat. We have a problem."

"We?" Christy spat tobacco juice into the dirt. "Thought you abandoned our partnership."

"I've had a chance to rethink things."

"Have you now? And what makes you think I want to share any part of my operation with you?"

"Shut up, Christy." Adam abandoned the pleasant tone. "I'm not asking you to share a damn thing."

"But you sure as hell want something." He raised his eyebrows. "Else you wouldn't have lowered yourself to meet me in an alleyway, now would you?"

"There is a certain element of security in dark places," Adam said, ignoring the barb, maintaining his superiority.

"So, what's your problem?"

"Our problem, Mr. Christy."

"Gee, I'm moving up in the world again. Mister, is it?"

Adam moved forward. "Shut up," he hissed.

"Look, Foster. I don't need you. You're irritatin' me."

Adam was annoyed by Christy's lack of

fear. He wasn't accustomed to this attitude from underlings. He stepped closer and peered down his swollen nose. "It appears your leverage is about to disappear."

"My leverage?"

"Lise Dupree isn't going to pay you a cent if Zach Spencer withdraws his candidacy, is she?"

Christy looked shocked. "Spencer's quittin'? How the hell did you let that happen?"

Bristling, Adam grabbed Christy by the arm and wrenched him so close they were touching. "Me? You and your greedy bumbling did that."

"Hell, Dupree ain't gonna pay me anyways." Christy twisted and Adam squeezed tighter.

"You'll get your money, you little shit. Maybe not as much as you'd like, but the payoff will be there." He relaxed his hold a little, until he felt Christy's tenseness fade. But he didn't let go. "All you gotta do is get her to convince Zach to stay in the senate race." He squeezed again, for emphasis, until Christy winced. "It's gotta be done tonight. Tonight. Threaten her family if you have to, that old lady with the Poncas. I don't care what you have to do, just get her to convince Zach not to drop the campaign for a few days."

"But she's an Indian!"

Adam grabbed Christy's other arm and shook him. "Right now, all I care about is keeping him in the senate race long enough to get to his bank, transfer some funds, and set him up good. He'll be withdrawing in disgrace inside of two weeks anyway. Understand?"

Christy peered up at him. "And I get my money?"

He shoved the little worm away from him, disgusted. "You'll get your money," he said, turning toward the street. "You and me both."

CHAPTER NINETEEN

Rufus Christy strode toward the library, muttering. All his plans had gone to hell, and he'd be damned if he was going to stand for it. Not in a thousand years.

Adam Foster could parade around in his fancy brocade vest and fiddle with his fine gold pocket watch all he wanted, but it didn't change the fact that Foster had almost let the whole deal slide out of their hands. For all his assurances that he had Spencer securely in hand, it was all poppycock in the end. A whole lot of poppycock.

Rufus aimed his worn boot toe at a pebble and sent it flying down the boardwalk.

Damn politician.

If Foster had let him handle things from the beginning, they'd both be sitting pretty right now instead of scrambling to repair holes. More strong-arm early in the game would have done it. Fast and tight.

Attacks were best accomplished without delay and with full force. It's what the Sioux had done to his family. They'd hit at dusk, at the end of a long, hard day of traveling. Like a wind, they'd sprung out of the ravine and poured into the camp. Women had screamed and dropped their cooking pots. Men had let loose of the livestock they were unhitching and scrambled for the rifles they'd left in the wagon boxes. Kids like him out on the prairie had abandoned the piles of buffalo chips they'd collected for fuel and run.

Within ten minutes, men and women lay with arrows through their chests and their throats cut, thick pools of blood saturating the ground beneath them. The children had watched the carnage in horror. The damned savages had scattered entrails in the grass and torn little girls apart with repeated rape. Then, they'd scalped them, slicing off broad sections of their skin and hair while they were still alive.

Rufus had watched from his hiding place in a buffalo wallow, unable to control his violent shivering. He'd wanted to save them, but terror had paralyzed him. Instead, he'd pissed his trousers until he was a muddy mess while he prayed the Sioux wouldn't smell him.

They'd found him in the wallow not long after. Already, the air was filled with the stench of decay. He'd tottered past the remains of his parents and vomited. His sister, Gertie, violated but still alive, had stumbled along with the rest of the captives.

They endured two years of hell with the Sioux. Until the day Gert died in childbirth at the age of twelve. On that day, ten-year-old Rufus had run, escaping by hiding in the bloated carcass of a dead buffalo.

Even now, the bitterness stewed in him. He'd taken his vengeance as an Indian agent. The government job had given him the chance to make Indians suffer. It didn't matter what Indians. Any Indians. He'd sat there in the courtroom while Standing Bear marched around in his war bonnet and demanded to be treated like a white man. No savage had that right. Bile had risen in his throat when he heard the verdict. He refused to accept it.

He'd heard the lawyers tell that damn librarian that they couldn't have done it without her, and dark hatred had boiled in his gut. It was boiling again now. He could have taken the money and lived somewhere far away from Indians and the stench of their villages. And *she* was about to take it all away from him. He'd be damned if he was going to let a half-breed best him. Foster had as good as told him what to do, said he didn't care what it took. Rufus slid his hand to his thigh, fingering the knife he had tied there earlier.

The Sioux bitch would pay for it. All of it.

Lise heard the door at the bottom of the stairwell slam shut and chided herself for not having locked it after the last patron. There often seemed to be someone who waited until the last moment to browse. Hopefully, the latecomer would already have a title in mind.

Late afternoon sun still lit one side of the room, but the light in the near rows was fading. She'd need a lamp if she waited much longer to put the books in place. She gathered the last of the books needing to be reshelved and sorted them according to Dewey's orderly system, then pushed the cart toward the shelves.

Heavy footfalls sounded on the stairs, and Lise sighed. It didn't sound like the patron was in much of a hurry. That usually meant they didn't know what they wanted. Less time to dress for dinner but hopefully, she'd still be ready on time.

The door to the main library room squeaked open, then shut. The unmistakable click of the slide bolt echoed in the stillness and Lise's mouth turned up, thoughts about the last time she'd been in a locked library filling her mind. She slid the last book onto the shelf and walked to the center of the room, thoughts of dinner gone. "Zach," she called. "Is that you?"

"It ain't Zach."

"Oh." Lise recognized the ugly voice of Rufus Christy, and her anticipation plunged into wariness. Then it registered: he'd locked the door. The weasel was trying to intimidate her. She swallowed her fear and emerged from the shelves with a couple of heavy books still in her arms. "I told you before, Mr. Christy. I don't have the funds to pay you."

Christy raised one corner of his mouth and sneered at her. "Then you'll have to find another way to pay, won't you?"

Lise shivered at the implication, telling herself to call his bluff. "There will be no payment."

"You ain't too bright, missy, for being a librarian. Must be that Injun in you."

She stared at him, despising him for his attempted extortion, for ruining Zach's dreams, for the evil that hung about him like a shroud. "You need to leave now, Mr. Christy."

389

"I ain't goin' nowhere." He licked his lips.

This time, the sliver of fear made her pause, her confidence sliding as she began to doubt that he was bluffing. The books in her arms would be little defense against him if he made the threat real. Her gaze darted toward the desk, and she remembered the scissors in the drawer. She glanced back to Christy and drew a breath. "Yes, you —"

"I said I ain't goin'," he shouted. "Now shut your trap and get over here."

Lise shook her head and took a step back, now truly afraid. In less than a moment, Christy was at her side, one hand reaching to grab her hair while the other slid a knife toward her throat.

"This is going to be my way, you hear? In a couple minutes, Zach Spencer is gonna be knockin' on that door. I already sent him a message you wanted to see him. You're gonna answer it and have a little conversation with him while I wait. I want you to talk him into staying in the senate race."

She twisted and his arms tightened. She felt the sharp point of the knife on her skin and stalled, shaking slightly. There was no way Zach was going to believe she'd ask such a thing. "I can't do that. He's already made up his mind."

"You can and you will. He can change his

mind. At least, ask him to think about it a few days, before he makes it official. That'll work for me." His lips neared her ear, and he whispered into it. "Think you can do that?"

"I think you're a pig."

The knife darted downward, under her collar, and white hot pain buckled her knees. Warm blood trickled down her shoulder.

"Now look what you made me do," he murmured. "You show me respect, or I'll slice your throat! Tell him to wait a few days before he withdraws. That's all you gotta do. Soon as he agrees, send him on his way."

Lise forced herself to think, to stave off the fear. If she could somehow convey to Zach that things were not right, they could overpower Christy. If she could convince Christy she was doing as he asked until Zach caught on. She nodded.

"Oh, and just so you know, you don't want to try no funny business. I got a partner waiting by the street door. He hears any ruckus up here, he'll be up here with a gun ready. So unless you want Spencer killed, you'll cooperate." He nicked her skin a second time.

She drew a breath and quelled her urge to scream a warning as the door at the bottom of the stairs creaked open. With a jerk, Christy pulled her to the door and grabbed her shawl from its hook, tossing it over her bleeding shoulder.

The instant he moved away from her, her hand flew to the bolt. Before she could slide it open, she felt the blade stabbing at her again, this time in the small of her back.

"You don't want to do that," Christy growled.

Lise panted, the surge of adrenalin still pumping through her, and fought for calm.

The door handle jiggled. "Lise? Are you in there?"

Lise drew an unsteady breath and stared at Christy. He stared back and nodded. "Open it," he mouthed.

Her fingers shook as she slid the bolt open. Christy stood to the side, hidden, knife against her as she peered around the door and offered Zach a nervous, wavering smile.

"Locked yourself in?"

She shrugged. "I had a lot to get done. Didn't want any interruptions."

"Not even me?" He cupped her head and kissed her, his breath clouding the glass of her spectacles.

The knife pressed inward, telling her Christy was angry. "You're fine," she said, drawing back slightly until Christy eased the blade away. She could almost feel his hot fetid breath from behind the door. "I . . . I wanted to talk to you."

"Sounds serious?"

"I need you to do something for me." For a brief second, she pointed toward the door, her gesture hid from Christy by her body.

Zach stared at her hand, then caught her gaze. "Lise?"

The knife ground into her back and she arched away.

"What's wrong?" Zach asked.

Lise drew a breath, remembered Christy's warning about his accomplice, and shook her head. "Nothing. Just . . . I . . . I've been thinking. I know you said you decided to pull out of the senate race but I'm not sure you should."

"It's not what I want any more, it makes me feel dirty."

"Could you think it through more? What about the opportunity for positive action, to make change? What about all the good you could do?"

"Good? I don't think anything good can come of politics. I used to, but not anymore. Do we have to talk about this now? Why don't I come in and you can lock the door again."

Deep brittle fear erupted inside her and she shook her head violently. "No!" Christy drew closer. "No," she said again, more calmly, waving her hand in front of her stomach and closing her eyes.

"Please, Zach. I need you to do this." She opened her eyes and swallowed as she looked into his eyes. "Tell me you'll wait a couple days before you take action. Talk to Tom Tibbles about whether or not he thinks you could have an impact. He knows the political climate as well as anyone, and certainly has a clearer perspective than Foster. Get his opinion. Figure out whether you could help legislate change if you went forward. Then make your decision."

Zach nodded, and mouthed, "Are you all right?"

"Please." She paused, and pointedly let her gaze shift to the side. "I want you to wait awhile."

"You're sure?" His face registered concern.

"Yes. Look at all the angles." She drew another breath. "Then, if you still want to pull out, I'll know it's for the right reasons, not just because of me."

"You are the right reasons."

"Please."

"All right." He nodded. "I'll think about

it. But you know I'm not going to change my mind. Let's just go now."

She shook her head again. "I can't. Mr. Christy asked me to do some research for him, and I have to finish it tonight." This time, she was ready for the knife point.

Zach's eyes darkened at the mention of Christy's name, as she'd expected. He scowled and stepped forward, fists balled.

"Please go," Lise insisted.

His eyes flickered and he paused. "I love you," he whispered.

"I love you, too." She stepped back and closed the door. Christy held the knife at her back until the door at the bottom of the stairs opened, then closed shut with a click.

"You done better than I thought," he said, lowering the knife but keeping it ready. "What the hell'd you mention my name for?"

Lise shrugged. "We were supposed to go to dinner. I had to get rid of him. It just popped into my head." She kept her voice slightly resentful, hoping a lack of fear would convince him. "I did what you wanted. Now, get out." She needed to keep calm and avoid upsetting Christy. If her efforts had been successful, Zach would return with help.

"We still got things to attend to." He slid

the bolt back into place and turned, a leer etched across his face. "We got lots more business to conduct."

"I don't have any money, Mr. Christy. I already told you that." She stepped toward her desk.

"Foster'll see to the money. There's other ways for you to pay, missy. And payment is long past due." He waved the knife at her and the blade shimmered in the lamplight.

She shivered at the unstated meaning. "Payment?"

"Nobody ever paid for what was done. Nobody but Gertie and the others." Rage reddened his face, and Lise backed away until her hips hit the desk.

"Gertie?"

Christy followed, waving the knife. "Shut up. You just shut up. All these years, I tried to make them pay. Did it all without bloodshed, I did. Ain't as satisfying but I reached more of 'em that way. They had their lives but they were miserable. Let 'em think about it every day their rations didn't get there, every day they were cold and starving. Every one of 'em that got malaria and smallpox deserved it as much as the others deserved watchin' 'em die."

Bile rose in Lise's throat as she thought how much suffering had occurred because of Christy. She fought the urge to spit in his face, instead staring hard into his eyes. "You're a wretched man. Wretched. Using your position of power to make people suffer."

Christy laughed. "See — that's just it. Injuns ain't people! And they haven't suffered enough." Christy's rage thawed, anguish filling his face, tears pooling in his eyes. "Ain't none of them suffered like Gertie did." His shoulders shook. "Ain't none of them paid for that."

Lise's senses warred. In the back of her mind, she recalled what she'd heard about Christy, that his family had been killed on their way West by a war party. Despite her hatred, despite her fear, a part of her ached for him. "Maybe we need to sit down and talk."

"We don't need to talk about nothin'." His hands were in her hair, yanking her forward. His knife gleamed above her forehead, his rage reignited. "Should I cut you? Cut you across your pretty half-breed face so others can see your brand?" The sting of the knife bit into her flesh, and blood trickled down her face. She froze, her heart pounding as she gasped for air.

"I could slice that mane of yours right off your head faster'n you could scream." His hot breath hung, foul, in front of her face. "But we're gonna save that. Bleeds too much. Let's say I cut you other places first."

He pulled her head backward, his knife hand jerking in front of her face as he moved. With a yank, he ripped her bodice open, then shoved her. She hit the edge of the desk and stumbled to the floor. He towered above her.

Lise's gaze darted around the room, seeking a weapon while Christy leered, drool hanging from his half-open mouth. Had Zach not understood? Her breath came in ragged bursts, her panic rising.

"Who is Gertie?" she asked, praying his memories wouldn't accelerate the rage.

He attacked in one fluid movement, sinking to his knees on either side of Lise, his body pinning her down, his rough hand grasping her upper arm. She struggled against him. He slapped her, and the sharp, biting pain stilled her.

"You killed her. You savages raped her repeatedly and killed her."

Lise searched her memory for the details of what had happened to him. He'd been taken prisoner, she recalled, with a sister.

"She didn't deserve any of it."

"No, she didn't."

She softened her voice. "I'm sorry."

"Sorry? That don't bring her back. It don't bring none of 'em back. Now, you get to pay for it."

His rough hands fumbled at her breasts, prodding them through her chemise. Terror clouded her senses and she struggled against him even as her mind distantly warned her against it.

"They done this to her. This and more." One hand whipped to her skirt, ripping both skirt and petticoat from the waist until they gaped open in front of Christy's hulking frame.

Tears pooled in her eyes and Lise swallowed hard. She couldn't think about this, not if she wanted to survive. She forced herself to lie still and think.

He slapped her again, and she arched in pain. They'd slapped the Sioux prisoners in Minnesota, slapped them and spit on them, beat them and hung them. Lise shuddered and the tears slid from the corners of her eyes.

The prisoners had paid. Gertie had paid. Vengeance and payment wreaked from the innocent while she and Christy had watched, each in a separate hell.

Christy shifted, fumbling with the buttons on his trousers, shocking Lise back to the present. She and Christy, unable to fix any of it. Then or now.

He pinned her down, his face contorted.

"It wasn't your fault," she whispered.

"Shut up."

Lise looked into his eyes. "You couldn't stop it. Any of it."

"Shut up, shut up, shut up!" he screamed.

A small glimmer of hope shot through her, and Lise drew a breath, the tears flowing down her cheeks as she comforted her enemy. "She never blamed you. None of them did. You were just a boy."

Christy sniveled. His body shifted, the forceful punitive pressure beginning to shake. "How do you know?" he whimpered. "How do you know what they felt?"

She slid her arm out from under him and touched him on the face. "You were a boy, Rufus. They were saving *you*."

He dropped the knife and slid away from her, curling into a ball, his shoulders heaving. "You damn yellow-livered coward. Pissed your pants and hid. You let them do it. You let them." His screams subsided until racking sobs overtook him.

Lise rose to sitting, fighting her own shudders and only dimly recognizing the sound of breaking glass.

And then Zach was there, gathering her in his arms and pulling her away from Christy.

CHAPTER TWENTY

Lise watched the two deputies who had manhandled Susette haul Rufus Christy from the library and shivered within Zach's strong embrace.

"Shhh," he whispered.

Though Christy was gone, fear and panic had caught up with Lise. The shaking seemed rooted deep within her. Even Christy's removal hadn't diminished them.

"Will they keep him in custody?" she asked now.

Zach hugged her close. "I'll see to it."

Another irrational spurt of fear rose within her. "But if the deputies could molest Susette without consequence, how do we know Christy will be charged for what he did to me?"

Zach cupped her face in his hands. "You know it's different."

"Because I'm passing for white."

He nodded. "That, and Dundy's decision

will have its impact. He established Indians are people, entitled to all associated rights and protections. Attempted rape of a person is illegal."

Lise drew a slow breath. "So, they'll charge him?"

"They'll charge him and they'll convict him. I'm still district attorney — I'll see to it. He has no defense. He should plead guilty and save himself the misery of a trial." He paused. "Should we get you to a doctor?"

"I'm all right." She shook away the panic, trusting Zach's assurances. "Just small cuts."

Zach eyed her tattered bodice, and pain surfaced on his face. "I should have pushed my way in," he said. "Between the two of us, we could have taken him. But you were so adamant that I leave."

Lise remembered Christy's warning. "He said there was someone else. In the alley. Did anyone —"

Zach shook his head. "The deputies checked. There was no one there."

"But he said there was someone waiting, that he'd shoot you if we tried anything." She heard the rising panic in her voice.

"A bluff."

She frowned, wondering if that's all it had been or if Zach was still in danger. "Or he left when you did."

Zach shook his head. "I should have come in. My God, look at you."

"I'm fine." She placed her hands on his chest. "You trusted me."

"You took a big chance." A hint of chastisement filled his voice. "If he'd seen what you were doing —"

"He couldn't. Not hidden behind the door like he was."

Zach's eyes clouded. "God, Lise, he could have —"

"But he didn't." This time, the panic stayed away, replaced by her common sense rationality. "I'm not sure he could have."

"But if I'd lost you . . ."

She laid her head against him. "I'm right here."

"I'm going to resign as soon as Christy confesses."

"I know." She recalled Christy's desperation, his bizarre insistence that she ask Zach to wait with his decision. "It was odd, Christy wanting me to convince you to delay. He was trying to blackmail me but I didn't have anything to pay him with. Do you think he was going to contact your supporters? He kept telling me I had to stall you for a couple days."

Zach pulled away. "He knew I was withdrawing?" He processed the thought for a moment, then his mouth dropped open. "Damn it to hell."

"What is it?"

"Foster," he said. "Foster was the only one who knew I was withdrawing, except for you and family."

Lise's heartbeat quickened. "You think Foster was part of this?"

"Not only part of it but very likely behind it." Zach scooped his hand through his hair. "He had a fit when I told him I was pulling out of the race."

"Was he part of the blackmail?"

Zach shook his head. "No, he was pretty upset when he told me about Christy. I don't think he was faking that. But asking you to get me to delay the campaign decision — that has Foster written all over it."

"But why?"

"Campaign contributions. The son-of-a-bitch was planning to steal the money." He rubbed his eyes. "I'll need to get those telegrams sent tonight."

Lise shot him a questioning look.

"I had a bad feeling things weren't right with Foster. I was planning to notify the contributors about my concerns when I withdrew."

"And Foster was trying to buy himself

more time before you did?"

Zach nodded. "Looks that way."

"Then you'd best get busy." Pushing aside her desire to keep him to herself for the remainder of the evening, Lise gathered her shawl tighter and extinguished the lamp on her desk. When she turned, Zach caught her in his arms again. She swallowed, remnants of fear still lodged in her throat, and leaned into him.

"You know he wouldn't have had any leverage to blackmail any of us if you weren't trying so damn hard to hide who you are."

She nodded, accepting the truth for what it was. "I wouldn't be here if I weren't hiding it."

"Are you so sure?" He stroked her cheek until she raised her gaze.

The painful memories tumbled through her thoughts. She was so tired of it all. "The town wouldn't let an Indian run their library. You know that." She moved toward the door.

Zach caught her arm, stopping her flight, his blue eyes refusing to concede agreement. "Didn't you notice those fine white people in that courtroom every day? You didn't read those letters to the editor?"

Lise shook her head, hope for the future

warring with past experiences. She didn't want to argue it anymore, didn't want to fight what wouldn't change anyway. "The Ponca are a peaceful nation, easy to accept. My people killed and murdered."

"Yes, they did." He sighed. "So did my people." He eased her back against the desk, then lifted her until she was sitting on it, unable to flee. "Maybe it's time to let that be. There's nobility in your blood, too. You should be proud of it. Let the shame go and maybe others will accept you."

Her stomach clenched so violently that her lips trembled. "I'm not ashamed."

He cupped her chin in his hand. "Aren't you?"

"I'm not."

"Then stop hiding it." He traced the line of tears on her cheek. "Lise, I love you. I want to know Aunt Rose and whatever cousins you have and to make them part of my family." He reached into a pocket and pulled a small box from it, opened it, and lifted out a gleaming golden chain. "I had planned to give this to you at dinner. I want you to wear it, proudly, with Aunt Rose's pendant on it where everyone can see it. I want to make you my wife and let you open my world. I love you."

Lise's heart pounded at the words, his acceptance and validation filling her. "I love you," she said, focusing on Zach's face, blurry through her tears.

The smile he offered back melted her heart. "Will you marry me?"

She looked away, then, as the doubt and fear returned. "And tell the world I'm part Sioux?"

"One-quarter Sioux."

"But Sioux nonetheless. You can't know what that will mean for you."

"I think I can." He caught her hands, his thumbs rubbing worry spots on them. "Though I'm not sure you do."

She drew a breath and sifted through his words. She thought of the gold chain, clutched in her hand, offering the beaded pendant for the world to see. "If we tell people, things won't be the same, for either of us."

"Then we embrace the change. I've spent my whole life living in a very narrow world, afraid to challenge what is in order to create what could be. We have so much out there that we haven't even imagined. So much that we can change together."

She wanted to believe him, but there was so much he didn't realize. She remembered the night her father's store had been burned, the frequent moves when whites refused to do business with him and he could no longer support his family. The pain of being fired from her past library positions still haunted her. How could she chance putting Zach through being shunned, being spat upon and called names, because of her?

"Say yes." His tone was light, encouraging.

Her heart thudded. Even if they weren't treated with cruelty, there would surely be repercussions. "You don't know how much your life could change because of me."

"My life has already changed, and it will change again. I take pride in that."

"But —"

"I don't think *my* pride is the issue, is it?"

Lise stared at him, her eyes pooling. For all the resentment she held for her mother's denial of their heritage, was she any different? Despite her verbiage in support of cultural pride, what had she done with hers? She rocked as the tears hit in rolling spasms.

She'd told herself if no one knew, no one could blame her. But that wasn't it at all.

She drew a calming breath, closed her eyes, and listened to Zach's words echo through her thoughts. He'd told her to let go of the shame, and she'd insisted she had none. But it wasn't true. It hung around her neck just as surely as Aunt Rose's pendant. She'd been ashamed of taking honor in who she was.

Finally understanding, she smiled at Zach and drew the pendant from under her bodice. The bright colors of the beads had begun to fade and the gold chain would alter its traditional appearance. It was no longer the same necklace as it had been when Aunt Rose had gifted it to her.

In truth, nothing was the same. Or ever would be.

"Han," she whispered, "yes." She lifted her head high as the joy overwhelmed her. "Yes. I will be your wife."

The following day, Rufus Christy hanged himself with a belt in his jail cell.

Lise read the news in the *Omaha Herald.* Hot tears stung her swollen eyes. The paper slid from her fingers, and she fled to the warmth of the library windows, shaking and unsure if she was relieved or sorry for him.

She let the sun surround her as she waded through the complicated emotions, digesting them.

It baffled her, feeling sorry for him when she should hate him. He'd blackmailed her, had nearly raped her. He'd been responsible for evicting Aunt Rose and the Poncas from their homeland as well as the arrest. He'd ruined countless lives, caused misery and death. He had been a cruel and vengeful man, and the world was well rid of him.

But he'd also carried deep scars that had ruled his life. Rufus Christy had nursed guilt most of his life, turning it into rage and blame, refusing to forgive himself for being unable to save others — for surviving. He'd spread out that blame, delighting in making life worse for everyone instead of working to change the situation.

Tom and Susette, on the other hand, embraced change. Already, they'd announced plans to travel to the East with Standing Bear on a campaign for Indian rights. Tom would arrange the venues and conduct the publicity, Standing Bear would speak, Susette would translate and add her own comments. They'd be a small party, accompanied by Susette's brother Frank and a few of Standing Bear's closest tribal members, with a mission of enlightenment.

And her? She fingered Aunt Rose's pendant, secure on its new gold chain.

For too long, she'd shunned the honor of her people. It wasn't disgrace over what the Sioux had done that had made her hide who she was. She'd accepted the violent acts her people had committed, blaming others for forcing them to it. And in doing so, she'd ignored the underlying reasons for the fears and biases of whites. Doing so had allowed her to embrace being a victim. Like Rufus Christy, she'd wallowed in her own casualty.

But today was a new day, a day to acknowledge the Sioux were neither victims nor savages. They were a dignified, noble people. Among them, as in all people, were those who had suffered and those who caused others pain.

She fingered her pendant, proud of what it proclaimed.

EPILOGUE

One month later

"Are you ready?" Zach called from the doorway.

Lise turned and walked across the main room of the library, then kissed him. She pivoted, letting her glance take in the shelves of books for the last time, already missing the legal volumes, the sun and the tables and her familiar oak desk. She breathed in the musty scent of old, well-loved books and fresh ink from the newspaper. She pulled her shawl from its hook and offered Zach a shaky smile.

"Scared?" he asked.

"A little. My life is suddenly very different."

"Mine, too." He grinned. "But we'll be fine."

He lifted her valise and followed her down the stairs, waiting while she exited and locked both sets of doors behind her. She'd turn the keys in to the mayor's office in the morning.

Warm sun still lingered, heralding spring's full arrival. Zach's confidence was evident in his purposeful stride. Having published his withdrawal from the senate race in the *Herald,* he'd shed that set of expectations. Shed it and left Adam Foster facing angry contributors and scrambling to avoid impeachment and arrest. His letter of resignation as district attorney would find its way to Lincoln tomorrow.

The spring in his step was as infectious as the warmth spreading through Lise as she acknowledged the rightness of their decisions.

Abigail Spencer met them at the front door, happiness animating her face.

" 'Bout time you two got here. Thad's been underfoot every time he comes in my kitchen to sniff at the roast, and I'm almost ready to wring his neck."

"Is Gramps ready?"

"Ready and then some. Everyone's here. Lise, you can change in here." She pointed to a small bedroom. "Zach, you go on back. I'll set that roast out on top of the range, and we'll all meet in Gramps's room."

Zach put her valise inside the room, winked, and blew her a kiss before continuing down the hall. She closed the door and drew a steadying breath, then opened the suitcase. Her mother's doeskin dress lay on top. She'd seen it only a few times before, a quick glimpse of it in the bottom of the trunk, buried beneath other items from the past. It had arrived yesterday, with her mother's note of congratulations. She picked it up, amazed that it had retained its suppleness all these years.

She shed her clothes and donned the dress. Its softness caressed her skin, and thoughts of Zach's nimble fingers filled her mind. She steadied her heart with another deep breath, changed footwear, and centered Aunt Rose's pendent between her breasts.

With nostalgic warmth, she sent out thoughts to Aunt Rose and her mother, and made her way down the hall. Thad's voice maintained a constant stream of conversation, punctuated at intervals by the Reverend Mitchell's deep baritone. Gramps's gurgling responses gave evidence of his merry mood. Susette, Tom, and George Crook added comments.

Zach waited at the doorway. Nervous anticipation bubbled through Lise as she slipped past him and realized all eyes were on her. She faltered, then stood straight and proud.

From the bed, Gramps turned. A lopsided smile crept across his face, stretching broadly on one side.

"Hello," she said, crossing to him.

Gramps nodded with slow, deliberate movements and reached toward her with his good hand. She placed her palm in his. His gnarled fingers wrapped around hers, and he squeezed.

"Can I show them now?" Thad asked, barely containing his excitement.

"Thaddeus Spencer," Abigail warned from the other side of the bed. "There'll be time later."

"Ah, Ma."

Zach raised one eyebrow in query.

"His wedding present," Abigail explained.

Lise watched him fight disappointment, a boy trying to act a man. "He can show us now, if that's all right," she said, unable to resist his barely restrained eagerness. "A few more minutes won't matter." She squeezed Zach's hand and he nodded his assent.

Upon Abigail's approval, Thad drew a piece of wood from under the bed and presented it to them. "Spencer and Spencer" was burned into it. Smaller lettering below proclaimed "Legal Research and

Representation, Specializing in Indian Rights."

"For the new office," he said. "I thought you'd want folks to know."

Lise grinned and hugged him. His effort was evident in the careful attention to detail, the uniform lettering, the centered words. And he was right, folks would need to know.

The enterprise had been Zach's idea, a mesh of their skills. Though the city council hadn't fainted when she explained her heritage, they'd been adamant that employment of married ladies was inappropriate. She suspected she'd spend a good deal of time in the library anyway. With their successful fundraising and purchase of the Niobrara island for Standing Bear, others had begun to seek their aid.

Zach cleared his throat and placed a shaky hand on Thad's shoulder. "Thanks, kid."

In his bed, Gramps rocked forward and back, drawing their attention. The lopsided smile was still on his face, and his jaw twitched as he spit out his thoughts. "G . . . g . . . g . . . gooooood."

A tear slid down Lise's cheek. Zach hugged her close, his face next to hers, and she felt the wetness of his tears, shared only with her. "I love you," he whispered.

"Lotancila mihignaki," she told him. *I love*

you my husband.

His hand pulled her body to him, his fingers brushing the doeskin dress, neither of them caring what anyone else thought.

AUTHOR'S NOTE

Although Lise and Zach are fictional characters, I chose to set their story into the historical trial of Standing Bear. I have endeavored to represent the events of the trial as factually as possible.

Standing Bear, General George Crook, Thomas Tibbles, Susette La Flesche, Joseph La Flesche, Andrew Poppleton, John Webster, and Elmer Dundy were real persons. I have attempted to be true to their roles and personalities in my portrayal of them. I should note that there are variations in the spelling of the La Flesches' Omaha names; I used those most frequently employed by scholarly sources. Krug's Brewery, the *Omaha Herald,* the Omaha Public Library, and the Wigwam existed as well, though the Grand Central Hotel was destroyed by fire in 1878, six months prior to my story.

Tom Tibbles's wife, Amelia, died suddenly in the fall of 1879. Tom returned to Omaha to bury her, then resumed his tour with Standing Bear. He and Susette La Flesche were married in June, 1881. History does not chronicle the nature of their relationship prior to their marriage, and it was my decision to portray it as one of unconsummated mutual attraction, based on respect.

Lise Dupree did not exist, except in my imagination, although the Omaha Public Library did employ a female librarian. Zach Spencer's fictional character replaced the real-life District Attorney Genio Lambertson. While Indian Agent Rufus Christy did not exist, he was inspired in part by Inspector Edward Kemble, an official with the Bureau of Indian Affairs, who played a role in the removal of the Poncas from their Niobrara homeland. Senator Adam Foster was completely fictional.

The Sioux Uprising occurred in Minnesota in 1862 after annuities were delayed for several months. A small uprising by a renegade band of Sioux also occurred in Spirit Lake in 1857.

The Trial of Standing Bear was a landmark case in Indian history and laid the groundwork for Native American citizenship, which was finally granted in 1924.

ACKNOWLEDGMENTS

This story, like all the others in my head, would never have found its way to paper without the support, guidance, and encouragement of many people.

Most certainly, it would never have been completed without Ken. I wasn't looking for him, I never expected to find him, I can't imagine living without him. He has been my confidence when I didn't have any, my rebuilder of dreams, my ever-present source of encouragement. He brings me joy, loves me without qualification, and makes me believe in myself anew each day.

I could not have continued without the support of my daughter, Katrina, and her husband, Shane (and Asher, too, even though he only babbles right now). And the rest of my family . . . Mom; Judy and Dave; Mike and Brenda; Ilka and Edgar, Luca and Enzo; Danika and Sergio, Kathia and Erik; Kendra and Kelly, Conner, Jacob, and

Makena. You have been there when I've needed you, celebrating my successes and commiserating with my setbacks, telling me you believe in me, asking me all about being a writer and writing your own "chapter books."

I am indebted to all of my critique partners — live and online, in Cheyenne and Denver — for continuing to teach me and hold me accountable for my craft, and to my soup-writing partners for keeping my nose to the grindstone. Liz, Heather, Mike, Mary, Jeana, Sharon, Sue, Janet, Robin, Peggy, Kay, Jessica, Steven, Thea, Denee, Carla, Cate, Heidi, Tasha . . . thank you all for being part of this journey. And I owe a mountain of gratitude to members of Rocky Mountain Fiction Writers for their lifelines during the months of loss, transition, and rebuilding. You know who you are . . . I'll never forget you were there when I needed you.

My appreciation goes out to Joanne Ferguson Cavanaugh at the Omaha Public Library and Joann Myer at the Douglas County Historical Society for responding to my questions when this story idea was a tiny germ. I also need to thank the staff of the Douglas County Historical Society and the Crook House at Fort Omaha for their detailed tours and information during my visits. And a hearty thanks to Dick Stewart who responded to me with information on the death of Amelia Tibbles.

Finally, I want to acknowledge my editors. Acquisitions Editor Tiffany Schofield showed extreme faith by contacting me when Five Star launched the new Frontier Fiction imprint — thank you, Tiff. And I hold nothing but the deepest appreciation for Hazel Rumney, my developmental editor. Her dedicated edits took this book to a whole new level — Hazel, I had no idea . . .

ABOUT THE AUTHOR

Pamela Nowak writes award-winning historical romance set in the American West. Her debut novel, *Chances,* was awarded the HOLT Medallion for Best First Book, was a WILLA Finalist, and was named one of the "Top Ten Romance Novels of 2008" by *Booklist.* Her second novel, *Choices,* was released in 2009 to glowing reviews and received a HOLT Finalist Award in Historical Romance. She was named the Rocky Mountain Fiction Writers' *Writer of the Year* in 2010.

Pam has been in love with history and rich characters all her life. With a B.A. in history, she taught history to prison inmates, served as project manager for the Fort Yuma National Historic Site, and ran a homeless shelter. Pam and her life partner, Ken, live in Denver.